MURDER ISN'T PRIVATE

★

To

BILL PÉRODEAU

★

JOHN GARDEN

★

*Murder
Isn't Private*

London
MICHAEL JOSEPH

First published by
MICHAEL JOSEPH LTD.
26 Bloomsbury Street
London, W.C.1
1950

Set and printed in Great Britain by Tonbridge Printers, Ltd.,
Peach Hall Works, Tonbridge, in Bembo eleven on twelve
point, on paper made by John Dickinson at Croxley, and
bound by James Burn at Esher.

Chapter One

*

AFTER Felicity was gone he was aware of no particular emotion of any kind. He certainly did not feel like a murderer. In fact, it did not occur to him then that he had committed a murder. If he had any feeling at all in that second he stood there in the darkness, listening, half-waiting for her to cry out, it was the defiance tinged with remorse felt by a spoilt child who, threatened with the loss of a precious toy, throws the toy away rather than let anyone else have it.

Then he stepped back from the stern of the launch, back into the flood of light that came from the saloon. The bridge players were still absorbed in their game, and Frank, the only one not playing, was still engrossed in the bridge players. During the last minute they had all ceased to exist. Dyke had to readjust his mind now to admit them back into his world. Or was he returning to theirs? The hand was finishing. The usual post-mortem was beginning:

'If you'd led hearts, partner . . .'

Dyke was looking at them, the lower half of his body in the light, the upper part out of it. He had stepped out of their sight for—what would it be—not more than a few seconds . . . and in that time he had killed his wife. The toy was gone.

He was Dyke Farne, who had destroyed his wife. He loved her, but he had killed her. He was rather clever. That was an understatement. He was very clever. Very. He had done, he thought now, in a flash of insight, what he was bound to do. He

5

had done it very cleverly. Nothing premeditated, nothing worked out. He had seen his opportunity and had acted, swiftly. It had been an opportunity that could never have occurred again. And he had been quick enough to seize it.

He moved forward a step or two, and the light, as if a shutter had been raised, moved up his body to illuminate him fully. Frank looked a moment, grinned, and returned his attention to the argument. Caroline's voice was now at the top of its after-bridge register.

Dyke suddenly realized he still held the gin bottle in his hand. He went to the door of the saloon and reached forward to put it on the table. Then he turned to look at the night, half his back out of sight, half still in. Behind him Harold was dealing again, and Caroline's voice fell slowly, lower and lower, with each dying rebuke.

The summer night was like a poem. It was so beautiful that for a moment Dyke was moved and he felt a lump in his throat. On such a night as this . . . The sky, dark as indigo, was dotted with pin-points of stars. The launch moved so gently that you could almost forget it moved at all. In its wake the water lay smooth; only the wide ripples the boat pushed out caught the diffused starlight in long converging lines. They were on Master-man's Reach. Dead straight behind, and dead straight ahead for the better part of a mile yet. It would be five minutes, no, nearer ten—before they ran aground. The boat would steer herself. They had been in midstream when Felicity lifted her hand from the tiller to take the drink he was holding out to her; they were still in midstream.

By the time they grounded—he shrugged his shoulders, turned and went into the saloon. Frank looked up and grinned again, but nobody spoke. He turned a chair, sat on the back of it and pretended to look down on the card-players. But he did not see them. They played with the intense concentration of the unskilled, but he was quite unaware of what went on. He looked down directly on to Alice's hand, but he did not see her cards, nor did he notice when she played them, or her fluttering indecisions as she half drew a card for her lead then substituted another. He was back in the cockpit, back in time at the moment when Felicity had stretched out her hand for the drink. Those few moments had become fixed in the time-consciousness of his mind, and he went over and over them.

Funny that it should have worked out exactly like that. What was the saying—the time and the place and the loved one altogether. He caught himself up at that . . . the loved one . . . Felicity gone! That was an aspect he had not thought of. Steady, he thought. He had to switch his mind swiftly from it.

She had been sitting there, curled up on the wide stern of the launch, steering. In the saloon the others were playing bridge. He had given them a drink and then brought out the bottle to give Felicity one. They had not spoken. They were weary of talking, both of them; weary, and, in his case at least, worn out. He had said everything he could say, pleaded, used every argument he could think of. And he knew then that there was no changing her. Her mind was made up. She really would leave him.

Nobody knew, of course. Everything very proper and private. No fuss. What would they say when they knew?

He heard them in imagination: 'Felicity—left Dyke? Never!' 'Good lor', they seemed to get on like a house on fire.' 'Poor old Dyke!' 'Silly ass, ought to give her a good hiding. That'd bring her to her senses.' 'Gone off with another man.' 'Well women get queer when they see middle-age coming. Game for anything.' And then Caroline's voice soaring in a crescendo of offended decency, 'I'll not have you being coarse.'

All the talking had been done over the last few days. There was nothing more to say. There was nothing he could say that

7

would have expressed the mixture of anger, sorrow and wounded pride which he felt. If she had died he would have been devastated, but that would have been unadulterated sorrow. He would have been left his pride.

And then as they passed the one spot on the river where noise reigned that night, the place where from the high left bank Gather's Mill poured in noisily, at that particular moment she threw back her head and drank off the neat spirit. There had been something purposeful about her drinking—as if she tried to drown a sorrow. There was not time to think; there was no for and against; there was no argument, no weighing of consequences. He did not even turn round to see if any of the bridge players was looking in their direction.

He made the one long step forward that took him completely out of the pool of light on the cockpit floor. As if the moment had been made for this he placed the flat of his hand against her chest. Perched as she was, precariously balanced, with her head thrown back, she fell. The splash was lost in the roar of the emptying mill-leat. He waited to hear her scream, wondering if she would clear her throat of the gin before the water overcame her. If she had cried out he would have done something to save her, though he could not swim any more than she could. They had been alike in that, loving to be on the water, but hating to be in it.

They would have fetched her out somehow, and afterwards he would have apologized. And she would have forgiven him, that was the funny thing. Spite was not one of her failings; she was generous and had a humorous understanding. She'd have said, 'You just loathed me in that moment, Dyke, and wanted to kill me. I can understand how you felt. I'm so sorry.'

Apologizing like that as if it were something *she* had done. He remembered that she was dead. She would never apologize again for being maddening.

8

I've really killed her, he said to himself.

'From dummy, I think,' said Alice coldly.

Frank laughed.

Dyke looked at his party: his sister Caroline; his brother Harold, who had married Alice Craven; Trent Farne, his cousin; and Frank Calvert. Except for Frank they were all related, and again except for Frank, who was in his early thirties, all middle-aged. Trent was almost another brother. In many ways he was closer than a brother. The friendship with Frank was of only a few years' standing, but in that time it had become very close.

Everything was still out of focus. In a way his mind was like this saloon with the smoke swirling thickly under the skylight. Every now and then the smoke would be dragged swiftly to the ventilator and the air would be clear and he would see plainly the grain of the wood in the ceiling, and then fresh smoke from Trent's cigar would swirl up and the air would grow thick again. In the same way his mind seemed to clear so that he saw something frightening, a vista that terrified him, the thousand aspects of the affair which he had not had time to consider. But these nightmares were indistinct and hazy. He was not yet able to hold on to them.

He was waiting for the launch to ground. It ought to run aground at any moment now. But it did not. One by one the players played their cards with slow, deliberate gravity, like actors in a slow-motion film. Dyke's nails clenched into his palms as he waited for the slight jar which never came.

Hell, he thought. We're bound to be at the end of the Reach by now. Why doesn't she go aground? The damn thing can't steer itself round corners, surely. Unless—unless—suppose Felicity were back on board. Suppose she had caught hold of something, a trailing rope or something like that, and had dragged herself in again, and were doing this to punish him . . . teasing . . . laughing at him.

9

He had such a clear impression of this happening that he stooped and looked out of the open saloon door. It would not have caused the least shock of surprise to see her there. He would have known she was mocking him. To have seen her would have been, in a way, a relief. But he could see against the sky only the darker mass of the hull and knew that whatever happened she would never, never sit curled up there again. What a silly idea to have had, anyway. . . .

He fought to regain that almost intoxicated exhilaration that had flooded his being in the first moments. The feeling nearly came—not quite. It was something just outside his grasp.

I'm clever, he told himself. I did that smartly. That was quick. I didn't have to think. I just acted. She deserved it. Really, it was the only solution possible.

All the time he was tensing himself against the jar that would come when the launch ran aground. His nerves tingled with expectancy. And then when it did come, it proved an anti-climax. There was no jar, no sudden lurch. The boat slowed in a dragging, sluggish way. The engine strained a moment like a tired heart struggling against extinction, then it was at a standstill and the lights flicked once and dropped a shade.

The bridge players looked up.

'Now what have we run into?' said Caroline, at once pleased that something had happened, and aggrieved that anything should interrupt the game.

They all sat frozen in an attitude with their cards fanned out in their hands, except Harold who was dummy, waiting to go on again, waiting to resume their game.

'Felicity!' shouted Trent. 'What the devil are you up to?'

'We've gone aground,' said Frank. 'Felicity's fallen asleep. It was that last drink. Ladies and gentlemen, you will go quietly to the lifeboats.'

Dyke had not moved from where he sat. He was at the same time very calm and very excited. Outwardly he showed no feeling. He might have been waiting for Felicity to restart the engine and put it into reverse, for the launch was very well designed as well as very expensive, and she could control it quite well from where she sat—or where she had sat. But he was waiting. . . . Now, he said to himself . . . now . . . now. . . .

Harold had risen from his seat and went past Dyke into the cockpit.

'Felicity,' he said into the night. 'Are you squiffy?'

Now . . . now . . . now. . . .

Harold's voice behind him: 'Where the devil are you? You've not tumbled in . . .'

Then he was at the doorway and his voice had changed.

'She's not there . . .'

Dyke spun round. He could stand no more. He pressed a switch and a small lamp outside the saloon doorway sprang into a thin, pathetic brightness.

They were crowding out of the saloon after him. Caroline still held her unplayed cards in her hand.

'Not there?'

'She must be.'

'She couldn't have fallen out.'

'She couldn't.'

And then Caroline cried out, 'Felicity! Felicity! Where are you?'

Only Dyke did not speak. He sprang into the stern, pressed the starter, and the engine awoke into life. He accelerated loudly before putting it into reverse. For a moment the mud clung to the hull as if loath to let go, then the launch moved sluggishly and almost immediately they were in deep water, swinging rapidly in an arc that threw the rest of the party against each other.

Caroline's empty hand pressed suddenly against her mouth as if forcing back a scream, and her voice came through her fingers. 'She's fallen in! She's fallen in the river!'

'Nonsense,' said Frank. His voice was frightened, swift in denial. 'She'd have shouted. Anyhow, the bank's not far——'

'She can't swim,' said Caroline.

The launch had backed into a half circle and now pointed downstream.

'Switch those blasted lights off,' said Dyke roughly.

Harold ran to the switch and the launch was suddenly dark, except for the small riding-lights, and became again a part of the night and the darkness.

'Frank,' said Dyke quickly. 'I'm going back downstream. There's the spotlight in the bows. You know where it is. Go and work it.'

A long, widening taper of brilliance shot down the river as Frank reached the bows, and the launch moved forward. In place of the murmuring tick-over of their journey upstream the voice of the engine rose urgently.

The others were thrusting against the gunwales, twisting to peer into that lane of light.

'Ease up, Dyke,' called Trent. 'You're going too fast. We might miss——'

The sentence stopped as if he had bitten it off. The pulse of the engine fell.

They stared. Silent now, Caroline still held those absurd bits of pasteboard in her hand, but closed up, not fanned out. On the bank the beam as it swung picked out a pair of lovers in a seat and they turned inwards to each other, clinging more closely, to hide from it. Only for a second the light flicked over them, but Dyke felt as if something in his stomach dropped. If anybody like that had seen . . . Something he had not thought of. There would be so many things he had not thought of. But they could not have seen—nobody could have seen. Not in that darkness . . . and he had even been outside the glow from the saloon.

But the passing glimpse of them had frightened him. He was in some danger. Or he could be. It was as well to be reminded and to remember.

They were opposite the mill-leat and the swirling, entering fall, and then in the broken water below it.

Dyke thought before he spoke. 'It's no good going any further. I handed her a drink, a good way above this.'

They had been watching the river, the banks, intent and anxious. Then Harold spoke for all of them:

'But this is ridiculous. She *couldn't* have fallen over.'

'She'd have screamed,' said Caroline.

Alice, Harold's wife, had thought of something else. 'Suppose she felt faint——'

'She'd have fallen *in*board,' said Trent.

'See if her glass is anywhere,' said Harold, then took his own order, and began striking matches and peering round the well under the stern.

'I can't see it,' he said. 'But there must be *some* explanation. she can't be—— she can't have——'

Yes, thought Dyke. There always must be some other explanation than the one that stares people in the face. The sick must be well, the infirm must become whole, the dead must be alive.

'I'm not going down any further,' he said.

The launch swung round towards the left bank as he spun the little wheel, then back and round to face upstream.

'Any good me going in?' asked Frank. 'I could swim upstream and you follow.'

'No good at all,' said Dyke. 'Plain damn' silly. We'd see nothing but you, and you'd see nothing at all. Work that light. We'll go up slower.'

13

'Suppose she did fall out,' said Alice plaintively. 'If she got to the bank——'

'If she'd reached the bank, she'd have let us know about it,' said Harold. 'She'd have cursed hell out of us. She had a voice.'

The beat of the engine was no more now than the throbbing murmur it had been when they last passed that way.

Alice said to nobody in particular, 'But she can't have . . . she couldn't possibly——' Her voice tailed off mournfully. She wanted to say Felicity couldn't be dead, but because she thought Felicity must be dead she did not want to say it in front of Dyke.

Dyke's smile was hidden in the darkness. He preferred the querulous tactlessness of his sister Caroline to Alice's well-meant ineptitudes.

They were nearly at the top of the Reach again. Patiently, slowly, Frank swung the spotlight, anxious that not a square inch of water should pass untouched by its beam.

'That's where we went aground,' said Dyke. Nobody had spoken since Alice's observation had dried up so uncomfortably, and his voice sounded unnaturally loud.

'Any good going down again?' asked Trent. 'One of us could walk down the path.'

'It's no good going back,' said Dyke. 'I'm going home. We can't do anything here.'

The motor raised its voice as he opened the throttle, but not so loudly that they could not hear the swish of water away from the bow as it cut its way through.

Dyke opened out still more. All at once he was tired. For his companions, though they were his best friends, he felt a momentary anger and contempt. They were both too moved and yet not moved enough. He felt they should have guessed his secret.

The launch rounded the last bend and Riverside Lodge came into sight—they could see it because a few lights had been left burning, and he wished at that moment that he too could fall so easily into the water so that everything could be at an end. At the sight of the house he remembered that he must enter it without Felicity, that she would never walk through its rooms again, that it would never hear her voice. The thought frightened him, and he even cast an eye at the pale swirl of foam in their wake. But that would not be any good. Either Trent or Frank would jump in after him and pull him out. Friends could be a confounded nuisance.

By the time he swung in to the landing stage the mood had passed.

Frank jumped on to the stage with a painter in his hand.

'I'll put her in the boathouse if you like,' he said to Dyke.

'No thanks. Tie her up. She'll come to no harm there. And the police may want to run down the river.'

'Police!' wailed Caroline.

They were all ashore and moving in an untidy huddle through the garden up to the house.

'Naturally,' said Dyke. 'We can hardly keep it to ourselves——'

Caroline snapped. 'This isn't the time to be facetious, Dyke.'

'She might be in the house,' said Alice weakly. 'She could be, you know——'

That was the sort of thing Alice would say. Alice would always proffer the last, unhopeful hope. It was too silly a suggestion even to consider.

Chapter Two

★

CAROLINE took possession as soon as they were in the house. She did this quite naturally, having taken charge often before, since Felicity, who had never been house-conscious or worried about her own position as mistress, had been glad enough, especially when they had guests, to delegate some of her authority to her sister-in-law. And Caroline in possession lost much of her spinsterishness. When she had charge of a house she blossomed, her angularity diminished, she became rounder and warmer. A house in her charge was a comfortable place to live in. She was a woman of whom her friends would say, 'Caroline ought to have married. She's a natural housewife.' Much of her time had been spent with Dyke and Felicity, so that Riverside Lodge was like home to her.

She switched on an electric fire, not for warmth as much as for the sake of the glow, made Harold get drinks out, went to make coffee for Alice who said she wanted something hot.

As she went through the hall she passed Dyke at the telephone. He was standing with the receiver at his ear waiting for his call to be put through. She went up to him and placed a hand on his arm.

'Dyke, I'm *terribly* sorry . . .'

He looked down at her but still with that vacant, waiting expression in his eyes. He was only a couple of years older than she, and at the moment was looking more than his fifty years while she was competent and, even with this tragedy hanging over them, comfortable in her charge.

'Terribly sorry,' she repeated.

He patted the hand on his arm, was about to say something, and then as a voice came over the wire lost contact with her.

'Is Inspector Brayton there?' he asked. 'Mr. Dyke Farne speaking . . . yes, I would rather like to speak to him if you can get him for me.'

He stood waiting. Caroline had gone to the kitchen. Apparently it took them some time to find the Inspector, for it was not until she returned carrying the cup of coffee for Alice that Dyke spoke again.

'Oh, is that you, Inspector? Dyke Farne speaking. Look here, something awful has happened . . .'

When he put down the receiver he realized he had only spoken the truth. It *was* awful. The house without Felicity in it was empty. He could fill it with people, but never again to him would it seem anything but empty. And yet, even if he had not killed her, it would have happened just the same. Wasn't that why he had killed her?

For a moment he stood there alone in the hall before going back to the others. His mind seemed split in two. One part of it was devastated and desolate that she was lost to him without the possibility of her ever returning; the other part rejected what he had done as incredible. He was, unconsciously, listening for her voice, her laugh; waiting for her to come through a doorway or down the stairs. He was not afraid of ghosts. If the wraith of his wife could have come in that moment he would have welcomed it and felt with relief that he had done the right thing. He could share the house with Felicity's ghost easily; what frightened him was the haunting that would have no connection with the living Felicity. Ghosts are better company than memories, he thought.

He looked at himself in the mirror over the hall mantelpiece. He was tall, greying, distinguished in appearance. He did not consciously study himself, but he noted that now he looked drawn and weary. There were dark shadows under his eyes. It struck him that that was exactly how he should look. He was a man who had lost his wife in tragic circumstances. He smiled slightly at his reflection. Felicity should have been there to say mockingly: 'Aren't you clever, Dyke!' He squared his shoulders. He *was* clever.

'I've poured a drink for you,' said Harold when he went into the lounge. He indicated the glass on the side table. 'Didn't put any soda in it Left that to you.'

Dyke picked up the glass, 'I'll have this one without soda, I think.'

It was a stiff drink, but he finished it in two gulps. It did something for him. He had slipped back into his rôle of bereavement. It did not escape him the way they all watched him while he was not looking at them. *How is Dyke taking it? Poor old Dyke! What a devil of a thing to happen.* And so back to—*But how did it happen?*

He picked up the bottle. 'We'd better have another, I think.'

'Not for me,' said Alice, sipping her coffee. Alice held a tiny, inadequate handkerchief in one hand. It was evident that she kept it ready for dabbing at her eyes when the time came. Not that her tears would be insincere. They were all fond enough of Felicity. There was no pretence in their sorrow.

'I've got all I want,' said Caroline, showing a half-filled glass. 'It isn't that I don't need it, but I get tight so easily.'

Dyke did not answer either of them. He went on filling the men's glasses. None of them protested or refused.

Dyke was the eldest of the Farnes. Caroline, at forty-eight, was the second of them. In her youth she had been good-looking, but she had never married. Dyke and Harold believed this was due to the fact that she spoke her mind too freely. The trouble was not merely that she did not suffer fools gladly, but that she did not suffer them kindly, and her interpretation of folly was wide and embracing. She was devoted to Dyke. Ever since childhood he had been her hero.

She had a wide circle of friends, male as well as female, who respected her if they did not always like her. She believed herself to be a natural leader and translated this belief into operation whenever opportunity presented itself, and making opportunity when it did not.

Harold, at forty-five, was a slighter edition of his brother, Dyke. He was prosperous, and ambitious to become more prosperous still. Curiously, he was still deeply in love with his wife. Alice had been beautiful, and in Frank's eyes she had lost none of her beauty. Married to a less thrusting man she would have been rather sweet and kind, but under the influence of the Farnes she had become ineffective and something of a nonentity. Caroline often referred to her as 'Poor Alice.' They had two children. Basil, the boy was in his last term at a public school—he was a year younger than Dyke's only son, Michael, and two years younger than his sister, Elizabeth, who in spite of a share in a cosmetic business in London was already very much in the marriage market.

Trent Farne was a first cousin. He was the same age as Harold, and unmarried. Like the rest of the family he was well-to-do, but in a quieter way. Trent's money seemed more of an accidental circumstance than a natural part of his life. He was quiet, never talkative unless he had something to say, and they were all fond of him. He had spent so much of his life in the company of the others that he was more like another brother than a cousin.

The Farnes had met Frank Calvert three years before at a fashionable Riviera resort where they had all been spending a holiday. Frank's wife had left him and he had been forced, much against his will, because he still loved her, to give her a divorce, and he was unhappy. They had taken him under their wings, and as he regained his spirits a friendship had grown up. A lack of sympathy with the other holidaymakers helped to cement the friendship. Also, they were slowing down into middle-age and he was still young. There was, when he forgot his troubles, a gaiety about him, something still boyish, that appealed to them, and the friendship continued after they had all returned home. At Riverside Lodge where the Farnes spent most of the summer when they were not abroad, he became a privileged visitor, came and went as he pleased. The Farnes were like that. Their friends were very close or very distant. And very few were very close.

They said nothing now as they drank the whisky Dyke had poured for them. It was he who spoke first.

'Brayton's coming over,' he said. He finished his drink and put his glass down rather hard on the table. 'I offered to meet him at the river, but he said he's going to send some of his men there, and he'd rather see us here.'

Caroline spoke in a decided, acid voice. 'I do not at all like this *police* business, as if it were something . . . something unsavoury.'

'Good heavens, Caroline, be your age!' said Harold. 'There's been an accident, hasn't there? Of course he had to let Brayton know at once.'

Alice put down her coffee cup, and dabbed at an eye. 'We don't know for certain there has been an accident.'

'The trouble is, we do,' said Trent.

'But——'

'It's no good looking for any other explanations, Alice,' said Frank. 'One moment Felicity's in the launch, the next moment she's gone. She was sitting just where it was easy to fall overboard——'

'But why *should* she——?'

'My dear Alice,' said Caroline coldly. 'All this is very distressing for Dyke. You know as well as any of us——' She looked at Dyke uncertainly.

'Let's not talk about it for the moment,' said Dyke. The

whisky had dulled his brain a little, and his misery was lessened, but this lessening made him more wary. He was safe, of course; he knew he was safe. But it would be so easy to say something stupid, something that it would be awkward to explain. There must be no suspicions. No suspicions ever. There was no reason why there should be. Unless he made any. Felicity receded into the background. It was himself he would have to think of for the present.

'We won't talk about it,' agreed Trent. 'But you'd better let Michael know, Dyke.'

'Time enough,' he said.

The funny thing was he had forgotten about Michael. He had forgotten about everybody, except Felicity and himself. There was Felicity's mother, too. She was over seventy. This was going to be a shock for her. He had a sudden feeling of sadness. What had happened—something that had been between himself and Felicity—must now begin to affect all sorts of other people. Something between themselves—only it could not remain between themselves.

As he thought about Michael, he felt uncomfortable. It did not seem incongruous that, having killed his wife, he should have this feeling of discomfort. At twenty his son was further from him than he had ever been. So far as Michael could be said to be attached to either of them, he was Felicity's, though she too, he knew, had often not understood him. The boy had gone his own way. When he left his public school he said he did not mean to go to the university. Not that he did not want to go, but plainly that he did not intend to. He had become involved with an artistic set, who lived, it seemed to Dyke, by taking in one another's washing. They wrote poetry that few read and still fewer understood, or composed music that nobody wanted to hear, or painted pictures that never represented the object painted. Michael could not write poetry or compose music or paint

21

pictures (Dyke thought that neither could any of his friends do any of these things for that matter) but he was connected with a film company that made films nobody wanted to see, so he remained well in the swim. He was an asset to his friends. Besides having the right ideas he also had money, and he was known and accepted by, and moved among, the right people. And the right people, however deplorable their views on art, could be useful at times. Dyke hoped that when he grew older he would turn his experience to some use and make money out of it, so he neither criticized, nor protested against what seemed to him a waste of time.

Michael as a baby had been all right; Michael as a small boy had been the grandest fun; Michael as a big boy had been at least understandable. But Michael as a young man was incomprehensible. To his father he was, at any rate. But Dyke had shrugged his shoulders, told himself wryly that, after all, sons are individuals separate from their parents and must be allowed to develop in their own way. But as he was fond of his son he hoped always for a new and more sympathetic development.

He supposed Michael loved him. He was sure the boy loved his mother. He had grown away from her, but in his way he was devoted to her, and could even, on the rare occasions when he was in an expansive mood, talk to her about his work. To himself, he was respectful—considering the size of his allowance it was the least he could be—mildly affectionate at times, and a little less mildly contemptuous of him as a Philistine and one whose higher intellect was completely undeveloped.

Dyke accepted the position philosophically, and now and then, remembering the chubby boy with whom he had played on summer sands and romped at bedtimes and sailed model yachts, felt sad that children could not remain perpetually below the age of ten.

He wondered would Felicity's death bring him and Michael

closer together, or would it be the excuse for his son to drift even further away. Whatever happened he had robbed him of something. And Felicity would no longer be a connecting link between them.

Remembering Michael, he felt vaguely that he had been cheated. One should not have the chance to kill somebody without an opportunity of weighing up all the arguments for and against.

He really did not know what he was going to say to Michael.

It's an awful business, he thought, and was appalled to realize how awful it was. For a moment he was frightened, then he packed the fear back into a corner of his mind. He imagined he was dismissing it, but it remained there, hardly realized, in the background, all the time.

There was the sound of a car swinging round the drive to the front of the house. The house faced the river, and the drive off the road made a wide sweep round it.

He put his glass down.

'There's Brayton,' he said. 'I'll go and let him in.'

They had no servants in the house. The two women who looked after them when they were at the Lodge lived in the village and went home every evening.

The coming of the Inspector gave them something fresh to consider. Alice moved her empty cup from the edge of the table where she had placed it, to another part where it was less in the way. Caroline altered the position of a chair slightly and patted some cushions into shape. Frank got up from where he sat and took another chair further from the fire. There was a sort of general post and they were taking up their new positions as Dyke brought in the visitor.

Inspector Brayton, who knew them all, nodded to the men, and spoke to Alice and Caroline. He was matter-of-fact in his manner, which made Alice stare at him reproachfully. She did not realize that he had to be casual. It was his work, even if on this occasion it was somewhat different from the everyday run of parking offences and petty burglaries, and he could not have afforded to indulge in dramatics even had he wished to.

Harold poured him a drink and took it to him.

'Thanks, Mr. Farne,' said Brayton.

'This is a rotten business,' said Harold.

Brayton had already expressed his sympathy to Dyke in the hall, so he only nodded at Harold's remark. He looked at Dyke.

'I suppose there's no chance of any mistake?'

Alice said eagerly, 'That's what I keep saying——' but Dyke interrupted her.

'Not a chance. How could there be? She was sitting on the stern. I went into the saloon. The launch ran aground at the end of Masterman's Reach—and she'd gone.'

Brayton had been drinking while Dyke spoke. Now he pursed up his mouth, looking very solemn. He nodded.

'We'd better go down there in a minute,' he said. 'But I've sent some of my men along. And Carstairs, our surgeon——'

'Ryder's our doctor when we're here,' said Dyke.

'Is he? Well, he's on holiday, anyway. So long as we do have a doctor. In case——' He stopped, then went on again. 'I thought I'd better come here first. To find out exactly what happened. You can't talk properly out there on the river bank in the dark. And I'm afraid there's nothing much we can do before day. You looked before you came away, of course?'

'We went down and up again,' put in Harold. 'With the spotlight on. But it was hopeless.'

'It would be,' said Brayton. He took a swift look at Dyke. 'I'm sorry to be so pessimistic, Mr. Farne——'

'It's all right,' said Dyke.

'She'd have sunk, naturally——'

Alice gave a gasp, as if this were news to her.

24

'Tell me what happened,' said Brayton. He was not looking at any of them.

'We were playing bridge——' Harold began.

'No, your brother, please.'

'I beg your pardon!'

'He was the last to see her alive—unless she still is alive, and I'm afraid there's no chance of that. He may have been more observant than the rest of you as he wasn't playing cards.'

'We were playing *bridge*,' said Caroline in the voice of one correcting a major error.

Brayton looked at her, puzzled. 'Yes, I know.'

Dyke spoke quickly. 'They were playing in the saloon. Except Mr. Calvert, there. He was looking on.'

Brayton glanced towards Frank, who nodded. 'That's right.'

'But I suppose you were following the game?'

'I was.'

'Closely?'

Frank grinned. 'Fairly closely. There was a chance Caroline would lose quite a packet, and since she hates losing I was interested.'

'Well, upon my word!' exclaimed Caroline.

Brayton motioned to Dyke to continue.

'I'd been in and out of the saloon.'

'Talking to your wife?'

Something in Dyke's stomach seemed to tighten up. That packed-away fear surged, then receded again. Not that Brayton was suspicious. But he would be soon.

'We didn't talk much.'

'She didn't say anything that would—explain what happened?'

'Good heavens, no!'

'Perfectly normal?'

'Perfectly.'

Suicide? Well, of course, Brayton would have to consider that.

Dyke's mind worked swiftly, trying to see if it would be a good suspicion to foster. But he abandoned the idea without even considering it.

'I poured some drinks.' He gave a vague glance round at the others. 'They all had one. Then I took one out to my wife.'

Brayton nibbled at the corner of his lip.

'Yes?' he said.

What's he thinking, Dyke asked himself.

'Then I went back into the saloon.'

'Immediately?'

'Practically. I—may have stood there a minute. I can't remember very clearly.'

'Did your wife have her drink before you went back into the saloon?'

Careful, warned Dyke. Careful. But what the hell! She'd had a few drinks already. Can't catch me there.

He knew quite well that Brayton was not trying to catch him. All Brayton wanted was a complete picture of what happened. That was his business. Only don't make him suspicious. Don't say anything, not *anything* to start him thinking. . . .

Dyke was standing there, his forehead wrinkled as if trying to remember.

'I really don't know,' he said. 'She may have taken a sip——'

Trent laughed. 'What, Felicity? Felicity didn't sip. She took her gin like medicine.'

Dyke was angry with Trent. Trent was only trying to help, but why the devil couldn't he keep his mouth shut? No harm done, but it showed you how careful you had to be—just when you were trying to be most careful. Unless Trent . . . He did not look, but he could see Trent smiling in his queer solemn way. Felicity hadn't told him who the man was. She had said that was immaterial at the moment. Could it have been Trent she was going to clear out with? Trent had always been fond of her. He knew

26

that. He took it for granted. But how fond? And now turning suspicion on him to punish him . . . but how ridiculous! Trent couldn't want to punish him, because he didn't know.

But the suspicion refused to die entirely. Punish him perhaps for having Felicity . . .

Brayton was looking at him.

'That's quite right,' he said. 'She wouldn't have sipped. She'd have drunk it straight off—unless it had been a very long one. I really don't know what happened—it was dark'—he was going to get his story right out; neither Brayton nor he should have time to think. He passed a hand over his forehead—'all I know is that I handed her the drink and a minute later I went into the saloon and stood watching them playing bridge——'

'You had the bottle in your hand,' said Trent. 'I remember looking up and seeing that.'

Anger again surged up against Trent. Why doesn't he keep his mouth shut? If he saw so much, let him tell it. What's he doing?

'You're quite right,' he said. 'I put it down on the table.' He looked at Brayton. 'We were on Masterman's Reach, as I told you. Then we ran aground. Somebody shouted to my wife to ask what she thought she was doing.'

'I did,' said Trent.

'There was no answer, so we all went out to see what was the matter. And of course she wasn't there . . .'

'You were pouring drinks from the bottle?' asked Brayton.

'Yes.'

They were looking at one another and Brayton raised his eyebrows. He and Dyke would hardly have claimed to be friends, but they knew each other well and were friendly acquaintances. That lift of the eyebrows was as good as a question.

Dyke shook his head slowly. 'We thought of the glass, by the way. We couldn't find it.' He added, 'She was perfectly sober.' Caroline made a clucking sound of disapproval.

27

'I didn't imagine otherwise,' said Brayton, but obviously, even if without meaning to, he had. That was what he *had* wondered. 'It would be one explanation, of course. But it isn't the real one.'

And the real one they couldn't know, and never should. Unless—— Suppose Trent *were* the man—and knew how he and Felicity had argued this—and were now suspicious?

'What a ridiculous thing to say,' said Caroline. 'Why, I've never known Felicity to show she'd had a drink—ever.'

Brayton revoked his earlier statement. 'I only wanted to make sure.' He caught Caroline's indignant stare. 'There must be *some* explanation, Miss Farne.'

'Obviously,' agreed Caroline. 'Felicity overbalanced and fell backwards.'

Brayton said slowly, 'Could anyone—a swimmer, say—have reached up and pulled her into the river?'

'Impossible. The launch rides too high out of the water for that.'

But now the suggestion was made that a murder might have been committed. Dyke's mouth suddenly felt dry. He took his glass over to the syphon, splashed in some soda water, and drank.

'Did any of you hear anything?' As Brayton asked the question he looked round from one to the other.

'I told you,' said Dyke. 'We were passing the old mill-leat. It makes a lot of noise.'

'That could explain not hearing a splash, I agree. But people falling into the water don't sink without a sound. They shout.'

'Suppose,' said Alice quickly, 'suppose she fainted?'

'Fainted!' Caroline sniffed. 'She never fainted in her life.'

'There's a first time for everything,' said Trent.

Every time Trent spoke, Dyke felt a rush of anger as if he already knew Trent was the man.

'That *might* be what happened,' Alice went on. 'If she fainted——'

'You're being silly, darling,' said Harold. 'You know quite well Felicity wasn't the fainting sort.'

'But as Trent says——'

Harold had gone over to her and now sat on the arm of her chair. 'Quiet, dear. Making up explanations won't help. You're only trying to get it tidied up in your own mind. It doesn't get us anywhere.'

'It's the one thing I can't make out,' puzzled Brayton. 'That absence of any sound at all. It's—it's very mysterious.'

He looked at Alice, then at Caroline, then at Dyke. But he was not seeing any of them. His mind was looking for something, calling up first one explanation, rejecting it, then another. . . . Of course, if there had been violence—a blow. Well, he'd know about that when they found her. Because of the shape of the launch she'd be bound to fall clear. There wouldn't be a mark on her she could have got from the boat. So that was all right.

'The doctor may be able to help us,' he said, looking through them. He had now reached a post-mortem, worrying in case they did not recover the body quickly. . . .

There was a drop of whisky left in his glass and he drank it.

'Have some more,' said Dyke, reaching for the bottle.

'No more,' he said quickly, then added, 'Thank you very much.' He got up. 'I'd better be getting down to the river. My men may have—something to report. Though I don't think—until it's lighter——'

'I'm coming with you,' said Dyke.

Brayton looked at him doubtfully. 'Are you sure you want to? There's no need, you know.'

'We can go on the launch,' said Dyke.

'I'll come too,' said Trent.

Frank got up. 'You'll be staying here?' he said to Harold.

Harold looked down at Alice. She had taken his hand in hers, and in a way her action had made him a prisoner. It was as if she had made her claim on him. She, or going down to the river. And she had first claim.

'One of us had better stay,' said Harold. 'You three go.'

'I don't mind being alone,' said Caroline. She corrected herself. 'Alone with Alice, I mean.'

Alice did not speak.

'There's nothing I could do,' said Harold. 'I'll stay here.'

Chapter Three

*

DYKE took control of the launch. He swung it into the stream and it moved quietly, the engine smooth and almost soundless, as if it had been urged by somebody not to make a noise.

'Go up and switch on that light, Frank,' said Dyke. 'We'll be able to see where the Inspector's men are.'

Frank went forward, Trent stood at one side near the saloon door, Brayton was close to Dyke in the stern. The whole affair now seemed to Dyke unreal. His earlier excitement had worn off. He could not realize that Felicity was dead, that there were policemen on the river bank searching for her body, that he was helping a police inspector in his enquiry.

The night was warm. Straight ahead the beam from the lamp in the bows slashed the water into a thousand segments of light, but when he looked to right or left or behind him, the trees lining the river paths loomed heavily against a sky almost as dark as they. It was so quiet. When he turned to look at the trees he had an impression that they leaned forward a little like silent spectators anxious to see what was going to happen.

Nothing was going to happen, he assured himself.

He was standing in the well as he steered. Brayton looked at the wide transom behind him.

'What made your wife perch up there?' he asked.

'She just liked sitting there,' answered Dyke. 'She must have sat there hundreds of times.'

Brayton made a noise—something between a cough and a grunt.

After a pause he said, 'Silly place to sit, really.'

'Oh, I don't know. As I tell you, she sat there quite often.'

Brayton's voice held a note of petulance. Perhaps he had just remembered that he should be in bed now, and was losing his sleep. 'People aren't careful enough when they're on the water. Not *careful*.'

The light shone on a group of men by the bank.

'There are your people,' said Dyke.

Brayton sounded businesslike again. 'Can you run close in? I want to speak to them.'

'I'll beach her. It's soft just there.'

'You know the river well, don't you?'

Dyke searched the statement for a hidden meaning, but either it did not exist or he failed to find it.

'I suppose I do.'

'You don't want to get stuck.'

'I shan't get stuck. I'll just put her nose on the mud gently. There's not enough current to move her and the engine will take her off without any trouble. We're only coasting, you know.'

There were four policemen, one a sergeant, standing at the edge of the water, staring into the beam of light. The electric torches they carried seemed faded and yellow in contrast. As the launch came in nearer they shaded their eyes with their hands or turned away. Frank swung the lamp round so that it no longer shone directly on them.

Brayton had gone forward to the bows and now he announced his presence.

'I'm here, sergeant. Have you found anything?'

'Nothing, sir. We were wondering who it was. Thought it might be somebody bringing you along.'

The launch's engine went softly into reverse as she touched the mud, and she grounded gently and stopped. The stillness after the engine was more an absence of vibration than of sound.

'Want to go ashore, Inspector?' asked Frank. 'There's a plank somewhere. I shouldn't jump, if I were you.'

'I've no intention of jumping. And you needn't bother about the plank. I can say all I've got to say from here.'

The sergeant had come closer. He was only a couple of yards from Brayton and he recognized him in the diffused, reflected light.

'No luck at all, sir,' he reported. 'Not much chance till daylight.'

'Seen anybody?'

'There was a courting couple about when we came down, but they've gone. Not a soul besides. It's late.'

As if the reminder had caused it, Brayton stifled a yawn.

'Yes, I know.'

'Bascombe here, he knows the river pretty well. He says there's not much current except where the old mill stream comes in, and there's weed well out into the river at the next bend. I expect we'll find her stuck there somewhere, soon's it's daylight.'

Brayton coughed noisily. 'Mr. Farne's here, Hamilton.'

'Oh!' said the sergeant. 'Sorry, sir.'

There was an awkward pause. Then Dyke spoke from the stern:

'It's all right, sergeant.'

'Thank you, sir,' said the sergeant. He apologized again. 'Sorry, I'm sure.'

Brayton lowered his voice to speak to the sergeant, though every word he spoke was perfectly audible.

'Two men had better stay on duty here until daylight, sergeant.'

'Very good, sir.'

'You'll get the dragging tackle and bring it back then. Better have a couple more men.'

'I'll bring Nash and Breene, sir. They're both good swimmers. You never know.'

'All right. I'll be back, but you can ring me if there's anything to report.'

'I'll do that, sir.'

'That's all.'

The sergeant stepped back, and Brayton went to Dyke where he waited in the stern.

'We may as well go. There's nothing we can do for the present.'

'Are you coming back with us?' asked Dyke.

'Yes. My car's at your place.'

'Oh, yes. I forgot that.'

He had started the engine, and a moment later they were returning upstream.

They were very much in the same positions they had been, coming down. Brayton spoke to Dyke.

'Don't hurry. There's something I want to work out. I wonder would you ask your cousin to switch on the saloon lights. And have that spotlight off. Get things as near like they were when—before your wife fell in.'

'Trent,' said Dyke, 'put on the light in the saloon, and you and Frank go in and sit down where you were for bridge. Frank, switch off first, will you?' He looked at Brayton who was now at his side. 'I'll have to slow down a good bit. There's enough light from the saloon windows to see the banks. It's plenty to steer by. Especially when you know the way.'

'Couldn't you run into somebody?' asked Brayton. 'Punt or skiff, or anything like that?'

'Not unless *they* were damned careless. There's room for a dozen boats abreast, and anybody can see us. We're rather fond of the river at night and I never did care for dashing about like a car with whacking great headlamps.'

Frank and Trent had gone into the lighted saloon.

'Do you want us anywhere special?' said Frank.

'No. Anywhere. Round the card-table if you like,' said Brayton. 'I only want to get the hang of things.'

He went to the raised thwart and sat on it, his legs dangling inboard. The saloon looked bright and warm, but its lights did not give much illumination, except indirectly, to the rest of the launch. Dyke and the Inspector, for all practical purposes, were in darkness.

'From here I can't see anyone in the saloon,' said Brayton. 'This is where your wife was sitting, isn't it?'

'Somewhere about there,' said Dyke. He was a little angry, and again a little frightened. There was sure to be some small point he had overlooked that would betray him. When he was on guard like this he forgot Felicity; he was thinking only of himself. He was sure there was a catch somewhere in the Inspector's questions. He said, 'She had her legs curled up on the ledge, you know.'

'Yes, quite.' Brayton was following a train of thought of his own. 'I can't see them, so they can't see me.'

'They would if they moved a little,' said Dyke. He spoke so that the two inside could hear him.

'Will you two try to see us without moving from your seats.'

Both Trent and Frank leaned forward and looked through the doorway.

'I can see you,' said Frank. 'Not distinctly. I can see you, knowing you're there.'

'The light's in my eyes,' said Trent. 'I expect Frank's eyes are better than mine.'

Frank came out to the door end of the saloon and leaned against it.

35

'I can see you all right from here,' he said.

'You aren't in a lighted room now,' said Trent.

'No, that's true.'

'All right,' said Brayton. 'Thanks very much.'

'I'll have the saloon lights off, and yours on again, please Frank,' said Dyke, and the engine purred a little more loudly as he increased their speed.

Brayton spoke to Dyke after a short pause. 'I have to get as complete a picture as I can,' he explained, then added sombrely, 'for the inquest, you know.'

'Of course,' agreed Dyke.

'It beats me, though. Beats me completely.'

'What does?'

'How she could fall overboard without making a sound.' He pondered a minute. 'If she fell out as you passed Gather's Mill you might not hear a splash. But why didn't she cry out?'

Dyke had no answer to the question. It was a factor which, until Brayton first mentioned it, he had not considered.

'Anybody falling into the water cries out,' said Brayton. 'Even suicides do.'

'You can dismiss that idea,' said Dyke.

Frank and Trent had come out of the saloon and had moved towards the forward end of it. They were smoking, and their cigarettes glowed brightly. In front of them Frank's head was outlined against the light he sat by.

'There are two other possibilities,' said Brayton.

'And they are?'

'That she slipped quietly into the river of her own accord.'

'That won't do, either,' said Dyke. 'She couldn't swim.'

'No. I know.'

'It wasn't suicide. I've told you.'

'I'm sorry, Mr. Farne,' said Brayton. 'I've got to consider every possible way it could have happened. She could have

36

gone over without thinking of suicide and without meaning to swim.'

'I don't follow.'

'If, for instance, somebody had been handy with a boat, either for her to get into, or to pick her up.'

'Ridiculous!' said Dyke. 'I'd have seen it, anyhow. Why on earth should she?'

'No *reason*. Only she could——'

'I don't think you need consider that, either.'

'If we don't find her body we'll have to consider it.'

Dyke was trying to see how this helped him, but he could not imagine that it was any help at all. But he knew he was not thinking very clearly. He was tired, the whisky he had drunk had made him drowsy. His eyeballs pricked and the lids felt hot and heavy.

'If my wife did a thing like that it would mean either that she was playing a practical joke, or was running away. If she'd been playing a joke we'd have known about it before this, and if she'd wanted to run away she could have done it in twenty easier ways. And I don't think for one minute that she did want to run away.'

That was not the truth. He had spoken again without thinking.

'I'm not suggesting she did. She could have done.'

'She'd have chosen a less spectacular way of going, I think.'

'Probably.'

'What's your other possibility?'

'The other is that she was unconscious when she fell.'

'You mean fainted——'

'I don't. She could have fainted, I know——'

'I doubt it——'

'But if she had, I think she'd have fallen into the boat, not out of it. No. What I mean is that somebody might have struck her.'

The two men were looking at one another in the darkness, their faces palely distinguishable now they had become accustomed to the subdued light. Dyke's drowsiness vanished. He forgot his tired, burning eyes and the ache in his limbs. The one mercy was that Brayton could not see his face. He was sure the alarm he felt must be written plainly on it. His mouth felt dry, and a few seconds passed before he could trust himself to speak evenly.

'What do you mean, Inspector?'

'Just that. Somebody could have hit her with something—causing her to fall into the river.'

Dyke's mind was screaming the enquiry: You mean I could have done it. But he forced himself to be calm.

His voice was not pleasant, though. 'I'm the only person who could have done it.'

Brayton was obviously taken aback. 'I wasn't thinking that, Mr. Farne. That would be nonsense, of course.'

He meant it, too. Dyke was so relieved he wanted to laugh. Or cry. He was not sure which. And then he wished he had not spoken. That's how you started people being suspicious.

'What I meant,' Brayton went on, 'is that someone might have been hidden somewhere in the boat——'

'Impossible,' said Dyke.

'You're sure?'

'Absolutely certain. It was daylight when we went out. We went down the river for a cruise. As a matter of fact it was at my wife's suggestion that we went. She loved the river—and this launch.' He broke off remembering. Poor Felicity! Why had she to insist on going out to-night? The others would have been satisfied to play bridge at home. But she knew there would be so few more of these evenings cruising on the river, and she was making the most of her opportunities. And so she had prepared the way for her death. It was ironic.

He went on. 'We were, one or another of us, all over the launch. It's impossible for anybody to have hidden. They didn't start to play bridge until we were coming back; until it was dark——'

'I see,' said Brayton. He sounded a little unhappy about it all. Not unhappy, thought Dyke, because a woman had died, but because he could not work out precisely the way she had died.

'I know it's accidental death,' he went on, after a pause. 'It's such a queer accident, that's all.'

'To you,' said Dyke.

'To anybody, I should think.'

'To us,' said Dyke quietly, 'it's a tragedy.'

And that, he thought, was the truth, not hypocrisy. To him more than any of them. Did all murderers feel like this, with remorse and fear of detection all mixed up so that you did not know where one ended and the other began?

Brayton apologized. 'I'm sorry,' he said. 'It's my job to see how a thing like this happened. When I can't see it, I get worried. But I'm sorry about Mrs. Farne. Honestly sorry. I mean that.'

'Thank you,' said Dyke. 'I quite understand.'

They were approaching the house and the landing stage.

'I'll let you know immediately there's anything to report,' said Brayton.

'Come into the house and have a drink?'

'Not now, thanks. There'll be a few formalities to fix up, and I want to go back to my men as soon as it's light. I shall probably see you tomorrow.'

'To-day,' said Dyke.

'You're right. I was forgetting. To-day.'

'Let me know if you want the launch any time,' said Dyke.

'That's an idea. I will.'

Frank had jumped ashore with the mooring rope, and they did not talk any more.

Chapter Four

*

WHEN they got into the hall the house had that intense quietness that marks the house of sleep.

'The others appear to have gone up,' said Trent. He stifled a yawn. 'I suppose we can't do any more to-night. May as well go to bed.'

'Yes, better get some rest,' agreed Dyke. His tiredness had returned again in the warm house. He longed for the others to go. He wanted to be alone.

They all looked weary. All, that was, except Frank. But Frank had more than ten years' advantage of them, and besides, he was not affected in quite the same way. Dyke, at that moment, was glad to have Frank there. His presence gave a reminder of normality. He was a reminder that nothing, no mood, no emotion lasted. In a year's time to Frank the happenings of this night would have become a faint memory, only recalled briefly at odd intervals. Perhaps in two years, in three, the same would apply to him.

Trent walked towards the stairs. He yawned again, noisily this time.

'Good night,' he said.

Although he yawned and went towards the stairs as if on his way to bed, he kept looking at Dyke as if he wanted to speak, but he glanced at Frank. Frank did not move; he had not even noticed Trent's uneasiness. Dyke was glad he stayed. Whatever Trent had to say, he did not want to hear it. During the last hour his suspicions of him had increased. He was not sure he could trust himself not to say more than he wanted to if they were alone together. Perhaps Trent was not the man Felicity had meant to go away with, but in his heart he felt he was.

'Good night, Dyke,' said Trent.

'Good night.'

Frank waited until they heard the door of Trent's room close before he spoke.

'Look here, Dyke, would you like me to leave in the morning?'

Dyke looked at him in surprise. 'My dear chap, why should you?'

'Well, I thought perhaps—people about—time like this——'

'Don't disturb yourself about that,' said Dyke.

'Of course, if there's any way I can help——'

'It's pretty rotten for you.'

'It's not that.'

'Do you want to go?'

'No,' said Frank bluntly. 'I don't.'

'Then stay. You'll help just by being here.' Dyke smiled. 'Families can be—a bit overpowering, even when you're fond of them.'

'All right, I'll stay,' said Frank. 'Thanks, Dyke.'

'Don't thank me. I thank you.'

'I don't need to say how sorry I am——'

'No, you don't.' He looked at Frank, grateful for the sympathy and warmed by it, and to his surprise Frank's mouth was trembling. He knew the younger man was fond of them—they had been his closest friends—but it was only now he realized how much. His feeling for Frank at that moment was what he might have felt for Michael—had Michael been receptive of such emotions. Frank's distress strengthened him, made him the comforter rather than the comforted.

'I should go up, if I were you,' he said. 'Like a drink first?'

41

'No, nothing, thanks. Good night.'

'Good night, old chap,' said Dyke.

Only it wasn't a good night. It was a hell of a night.

He went into the lounge, switching the light on as he went in. He looked round doubtfully. He was thoroughly weary. His nerves, losing their tautness, cried out for rest. He too had better go up. Then his eye caught the tray of drinks. He might as well have a final one. Help him to relax.

He crossed to the tray and poured out a stiff whisky. As he was adding soda his ear caught a sound from the hall, and then Caroline came into the room. She was in a long white dressing-gown of some thick material, and her hair hung over her shoulders in two plaits. She looked younger. Her face was placid and at rest. He knew why, too. She had him to herself for a while, and always when that happened—though it had happened seldom enough during the years of his marriage—she shed some of her self-protective shell of angry capability and became softer and younger.

He smiled at her. 'Not asleep then, Caro?'

'I was waiting for you, Dyke. I heard the others come up. Since you didn't follow, I came down.'

'You ought to be resting.'

'So ought you.' There was a fierce protectiveness in the quick way she spoke. She was looking at his drink. 'Pour me a small one.'

When he brought it to her she sat on the wide arm of a chair. 'I rang up Michael,' she said.

He was conscious of a rush of gratitude. This was a duty he had flinched from. If he'd known how deeply Michael's feelings went he wouldn't have minded so much. He wished he understood Michael better. Perhaps he'd get to know him better now.

'You didn't want to do it, Dyke, did you?'

'I loathed having to do it.'

42

'I guessed that. Anyhow, it's done.'

'How——' Dyke stared down into his glass. 'How did he take it?'

'The telephone is a rather unemotional instrument,' said Caroline. 'It's use in drama hasn't made it dramatic. I broke the news as gently as I could.'

'I know—I know——'

'I can only answer for my end of the line. He'll be down in the morning.'

'I see.'

'He said don't bother to meet him. He'll get a taxi over from the station.'

'Right.'

Caroline finished her drink, and then put the glass down and came across to put a hand on his arm.

'Michael will be all right, Dyke. Don't worry about him.'

'I'm not worrying about him.'

'But you do worry about not understanding him better, don't you?'

He was not surprised when she said that. If anyone understood Michael it was his aunt. Perhaps that was because there were no close emotional ties between them. They expected nothing of one another. This father-and-son relationship was the devil. You could understand other men's sons, but never your own.

'Don't worry,' said Caroline again, 'everything will be all right.'

Yes, for Caroline everything would be all right. She would shed a few tears for Felicity and then settle down to making herself indispensable to him. He would be for her the husband she had never had and the children she had never borne. Better than that, for there would not be between them the strange antipathetic relationship she had sensed between him and Michael. He was not sure the prospect pleased him. He remembered Frank.

43

'Frank offered to clear out in the morning,' he said.

She looked at him quickly. 'It might be a good idea——'

'How ridiculous! He's—he's like one of the family.'

She used Frank's own words. 'At a time like this——'

'At a time like this,' he said, 'it's nice to have your friends about you.'

'It won't be much fun for him,' she said.

'It won't be much fun for anybody. This isn't a time we're expecting fun——'

'Dyke,' she said quickly. 'Let him go. It will be much better——'

'You don't like Frank much, do you?' he asked.

'I like him, but——'

'No. I don't think you ever have liked him.'

'Listen, Dyke,' she said, and she was unexpectedly earnest. 'I think it would be far wiser if Frank did go. He has nothing to do here—it's only spoiling his holiday—and we'll be better off without strangers for a while——'

'He isn't a stranger. He's my friend.'

'I think he should go,' she said. She was persistent, and it was not like her to be persistent in such a matter. 'Honestly, just for the present, I wish you'd get rid of him——'

He interrupted her. 'My dear Caroline!' and she stopped suddenly. 'I've told him I'll be glad for him to stay, and he says he wants to. I can't ask him to leave after that, can I?'

'I still think you're wrong,' she said obstinately.

'And I think you're being silly.'

She found a new argument. 'Michael doesn't care for him much.'

'Michael isn't home often enough to have seen much of him. The fact that my friends aren't Michael's isn't a good reason for turning them out.'

She walked away from him uneasily. She really was uncomfortable about this. He was surprised. Caroline was usually too level-headed to let whims upset her.

'I hope you don't regret it, that's all,' she said moodily.

'I think I'll go up now,' he said. 'We're both tired. And no wonder.'

She was at the door when he was finishing his drink, and turned and waited for him to put his glass down.

'I forgot to ask you whether anything happened when you went back down the river?'

He shook his head. 'Nothing at all. Brayton's men will patrol the bank until morning, that's all.'

'What did Brayton say about it?'

'He thinks it's a queer thing to happen. He has a wide choice of theories. Felicity committed suicide, or she was running away, or somebody knocked her on the head and she fell in. He doesn't know which to pick. I'm afraid he's not quite happy about it.'

'Happy!' she exclaimed.

'When Brayton knows exactly why Felicity fell in the water, and *how* she fell—everything explained and tabulated and put away in the appropriate pigeonhole of his mind—then he'll be at rest. Anything he can't explain is an insult to his intelligence. He did, as an afterthought, remember to say how sorry he was. But he isn't a comfortable man.'

'That's a pity,' said Caroline sarcastically.

'Yes,' agreed Dyke. 'It's a pity.'

Chapter Five

*

HE had steeled himself to face the bedroom, with the reproach of its twin beds, its loneliness, its emptiness, its silence—but it still was like a blow when he closed the door behind him. Always, from now, he would be alone at night. For the day there would be people, voices, laughter, but always, for the nights, silence. Silence, except for the unending clatter of his own mind.

Resolutely he forced himself not to think about Felicity. For a moment he realized that if he relaxed and opened his mind she would be back. If she had merely died this is what he might have done, but when he thought of what she had planned, he felt that having her there, though only in memory, would be misery. It was going to be hard enough, anyhow, to keep her out. He had only to let her, and she would return. But his sullenness with her was still in his heart. It was as if she had gone with that other man. He smarted under the desertion and would not have her back.

He went over to the window and opened it. For a few minutes he stood there breathing deeply, not thinking, forcing his mind to be blank.

Then he undressed and got into bed.

For a while he lay perfectly motionless. His mind was still empty. He went on breathing deeply, relaxing, waiting for sleep, revelling in the luxury of rest. But thoughts were creeping back. Like maggots that have been pushed off a plate, they came crawling back over the edge. He found himself listening to see if he could tell if Felicity were awake.

Then he became restless. He tried one position after another. The sheets were no longer a cool refuge, and grew tangled and hot. The weariness that like a benediction had promised sleep, began to recede. He was hot, and his mind was alert, going back to Felicity, back to what he had done, working things out—he would have to be careful with Brayton—the man was bed-fellow to suspicion—he would have to watch what he said. Not that Brayton, even if he guessed, could do anything, but——

He tried to force Brayton out of his mind, and then Felicity was in full possession of it . . . Felicity . . . Trent . . . was Trent . . . Michael . . . Frank . . . Caroline. . . . Why didn't Caroline like Frank? For a moment she'd been near hysteria. Jealousy, of course. . . . Caro would stay with him now . . . she'd be devoted . . . he wasn't sure he wanted devotion. He might grow to hate it; perhaps hate Caro with it.

The curtain blew inwards on a breath of night air, and he had a glimpse of the sky, clear and purple as a royal robe and brilliant with stars. Soon be dawn. Oh damn! he thought. I'll never sleep to-night. It was mad to try. I should have dozed in a chair.

He got up, and without making a light picked up a dressing-gown and put it on. Then he found a cigarette and lit it, pulled a chair over to the window and, drawing the curtains, sat there, his bare feet crossed on the sill, staring out into the night.

'On such a night as this . . .' Why did quotations creep back into your mind? And right out of context. A line that was written for mounting passion attaching itself to a night of treachery and violence and death. Like a picture through a swiftly-passed window he saw momentarily Jessica and her Lorenzo. Love reaching out to love, eager and yearning. Something he had never known. It came back to Felicity all the time. Wherever he started, sooner or later, always to Felicity. And so to the beginning.

She had never cheated. He had to allow her that. Not from the very beginning. Felicity, young and lovely, so desirable that he, sane and level-headed as he had imagined himself, would tremble with the force of his desire for her. Felicity, so sweet, and a little pathetic in her poverty, never having the things that should have been almost a birthright—the things that he could give her. A strange, self-contained family they had been, a kind of circle into which it seemed impossible to break: her mother, rather fine and handsome in those days, a woman you could never quite understand, whose thoughts you never read, kind enough, but aloof and apart; Felicity's adored, semi-invalid father, the retired, broken-down clergyman; and Felicity herself, of course, Always Felicity.

They were so abominably poor. In a way it was pitiable, yet the strange thing was that neither of the older people seemed to realize their poverty. It was left to Felicity fully to understand it; hating and resenting it, and realizing that there was no escape. The other two in that curious, self-sufficient way they had, owned a contentment almost like a personal possession. Poverty was often inconvenient, but it could not destroy their satisfaction in each other and in life.

Felicity at seventeen, too adult and developed, seeing the stratagems to make a shilling do the work of a pound, rebellious and resentful. That had been a weapon in Dyke's hand, a gap in her armour.

'I don't love you, Dyke,' she had said.

'Perhaps you will in time.'

'I don't think so.' Even then she saw clearly. 'I don't think I ever shall. I like you tremendously. I think I like you more than anybody I've ever met, except Father and Mother. But that's not love, is it?'

'You never know,' he said.

She did know, though. 'It's an awful risk, Dyke.'

'One I'll be very glad to take.'

She had shaken her head. 'That shows you don't really understand it.' She added, rather naïvely, 'I'd try never to fall in love with anybody else.'

'Fair enough,' said Dyke. He felt he was winning her and pressed her harder. Subconsciously he realized that if love had stirred in her, even for the butcher's boy or the sweep, he would never have had a chance, and—again subconsciously—he feared her awakening to someone else, and gave her no rest.

You could not say their marriage was unhappy or unsuccessful. There was much in it that could not have been bettered. As a friendship it would have been almost perfect. Only one thing it lacked. Felicity had no answering passion to match his ardour. Physical love was to her something at first feared and resented, then later tolerated, finally accepted. In the end she gave herself kindly, could even pretend warmth, but in his heart he knew that never once in their years together had love been something she waited for and reached out for eagerly. He had tried to be patient, tried to be kind, tried to wait for the heat in him to kindle an answering spark, but either the trial was too hard for him, or the fire had not been in her for his lighting.

She had not been the only woman he had wanted in his life. But she had been the only woman he had wanted to want him.

What it came to in the end was that she would never have married him but for his money. She liked him, and she liked him enough to let him buy her so that she could give her mother, and especially her invalid father, all the things she felt they ought to want. And fate struck at her, and perhaps also at all Dyke's hopes of ever making her love him. Just before they returned from their honeymoon her father died. She made no reproaches, but he had a feeling that she was thinking she had sacrificed herself for nothing.

Sometimes, in later years, when passion had not been so demanding, and tolerance had taken the place of frustration, he wondered if Felicity's devotion to her father had been what defeated him. She had been young and resilient, and she had soon recovered from the ironical blow. But nothing, it seemed, not even the baby, born in the first year of her marriage, ever quite filled the gap left by the quiet scholar who had not waited to receive the gifts she had won for him

As they were, so would they ever be. That was how it appeared to him. When he came to forget his resentments, and the pain of his longings, he grew satisfied. He had so much. Youth's a stuff will not endure. There is more in life besides youth: warmth is, in the end, more pleasant than heat; contentment lasts longer than ecstasy. But, he had not grown entirely beyond an occasional hope that even yet she might become one day unreservedly and completely his. And the death of that hope added to the weight of the blow when she said she was going to leave him.

At first he could not believe she meant it. It was just impossible. He had laughed at her, thinking it a threat, something to frighten him, something she would never be able to do. It was hysteria, though he knew she was sane enough and not given to vapours or posturings; it was a woman's foolish whim. And then, with dismay and something akin to despair he realized it was neither hysteria nor whim. She was in earnest, and he had to accept the fact that he was really going to lose all in his life he cared about. He had pleaded with her, mocked, argued, threatened; he had been patient, he had been angry; he had shown her the enormity of what she was going to do, the impossibility of it. And nothing had made the slightest impression on her. She was a friend refusing to listen to a friend. She was another Felicity. What was going on in her mind was something beyond his knowledge. It was the part of her he had never reached. She was someone he did not know, over whom he had no influence. She was in love.

He had not forgotten the promise she made before they married.

'You said if you couldn't love me you'd never fall in love with anybody else.'

Her memory was more exact than his. 'I said I'd try never to, Dyke,' she sighed, a little wearied by his pressure. 'And you must admit I've not done so badly. The trouble is I grew careless. I forgot to try.'

He did not know her any more. He realised dimly that a change had taken place.

'I'm sorry, Dyke. Very, very sorry for doing this to you.'

She was not the woman he had watched develop from girl-hood to maturity. In spite of what she was doing she did not lose her poise or sanity, nor even her humour. But she was nearly forty, and she believed something was within her reach that had never been in her reach before, and almost certainly never would be again, and it was stronger than she was.

'I like you just the same, Dyke. Not a bit less. I'm terribly worried about you.' She smiled at the politeness of it all. 'This won't last, and I'll come back penitent on my hands and knees before the end of a year, begging you to take me in.' Then the smile disappeared and he felt the strength of her urge, the hopelessness of his own position. 'But I can't help myself. I *can't*.'

She would not tell him who the man was. He would have to be told eventually, of course, but she did not want to discuss it. It might be someone he knew—or someone he did not know. He felt it must be one of his friends, for she seemed, in a curious way, ashamed. Anyhow, at that stage it did not, in comparison with the fact that he was going to lose her, seem so important, and seeing how discussion of that side of the affair distressed her he forbore from pressing her. Even with things as they were he had a strange desire not to give her pain.

Another curious side was that she did not seem to want her freedom.

'I'll not divorce you, Felicity,' he had threatened during one of their interminable arguments.

'No, Dyke, I don't expect you to.'

Something in the tone of voice made him regard her closely. 'You don't sound as if you very much want me to, either.'

'I don't think I do,' she said slowly.

'But—you must.'

She looked at him solemnly. 'Why?'

'Why?' he exploded. '*Why?* Damn it, don't you want to marry him?'

'I don't know. I haven't thought about it.'

She hadn't thought about it!

'But you must have. Anyhow, he must want to marry you!'

'Marriage,' she said, turning the word over as if she examined it for the first time. 'Marriage? Marriage is what we've had, Dyke. It's been—good, in its own way. This is the other thing. It's something entirely different.'

'You're mad!' he said. 'Mad!'

'Perhaps I am. Why don't you let it go at that, Dyke. Mad people aren't responsible. They aren't themselves. I'm not the person you married. I'm somebody else——'

She searched for words to console him. Even while she planned to leave him she tried not to hurt him. She was right. She was someone else. But the damnable part was that she was still the someone else he had wanted all his life to find.

They had wearied themselves and each other. Outwardly they were the same as usual. Trent and Frank, Harold and Alice and Caroline had been due to visit Riverside Lodge, and they had come and Dyke and Felicity had given them hospitality and entertained them, and everything was as it always had been. The truth was that it was easier for them to be as they always had been because, more than anything, they had always been friends, and, curiously, they still were friends. In private, Dyke could not let the matter rest. Except when they were alone together the threat became a nightmare that he pushed to the back of his mind. He did not even know when she would go, so that an hour away from her was a torment. He could not turn his back on her without wondering if he was ever going to see her again.

He stirred in his chair before the window. Turning his head he was suddenly aware of the indistinct shapes of the contents of the room. Outside, the sky was losing its clear lambence and fading to grey, except over the horizon where a single star blazed brightly against a transparent pearliness, blazed in loneliness as if it defied the coming day.

Suddenly a blackbird in the garden sang a sad, almost tired note, not greeting the dawn, but sorry that the night was gone. Other birds joined in with their fluting; lacking the ardour of spring they sang reluctantly, regretting that each new day brought them nearer to the end of summer.

A thin, transparent breath of mist moved lazily up over the river and the rising hills on the opposite bank began to reveal their details. Trees detached themselves from the general mass of darkness into individuals; fields became lighter and dissolved the night-time partnership with their hedges, and cows were grazing in them; a gate appeared where no gate had been, a cottage seemed to rise out of the ground, colours separated themselves from the even monotony of night. When he looked from the picture spread before him to the star that had burned so fiercely, it was no longer there. Somewhere in the distance a dog barked.

His mouth was dry from too many cigarettes, and his eyes burned. He pressed his hands over his eyelids and felt hot tears creep out to wet his fingers. But they were tears of weariness, not of sorrow. He ought to be weeping for Felicity, weeping for loneliness, for all he had lost. He wished he could weep, longed for the relief crying might bring. But the whole affair now had become invested with unreality. It was something that should never have happened. He wondered if he wished hard enough into the past, it could be wiped out. Felicity still alive. Felicity not even wanting to leave him. As he had done when he had first come into the house from the river, he felt her nearness and her reality again. He forgot the resentments, the pain, the hopeless longing. His hands were still over his eyes. If I stay like this, he said, I can bring back the past. Everything can be as it always was. There have been twenty years of close companionship between us. That cannot be wiped out in a second of time because one of us has ceased to breathe. Just as she, if she had left him, would have had to carry always a part of himself in her, so he would always have something of her in him. She had not wholly gone. He had not completely killed her. Something distilled from her was still in the house, was in himself. She was not dead. He had not been able to sleep and had come to sit by the window to watch the dawn, and she lay in her bed behind him, sleeping quietly. He listened to hear her move, to catch the sound of her breathing, alert for when she should awake so that he could turn round and meet her eyes and catch her first sleepy smile.

But the sound when it came was not from the bed. At the front of the house a gate slammed, startling him, making him jump up in his chair and drop his hands from his face.

In the few minutes he had dreamed, the day had crept fully upon the world. The river, grey and sluggish, tired in the morning light, crept past the end of the garden.

There were footsteps on the gravel. They were coming round the house. He stared, wide-eyed, at the drive beneath the window. He could hear his heart beating rapidly. He was, for no reason he could explain, very frightened.

And then they had rounded the house and he could look down on them. Four policemen walking awkwardly, out of step, carrying a stretcher. And on the stretcher a form covered with a sheet of some grey material.

They were bringing Felicity home.

Chapter Six

*

LATER in the morning he slept, falling asleep in an armchair in the lounge. When he woke, he wrote a few letters and then walked down to the village to post them. The day was fine, sunny, but not too hot, with a breeze coming off the river.

The sleep and the walk refreshed him. Life seemed normal once more. The happenings and the thoughts of the night were far away and unreal. At the same time he grew wary again, alert and watchful. He was two people, really. There was the self sorry for Felicity and bitterly regretting her death and his loss, and there was the self determined not to be caught and punished for what it had done. There was nothing to connect him actively with Felicity's death, yet he knew how easily he might make a slip that would give him away.

When he arrived at the house from the post office there was a car standing outside. Caroline met him in the hall.

'Michael has arrived,' she said. She was looking at him anxiously, and added before he could speak: 'He's brought a girl with him.'

'A girl!' exclaimed Dyke. 'At a time like this?'

'Not too loud,' she warned. 'She drove him down, I think. That's her car outside. She's in the lounge. You'd better come in and meet her.'

For a moment he felt cheated and angry. He did not want to see anyone. This was a time when they could do without strangers in the house. What the devil was Michael thinking of?

Though he was not looking forward to the meeting with Michael, he wanted to get it over. He both wanted it and dreaded it; wanted it because he thought Felicity's death might bring them into a new intimacy; dreaded it because of what was hidden in his own mind.

But there was not much choice as to what he should do.

'All right,' he said. 'Come and introduce us.'

The girl, whose name was Dinah Carstairs, was about twenty and was strikingly beautiful. She was very sure of herself, self-possessed and not at all shy; but she did, Dyke realized, dislike the position she was in.

'I'm terribly sorry to descend on you to-day,' she apologized, 'but Michael insisted on my coming.'

Dyke did not know what to say to this. He could not very well pretend that he was glad to see her.

'Actually, I'm being a sort of chauffeur for him. He was going to come by train, but there wasn't a convenient one running. I offered to lend him the car, but you know how he hates driving, and he's been rather cut-up about what's happened. He really insisted on my coming.'

'It's very kind of you to have brought him, Miss Carstairs,' said Dyke.

He had given her a cigarette now and she was smoking.

'You'd better call me Dinah,' she said.

He smiled. 'Shall I?'

She was looking at him in inquiry. 'I suppose you know I'm going to marry Michael?'

His eyebrows went up. 'Are you?'

She could see how surprised he was. 'Michael hasn't told you! Oh, he's the limit! I shouldn't have sprung it on you like that. I'm so sorry.'

'There's nothing to be sorry for,' he said. 'I think Michael's very lucky. And when I've got to know you, I'm sure I'll be pleased. I only wish—we'd known you earlier. Before—what's happened.'

'Let's not talk about it now,' she said. 'I wish I hadn't blurted it out. I just took it for granted you knew.'

'Michael doesn't tell us much of what he does,' said Dyke. 'But that doesn't matter at the moment. I'm glad you're going to marry him. Now I'm going to ask you to excuse me. I'd like to go and speak to him.'

'Yes. Try not to mind my being here,' she said. 'You haven't to entertain me to-day. I shall be going soon, anyhow.'

He met Caroline in the hall again. He nodded towards the door he had just closed.

'The future Mrs. Michael Farne,' he said in a low voice.

'Oh, that's it?' said Caroline.

'The poor girl blurted it out, thinking I knew. You'd better go and be nice to her.'

Caroline did not seem to be surprised. 'I noticed she had an engagement ring. I wondered if that could be the explanation.'

'You're remarkably astute, Caro,' said Dyke.

'Well, there had to be some explanation. Even the most casual young man doesn't blow in with a visitor when his mother has just died.'

'Where is Michael?' asked Dyke. 'I'd like to see him.'

'He's probably in his own room by now,' said Caroline solemnly. 'He wanted to go up alone. He went in to look at Felicity, but I think I heard the door of his room close afterwards.'

Michael was in his room. He was tall, good looking and gracefully thin, but a little effeminate. Dyke noticed as they shook hands that his eyes were red as if he had been crying. Once they had shaken hands neither seemed to have anything to say. Michael went across to the window and stood, his back half turned to his father, looking down at the river.

57

Dyke felt bound to speak.

'This is a wretched business, Michael.'

Michael thrust his hands into his pockets and his shoulders hunched a little. He did not answer, nor turn round.

'I suppose you know how it happened?'

'Yes,' said Michael. 'Aunt Caroline told me.'

'She must have lost her balance and fallen backwards,' said Dyke. 'We were all in the saloon——' He stopped. He couldn't go on like this. He had an awful feeling of being a hypocrite, yet anything he said from now on about Felicity's death couldn't be anything else but hypocrisy. He wondered whether Michael would have minded so much his mother running away with another man. It would be a consolation to imagine he would, but probably he wouldn't. Probably he wouldn't have minded at all.

'Of all the damnable things to happen!' Michael burst out. 'What did she want to sit there for? Why couldn't you have heard her? Why couldn't it have happened when somebody was there to pull her out?'

He turned now and Dyke could see the tears streaming down his cheeks. His face was puckered a little. Dyke had not seen him cry since one of his birthdays when he was a child and somebody had trodden on a toy train he had been given for a present. The sight of this new Michael, grief-stricken and in tears, moved him to a compassion he could not put into words. He wanted to say something, but between his thoughts and his words was his secret knowledge of what he had done. He was the cause of his son's sorrow. What had been between Felicity and himself couldn't be kept to themselves. More or less, everybody who knew them was concerned.

Michael was still standing facing him, still had his hands thrust into his pockets, as he cried. Then he seemed to realize himself, found a handkerchief and wiped his eyes. Dyke wished he had not come. He wished he had met him in front of the others.

Alone like this, there was an awful terrifying nakedness about the boy's emotions. And he was powerless to clothe it. Michael's face still worked spasmodically. He seemed to be fighting back a fit of hysteria, but Dyke could offer no words of comfort, find nothing to say that would bring them closer together in their grief. The only thing he could do would be to tell the truth. And the truth would be no help at all.

His heart sank as he realized that Felicity's death would not bring them nearer together. This was the last opportunity he would ever have of establishing a bond between himself and his son, and it was no use to him. In fact, all that had happened would now force them further apart. It had become an obstacle between them. An obstacle he would never be able to surmount.

There was nothing else Dyke could say. Neither would Michael, who now had his feelings under control, say anything of what he felt. Something which normally might have been a point of contact had become a gulf. If Dyke had thought about it, he must have known it would fail.

He said, 'I've just met your friend, Dinah. She says I'm to call her Dinah.'

Michael corrected him. 'She's my fiancée.'

'Yes, I—gathered as much.' Any sort of reproach seemed pointless. 'You haven't mentioned her before.'

'I'm sorry,' said Michael. 'I ought to have done. But we only fixed it up a few days ago. I was going to bring her down as soon as I could manage it.' Tears started to his eyes again. 'I wish I had now. But there didn't seem any hurry.'

'Well,' said Dyke. 'This is hardly the time for congratulations and all that sort of thing, but she seems a very lovely girl. I'm sure you're lucky.'

'Yes,' said Michael. 'Thanks, Father.' He came out with a sudden burst of confidence. 'As a matter of fact, it's been the very devil of a job getting her to say yes. She's an only child and her people are rather stuffy. County and all that.'

'You know them well, of course.'

'Not very well. I've met them a few times when they've been in town.' He looked at his father doubtfully. 'I've an idea they don't think a lot of me. In fact, I'm sure of it.'

'Because you aren't county?'

'I don't want to be county. The middle classes count for a lot more to-day, I reckon. They do the only things worth doing. But the Carstairs are poor and stinking with pride.'

'If they don't like you it's a pity, but it's something that can be put right. It's what Dinah thinks that matters, isn't it?'

'Yes, of course. But she's been brought up as closely guarded as if she were royalty. She's got a—what is it—dutiful streak. I suppose that's why she wasn't too keen at first.'

Michael's own streak of duty being so nearly non-existent, he gave the information as if it were a complaint. Dyke's heart sank. Youth was not often dutiful to a fault, especially when in love. His son was known to be the heir to a rich man. He hoped history was not in process of repeating itself. But he could not very well say so.

'She's going back to town soon, I gather.'

'Yes. We shall have to leave after lunch.'

'We?' queried Dyke.

'Well, I can hardly ask her to stay now, can I?'

'But have you to go as well?'

A look of spoiled sullenness came into Michael's face. Dyke had seen the same look before when Michael had thought himself in danger of losing anything he particularly wanted.

'I can't very well let Dinah go back on her own.'

'But you could return.'

'I shouldn't be any use here, I—in fact, I'd rather not be here.' He added gracelessly, 'If you don't mind, Father?'

Dyke felt a sense of bitter disappointment. Whatever the distance between them, he and Michael could at least appear united and side by side for these few days.

'I couldn't do anything,' Michael went on. 'If I were any help—— And I've got a good bit to see to. I'll be back, of course. I'll be back before—— I'll be back in plenty of time.'

'I'm sorry,' said Dyke. 'I'd have liked to have you here, but of course you must go if it's necessary, and, as you say, there's nothing you can do.'

Michael did not reply. Once again they were at a dead end, each on his own side of a blank wall There was nothing more to say.

'Shall we go down?' he asked.

'Yes, you go. I'll come in a minute. I'll have a wash first, I think.'

Dyke went slowly towards the door. All the time he hoped for some word from his son that would indicate a sympathy between them. He no longer expected miracles—just one word that would bring them closer for a moment. But Michael did not speak.

Dyke longed for kindness and understanding. He longed to be able to tell his disappointment to someone who would know how he felt. And Felicity was the only one to whom he could have explained. He smiled to himself, but it was a twisted, painful smile.

Chapter Seven

*

AFTER Michael and Dinah had gone the house seemed very quiet and empty. Alice went to lie down, the other men went out for a walk. They asked Dyke to go with them but he could not very well have gone if he had wanted to, because Brayton had telephoned that he would be calling sometime during the afternoon. Caroline stayed with Dyke and they sat on the porch, for the day had turned out hot and sunny and the porch was the coolest place.

'What does the Inspector want?' Caroline asked. She had some sewing on her lap and her materials were spread out on a small table at her side. She did not look at Dyke as she spoke.

'I don't know what he wants,' said Dyke. 'I suppose he'll be backwards and forwards now until—until it's all over.'

'Isn't it all over?'

'It's all over from our point of view. It isn't for Brayton until after the inquest, I suppose.'

'It all seems very pointless to me,' said Caroline. 'We all know how poor Felicity died. It's obvious. I think Brayton's being officious.'

'It's his business to be officious,' said Dyke.

'Not unless there's some reason for it.'

Dyke came to a sudden decision. He knew there was one secret that would have to stay locked up in his heart for ever. He could never share it with anybody. That made it all the more imperative that he should share as much as he could. Now Felicity was gone he had nobody but Caroline. To tell her would break a little into his awful inner loneliness.

'There's something I'd like to tell you,' Caro,' he said.

The tone of his voice made her look at him in enquiry.

'Secrets?' she asked.

He nodded. 'Secrets.'

It took them both back thirty years to the days when she had been his early confidante, as she had been always before Felicity came.

'What is it, Dyke?'

'Just this. Felicity was going to leave me.'

She did not speak for a minute, but she put her sewing down on the table and sat up straighter in the cane chair.

'*Leave* you?'

'Yes.'

'But—why? You hadn't quarrelled or anything.'

'No, we were as good friends as ever. She was leaving me for another man.'

Caroline relaxed a little. It was as if something incomprehensible had been made clear suddenly.

'Are you sure?'

'Quite sure.'

'She told you?'

'Yes.'

'Who was the man?'

'She wouldn't say.'

Again there was a short silence. Dyke broke it. He was admitting a painful truth that he had never confessed to anyone. It seemed as if ever since he married there had been secrets he could not share.

'You know, Caro, Felicity never really loved me. She liked me to start with, and I believe she had a very real affection for me. But not'—he glanced at his sister to see if she understood—'not

63

love. But I didn't expect this. I thought we were too close to each other.'

'Dyke, I'm so sorry——'

'The whole thing has been—horrible. A nightmare. I couldn't believe she meant it. But she did.'

Caroline was staring hard in front of her. 'It's very strange.'

'Strange?'

'You were about to lose her in one way—and you lost her in another.'

'Yes,' agreed Dyke. 'Oh, it's strange all right!' He wished he could tell her how strange. 'The whole damn' business is more than strange. Why, at this time of day, she should——' He stopped, then said, as if trying to make allowances, 'If she'd been younger——'

'You're more sensible when you're younger,' said Caroline.

'I thought it was the other way round.'

'It's supposed to be, but often it isn't. You see, Dyke, when you get older you're likely to make a fool of yourself because you feel your chances of doing so are growing less. Felicity was forty, wasn't she?'

'Nearly. What's that got to do with it?'

'Probably a lot. Forty's a nasty age. What you haven't done by then you feel you'd better hurry if you're ever going to do it.'

'That's rather a silly theory,' said Dyke.

'It is. And a dangerous one. But it's true enough. If Felicity felt there was something she'd missed with you and there was a chance she could still find it with somebody else. . .'

Dyke pondered. 'I don't think Felicity was that sort.'

'We're all that sort, Dyke. No fool like an old fool.'

He looked at her sharply. There was an unhappy note in her voice.

'We find we're getting on and we think of the things we haven't had and haven't done and we get reckless. We jump at the chance of a last fling.'

64

'I can't say I've noticed it much myself,' he said drily.

'You were in love. That makes a difference.'

'All right, I see what you mean. We won't talk about it any more. I just thought I'd let you know.'

He felt relieved now he had told her. Lighter, as if he had got rid of part of a weight.

'You don't know who the other man was?'

'She didn't say. I didn't press her. I would have known eventually, of course.'

'And now you won't?'

He did not answer.

'Or do you think you do know?'

'I think I do,' he said. He had not meant to say this, but it came into his mind that from now on he and Caroline would be much together. Nothing had been said yet about their future plans, but obviously she was the one to run his home for him. It would be better if she did know.

'I think it's Trent,' he said.

The announcement startled her. 'Oh, Dyke, no!'

'I don't know, of course. But that's what I think.'

'You've nothing to make you believe——'

'Nothing. It's just—call it an instinct, if you like. He's always been very fond of her. He's known her as long as I have. She liked him——'

'*Liked* him, yes, but——'

'For all I know, she might have married him if she hadn't married me.'

'If she'd wanted to she'd——'

'Caro,' he said. 'Let's be honest. Felicity married me for my money. She liked me, but she'd never have married me if I hadn't been rich. Trent is comfortably off, but he's never had too much money.'

'Listen, Dyke,' said Caroline. 'You may be right about Trent.

But I don't believe you are. Don't be too sure. I don't know much about what Felicity meant to do. Only what you've told me now. But I don't think she'd have left you for Trent. Trent's nearly your age——'

'Age hasn't anything to do with it——'

'In a case like this, age has a lot to do with it.' She spoke quickly, her eyes bright, and her face had coloured. 'When we get middle-aged we get silly. But silly with somebody half as old as we are. We try to reach backwards into youth. It's not the sort of thing that lasts. We know it won't last, it isn't meant to last.' She laughed. 'I know I couldn't ever make a fool of myself over a man as settled as Trent—but if somebody about Michael's age thought he'd fallen in love with me——'

'That's ridiculous!' said Dyke.

'Yes, it is, isn't it? Only I don't want you to be sure about Trent, until you *are* sure.'

'I've no doubt at all in my own mind. But we shall have to drop the subject. There's a car slowing up. I expect it's Brayton.'

Brayton, in spite of an effort to appear normal, was not at ease. He took the chair Dyke offered him, but refused a cigarette, saying he preferred his pipe.

'I can't stay many minutes,' he said. 'I've come to make a request.'

'Yes?' said Dyke.

'I'm still worried about how your wife came to fall.'

Caroline, busy at her sewing again, put in a word quietly. 'We are worried, too, Inspector.'

He looked at her, then sat inspecting the bowl of his pipe. 'Yes, yes, I know, Miss Farne. I'm sorry, sorry for you all, especially for Mr. Farne. Personally, I mean. But whatever my personal feelings are, I'm bound to take the official attitude as well. There's the inquest, and the coroner will ask some awkward questions. Old Crowther's got an idea he's no fool, and he likes to live up to that.'

'This request of yours?' said Dyke.

'Just this. I would like you to take me on the river in the launch to-night.'

Caroline, lowering her work into her lap, sat up suddenly in her chair.

'Go on,' said Dyke.

'I want to reproduce the conditions of last night as nearly as possible——'

'You mean you want us all——'

'No, no, not that. There's no need for any of them to come. In fact, it will be better if none of them do. Except you——'

'Inspector,' said Caroline. 'Don't you think my brother has endured enough already?'

'I'm sorry——'

'It's all right, Brayton,' said Dyke. 'Of course I'll come. What is it you want, exactly?'

'Well, I shall bring a few of my men. At about the spot Mrs. Farne must have fallen, one of them will slip into the water.'

Both Caroline and Dyke were watching him closely.

'As a matter of fact, he will sit exactly where your wife sat, and he'll let himself fall something like she must have fallen.'

'Where does that get us?' asked Dyke.

'We shall establish two facts. Whether anyone could hear a splash, and whether anyone could hear a cry.'

'But we didn't hear either,' said Caroline.

'I know——'

'There were six of us, and none of us did.'

'I know. I think Crowther will ask if it was possible, though.'

'Really——' began Caroline. Dyke interrupted her.

'All right. I'd never thought of that. You come round here and we'll do as you say. Unless you'd like me to pick you up somewhere along the river.'

'No, we'd better start from here. About dusk, I should think. Will that do?'

'Yes,' said Dyke. 'I'll be ready.'

'I know this is painful for you.'

'Everything is painful,' said Dyke. 'Doing this or that won't make any difference now. It won't bring my wife back, but if it helps you at all I don't mind.'

'Thanks,' said Brayton. He put his hands on the arms of his chair as if to rise, then, in the act of getting up, he paused.

'There's one more small matter.'

'What is it?' asked Dyke.

'When our surgeon examined your wife's body he found a slight bruise across her head. Have you any idea how that happened?'

Dyke looked surprised. 'None at all.'

'She didn't have a blow at any time that you know of?'

'No. Look here, are you sure about this? I'd have been bound to know——'

Brayton stood up. 'Yes,' he said. 'That's what I thought. It wasn't a bad bruise. Not much more than a mark. But rather long, across the skull, about two inches above the forehead, and definitely recent.'

Dyke looked mystified. 'I can't think of anything.'

'I can explain,' said Caroline.

They both turned to her.

'She hit her head against a bough of a tree yesterday.'

'A tree?' repeated Brayton.

'Yes. We were walking across the garden. Look, I can show you the spot where it happened.' She got up and they all moved towards the front of the porch, and she pointed down to the side of the lawn where a number of trees grew close together. She said to Brayton, 'You see—that one there?'

68

Brayton was looking. He did not appear very pleased. 'Yes,' he said.

'You see how the branches sweep low, don't you?'

They could see the tree she pointed to. The path running parallel with the river across the garden went straight under the sweeping branches.

Caroline went on. We were walking along the path there. I was in front. I heard Felicity exclaim and when I turned round she had her hand on her head. She'd hit it against that branch.'

'Did she hurt herself badly?' asked Brayton.

'Oh dear, no! We both laughed about it.'

'But surely you stoop to go under the branches when you're walking along that path?'

Caroline laughed. 'Not always low enough. Haven't you ever hit your head against something you knew was there?'

'You think she hit herself hard enough to—well, to raise a bruise?'

'I didn't think about it. But evidently she did.'

Brayton was probing at his pipe. He seemed discontented and sulky, but when Dyke spoke he looked straight at him.

'You're not still on that theory that somebody hit my wife——?'

'It wasn't a theory. It was an idea.'

'But I've told you. It's ridiculous.'

'Oh, quite. As long as she did hit her head in the garden here——'

'Bruises and marks came up very easily on Felicity,' said Caroline.

Brayton turned his gaze on her. 'Tell me, Miss Farne?' he said in a slow, deliberate way, 'did *you* know that I'd suggested to Mr. Farne that his wife might have been hit in the head by someone?'

There was a pause. Then suddenly she went very red. She looked at Dyke uncertainly.

69

Dyke spoke. 'I mentioned the fact when I came in last night.'

'I—see,' said Brayton. His manner changed suddenly. He smiled, put his pipe in his pocket and seemed brisk and wide-awake all at once. 'Thank you. Well, I'd better be off. I'll see you this evening, then. Good-bye.'

'Good-bye,' they said, and they stood at the top of the porch steps watching him as he went, before they returned to their chairs.

'Isn't he a little—peculiar?' suggested Caroline.

'All policemen are a little peculiar at times,' said Dyke.

'He was almost—questioning us.'

'Yes. You see, he wants to find out how Felicity died.'

'But it's obvious, isn't it?'

'I suppose it is. Probably that's why Brayton is suspicious.'

'Suspicious?'

'Well, wondering if he ought to be suspicious.'

'But who can he be suspicious of?'

Dyke took his time before he replied. 'I suppose he might be suspicious of me.'

When he had said it he wished the words unspoken. He had told Caroline about Felicity and Trent. Now this suggestion. She would think about both, and sooner or later would connect the two and begin to wonder. That would make her unhappy. She would wonder whether he could have killed Felicity because she was leaving him. Then she would dismiss the idea as preposterous —but it would return—perhaps again and again. He wished he could tell her everything. If there was one person he could confide in safely it would be Caroline. But it would not be fair to her.

'I think the Inspector is a very stupid man,' she said.

'No, Caro, he's not stupid.'

'Silly, then.'

'We're all silly at some time or another,' he said.

Chapter Eight

*

THE light was fading as they set off in the launch. At the last minute Brayton had suggested that perhaps one of the others had better come along, not, he said, to corroborate Dyke's statements, but as an aid to his memory. Caroline wanted to be the one to go, but Dyke had chosen Frank.

Brayton had brought three of his men with him, a sergeant and two constables. As soon as they had started, one of the constables stripped and put on a bathing costume. He then took an overcoat which the other constable was carrying and slipped it round his shoulders, for the day, so hot in the afternoon, had become cool. The sky by evening had become cloudy and overcast and the river was grey, and a cool wind whipped it.

Dyke was at the wheel as they went down and he explained the controls to the sergeant, since Brayton had asked him to hand over on the way back. Brayton and Frank stood near them. The constables were by the saloon door.

'This is what I want,' said Brayton when Dyke had finished his instructions. 'You'll turn where you turned last night. Then perhaps you'll let Barclay take over. I'd like you to put young Frame there as near as possible to where your wife sat. Mr. Calvert and I will go into the saloon. All right?'

'Yes,' said Dyke. 'What then?'

"You could stay out here until we get to the place where you poured the drinks, then join us.'

'I don't know whether I can repeat my actions exactly,' said

Dyke. 'I've an idea—I know we were somewhere below Gather's Mill.'

'That's near enough,' said Brayton. 'Come into the saloon then. When we're passing the mill, Frame will topple himself backwards into the water——' He looked at Dyke, seeming suddenly a little ashamed. 'You know, I'm sorry about this.'

Dyke's nerves were taut, but he swallowed back an irritated reply. 'Don't worry. Anything to help.'

'What about the constable?' said Frank. 'Chilly night to go bathing.'

'We needn't worry about Frame,' said Brayton. 'He's a first-rate swimmer. If he never goes in on a colder night he'll be lucky. He'll go under, of course. When he comes up'—he looked anxiously at Dyke, but it was growing too dark to see features clearly—'he'll shout out.'

Dyke was looking straight ahead. He did not speak.

'We don't stop to pick him up,' continued Brayton. 'After that one shout he'll swim to the bank. I've a man posted with clothes for him.'

'What's the object of all this?' asked Frank.

Brayton repeated what he had told Dyke and Caroline in the afternoon.

'I want to find out two things. Whether we can hear the splash, and whether we can hear the shout.'

'Does that get us anywhere?'

'Well, it might establish the fact that Mrs. Farne could fall overboard and neither be heard fall, nor be heard calling for help.'

'But she couldn't—obviously.'

'Quite. Only I need evidence for the inquest. Coroners some-times like these details proved.'

'I—see,' said Frank.

'Is there anything else?' asked Dyke curtly.

'I think it would be a good idea if Sergeant Barclay let go of the controls then. We'll be in Masterman's Reach by that time. We could just check up on whether the launch will behave in the same way.'

'No good,' said Dyke. 'She won't.'

Brayton sounded aggrieved. 'Why not?'

'Because the weather isn't the same as it was last night. She'd probably go ashore in twenty yards. Or turn right round. On the same throttle, anyhow. Last night it was dead calm. Now there's a cross-wind.'

'Oh,' said Brayton unhappily. 'I see.'

'Does it make any difference?'

'Quite a bit, really. So far, we're assured that your wife fell off the launch somewhere about Gather's Mill. We've no proof of that.'

'But look here,' said Frank. 'She must have done. If she'd fallen out anywhere else we'd have heard something.'

'We've no proof of that, either.'

'No,' said Frank slowly. 'I suppose we haven't.'

'Actually, she could have fallen at any time before you grounded.'

Dyke sighed and passed a hand wearily across his eyes. He hated this trip. He had not liked the prospect of it, and the reality was proving worse than the expectation. He tried to take as little notice as he could of what passed. Listening to Brayton's eternal theorizings over what he could have explained in a dozen words made him dejected and depressed. At the same time he was afraid; Brayton's persistence worried him, touched on his nerves like something nagging the exposed nerve of a decayed tooth. The alternative to fear was anger. Had he nothing to fear, he would have given way to anger long ago. He would have cursed the police, refused to co-operate with them and had a first-class row with Brayton. But he dare not risk that. Anger made one careless.

73

'Well, it's a pity, but if the launch won't steer herself, she won't,' said Frank.

'She won't,' said Dyke definitely.

'We could try again on a suitable evening,' said Frank.

'Spare us!' said Dyke quietly. 'This isn't a pleasure trip, you know.'

'Sorry, Dyke!'

'It's hardly necessary,' said Brayton.

As it grew dark, Dyke's spirits sank still lower. When he turned the launch and handed the controls over to the sergeant, Frank and Brayton went into the saloon, and he felt deserted and forlorn. Frank switched on the saloon lights, at Brayton's request, exactly like they had been for the bridge players. Dyke stood half-way between the stern and the saloon door.

'Switch the wireless on,' Brayton said to Frank. 'We're all concentrating too hard.'

The saloon and the launch and the night seemed filled with music. An orchestra was playing dance music, a jingling-jangling quickstep, through which a trumpet brayed unmusically with the persistence of a cow calling for its calf. Dyke clenched his fists, hating it, hating Brayton for wanting this miserable masquerade, hating the launch, hating himself. Then suddenly, without any announcement, the tempo of the music changed. They were playing a waltz, an old-fashioned tune, slow, dreamy, that swung in a triple arc from side to side.

The relief was immediate. Dyke was soothed. He relaxed. Imperceptibly his body moved slightly to the rhythm. He knew the tune, too. Strauss? No. Some other chap. But Austrian, definitely. Only Austrians could write exactly those tunes, sweet, treacly, but pleasant, nostalgic. There was that holiday in Vienna, with Felicity so excited and happy that he hardly noticed she did not love him. Grateful to him, very fond of him. Why, they had waltzed to this very tune in the Winter Gardens. He could

74

remember it clearly now, Felicity in his arms, the scent of her hair, her face turned up a little to smile into his eyes, the feel of her under his hands, the warmth of her flesh where it met the edge of her dress, his fingers touching the young firmness of her back. He had wanted her so badly. Let's go, he whispered, and her eyes clouded a little. Oh no, not yet, Dyke. I want to dance for hours and hours. I'd like to dance all my life. The quick feeling of disappointment and then not minding much. Not minding at all. Grateful that she was his. His, and liking him, even if not in love with him. And she seemed so near loving him.

How many, many times they had heard the tune since. And she would turn to him quickly: Oh, Dyke, listen. Our waltz. Do you remember Vienna?

Never again. Never again. He stood there in the well of the launch under the stars, and there was nobody near but damn policemen wanting to know how the wife he had murdered met her death.

One-two-three, *One*-two-three, *One*-two-three, reproached the tune, and Felicity's voice: I want to dance for hours and hours. *All*-my-life, *All*-my-life, *All*-my-life, *One*-two-three.

He could feel tears pricking his eyes.

'Get another station,' he called roughly to Frank.

Frank's head dropped to get him completely in view. 'What's up, Dyke?'

'I can't stand that damned tune . . .'

The set whistled and grunted through half a dozen stations and came to rest at a recital on a cinema organ. As Frank adjusted the volume control Dyke could hear him talking in a low voice to Brayton. Explaining about the waltz, probably. Frank had heard them speak about it more than once.

The organ was a tiresome noise, but an inexpressible relief. Dyke lit a cigarette. He could see Frank from where he stood, and a wreath of pipe smoke curling out of the doorway showed where Brayton was sitting.

Then Brayton leaned forward and spoke. 'I'd be grateful if you'd reproduce last night's movements as near as possible, Mr. Farne.'

'I'll do what I can. I wasn't noticing particularly——'

'Not exactly, of course. But if you'd go towards the stern about when you went to give your wife a drink, and then come in here—like you did then.'

'What about your constable?'

'He knows what to do and when to do it.'

Dyke smoked his cigarette. He looked away, out of the launch, into the darkness. They all faded out. There was the throb of the motor and the slight undulation of the launch over the water. He flung his cigarette from him and imagined he heard the hiss as the glowing end struck the water. Then there was another sound in his ears, the roaring splash of Gather's Mill leat as it hurled itself into the river. The turbulence made the launch dance slightly. The mill-race grew stronger, louder and louder, exactly as it had been last night . . . exactly. . . . He took a few steps towards the stern and the young policeman sitting motionless, and turned as to Felicity. Felicity too tired to argue any more, and she held out her glass and he poured the gin into it from the bottle in his hand and she raised it and drank . . .

He stumbled on his way back to the saloon, stumbled over nothing, felt the neck of the bottle clutched in his hand, stood by the saloon door, lowered his head and stepped inside. Frank and Brayton might not have been there for all the notice he took of them.

'I say, old man, you do look rotten——' Frank began, and then broke off.

Brayton sat on the settee by the wall, absorbed, intent, concentrated. Brayton was trying to catch him. Brayton knew, or

76

guessed. And yet Brayton was not there. Nobody was there, not Brayton, nor Frank, nor the policeman. Only Felicity was there. She was there. She sat on the stern, her long slim legs tucked under her, too absurdly beautiful for a woman approaching middle age. She sat there and she always would sit there. The launch was alive with her, he could feel her, hear the rustle of her dress as she moved, smell the faint perfume that always hung on her lightly like a garment. She was not angry or avenging or menacing. She was as she had always been, laughing at him kindly, mocking a little, always just out of reach . . .

Out of the darkness and through the roar of the falling mill-water came a shout. It was not loud, but it was distinct, so distinct that even Frank jumped and looked startled. But Dyke moved so sharply that he almost struck his head against the beam of the door behind him. Only Brayton was not startled. He nodded once or twice, smiled secretly to himself before he looked at his companions.

'You heard that?'

Frank wrinkled his face in a distaste that was almost disgust. 'Phew! It made me jump. I'd forgotten what we were waiting for.'

Dyke did not speak. The experience of that unexpected shout had been horrible, yet it had broken the spell that had nearly grown into a halucination. It had banished that terrifying near-ness of Felicity. He was not sure whether he was glad or sorry, but she was gone. The others were there again, real people: Frank, his friend; Brayton, the familiar acquaintance; a stolid police-sergeant; a silent, obedient constable trying to see where his comrade swam towards a flashlight held in the hand of some-body on the bank.

'I didn't hear the splash,' said Frank.

'I did,' said Brayton. 'At least, I'm pretty sure I did. It wasn't clear, not clear like the voice. It was jumbled up with the noise from the mill.'

'I'd forgotten about the splash,' said Frank. 'Did you hear it, Dyke?'

'No,' said Dyke. He was pale and grim as he turned to Brayton. 'Have you finished?'

'Why, yes, I think so——'

The sergeant's voice came from outside. 'Frame's all right, sir. They've signalled.'

'Good,' said Brayton.

'Frank, go and put on the spotlight. I'll take the wheel. I'm sick of this——'

Brayton was looking slightly ashamed, as if he had played a mean trick on someone and now was sorry for it. 'I'm sorry it's been such a strain for you.'

'You've apologized before,' said Dyke curtly. He said to Frank, 'Hurry up with that light. I want to get home.'

Chapter Nine

*

WHEN the launch ran alongside the landing-stage, Frank jumped off and made her fast. Dyke stepped after him.

'See to everything, Frank, will you?'

'Yes, of course. You go on up.'

Brayton by now was standing immediately behind Dyke.

'Will you come in for a drink?' Dyke asked him.

'I was going to ask you if I could have a word with all of you before I go.'

'Come along then.'

They set off up the path to the house. Brayton's sergeant and constable had discreetly got out of the way. There was a light shining in the windows of the lounge, and as Frank switched off the launch lights it shone down the path and showed the way to Dyke and Brayton.

They were all in the lounge—Trent reading a book, Harold absorbed in a game of patience, and Alice knitting. Only Caroline was unoccupied, and she looked anxious as the two men entered.

'We want a drink,' said Dyke after the Inspector had said good evening to them all.

'A very small one for me,' said Brayton.

Both Caroline and Alice refused anything, so Dyke poured whisky into four glasses, and set a fifth glass ready for Frank as soon as he should come in. The strain and fear he had suffered had, in spite of his determination to remain calm, turned to anger.

He was angry in general rather more than particular, but mainly with Brayton. Why should Brayton go on worrying him like this? Either he should come out with what he had on his mind, or let the matter drop. It wasn't even as if he would ever be able to find out anything. But what fanned his anger most was the sight of Trent sitting there calmly reading. After all, Trent was to blame for the whole wretched tragedy. Trent had looked up from his book to answer the Inspector's greetings; he had accepted the drink Dyke offered him. Apart from that he had taken no notice of them. Dyke could feel the anger surging up in him; he could feel it localizing itself on Trent. He did not hate Brayton, but he hated Trent.

'I'm sorry I didn't ask your men to have a drink,' he said to Brayton. 'But the fact is I'm not feeling in the mood to be hospitable.'

'Don't worry about them,' said Brayton. 'Anyhow, they're on duty.'

Harold laughed, not offensively, but as if, sensing the strained atmosphere, to lessen the tension.

'Aren't you?' he asked.

'Well, I am,' said Brayton amiably, 'but I'm able to allow myself a little latitude.'

Harold pushed his cards away from him. 'Won't come out again.'

'You should cheat, dear,' said Alice.

'I generally do. It would be nice if it would come out for once without, though.'

Dyke had given Brayton a chair, but remained standing himself. Caroline came up to him.

'Dyke, you look absolutely fagged.'

'I am.'

He had hardly realised how tired he was until Caroline reminded him. If he were not careful his weariness would swamp the anger he was nursing. He did not want that to happen. He was saving the anger until he could use it.

'Can I get you anything?' asked Caroline.

'No thanks, Caro.'

She went and sat down again, but she still glanced at him uneasily from time to time.

'Will Mr. Calvert be coming in?' Brayton asked Dyke.

'Yes, any minute now. I think I can hear him.'

A moment later Frank entered the room.

Dyke indicated the glass. 'Help yourself, Frank.'

'Thanks,' said Frank, pouring a drink.

Alice had been watching them curiously, looking from one to the other.

'Well,' she asked. 'Did you find out anything?'

Brayton looked at Dyke before he answered.

'We discovered that Mrs. Farne could have fallen off the launch without anyone hearing,' he said. 'But if she had shouted for help she must have been heard.'

'Then she couldn't have shouted,' said Frank.

'Exactly.'

No one spoke. Brayton looked at them. He knew them all pretty well; he had known them for years. At best they might have called him a friend, in less expansive moods at least a friendly acquaintance. But at this moment he realized that their feeling towards him was verging on the hostile. He finished the whisky in his glass and stood up. Standing, he was at better advantage. Only he and Dyke were on their feet, for Frank had gone to the settee where Alice was sitting.

'I must be going,' he said. 'But before I go I want to say something to all of you.' He looked at Dyke, then away again. 'I know this is painful for Mr. Farne, so I'll keep it as brief as I can. But the truth is I'm not satisfied. Obviously Mrs. Farne was unconscious when she fell into the water. But we've no idea how

81

she became unconscious. She may have fainted, though there's no apparent reason why she should have done. Or she might have been made unconscious.'

Trent broke in. He was sitting with his book closed on his lap, his forefinger in the page he was reading. 'Here, steady on, Inspector. How the devil could she be *made* unconscious?'

'By a blow, Mr. Farne. I saw the possibility of that at once, and there *was* a bruise on her head——'

'But I told you how that happened,' exclaimed Caroline indignantly.

'Yes, I know. And your explanation may be correct. But I suppose you haven't any witnesses to prove it *was* correct?'

'Well——!' Caroline half rose from her chair, caught Dyke's eyes, and subsided unwillingly.

'Did Mrs. Farne mention to any of you the fact that she hit her head against the branch of a tree?'

Nobody spoke. Brayton looked at Caroline.

'Please understand I'm not casting any doubts on your word at present. But an uncorroborated statement isn't the best evidence. I'm not saying the blow was enough to cause unconsciousness——'

'It certainly was not,' stated Caroline.

'—but on the other hand it could be. It's one of those things very difficult to judge. And there is one other point We have no evidence of when Mrs. Farne *did* fall off the launch. It could have happened at any time between when Mr. Farne gave her that drink and when the launch ran aground.'

'Hardly,' said Trent. 'Any other place except opposite Gather's Mill we'd have heard the splash.'

Brayton shrugged his shoulders expressively. 'I should imagine so,' he said drily.

'Look here,' said Harold. 'What the devil are you getting at, Brayton?'

'I'm not getting at anything. I daresay what happened was an accident. But an accident nobody can understand. And that's a most unsatisfactory accident.'

They were all openly against him now.

Alice's voice was as sharp as acid. 'All other accidents being *most* satisfactory.'

'If this accident had happened on anybody else's launch, knowing exactly what you know now, what would you think?' demanded Brayton. The antagonism was not unexpected, but he resented it. He fixed his eyes on Harold. 'Come on. Somebody falls overboard and it isn't noticed for a couple of miles. What would you think?'

His attack discomfited Harold.

'What *would* you think?'

Harold grumbled and grunted over an unwilling answer. 'I suppose—well—I might ask what they had been drinking.'

'Exactly.' Brayton was human enough to show a moment's triumph. 'There you are.'

'We were all stone cold sober,' said Trent decisively.

'I don't question that for a moment. Are you sure Mrs. Farne was? Had what she'd drunk made her sleepy, drowsy—anything like that?'

Dyke's answer snapped back, 'No!'

It would have been so easy to have allowed a doubt about this to remain in Brayton's mind. And the fellow might have been satisfied. But he could not do it. It was a course he could not even consider.

'Very well, then. What *did* make her fall in?'

'Lost her balance,' suggested Harold.

Brayton looked at him contemptuously. His grin was not free from a gamin-like vulgarity. 'There's a one-syllable word for that theory,' he said. 'But ladies being present—— Anybody losing their balance would let you know soon enough.'

'Brayton,' said Dyke. 'Why don't you say what you think?'

'I'm not thinking anything. I want to know.'

'You mean you think we're hiding something from you?' said Harold wearily.

'I don't mean that at all. I mean I *want to know*.'

Alice spoke in a very dignified voice. 'You know as much as any of us know.'

'Hardly,' said Brayton. 'You were there when it happened. I wasn't.'

All Dyke's anger drew together, concentrated itself into one towering peak of rage, trembling like a wave at breaking point. He drew in his breath to speak, felt his lip quiver uncontrollably, and had to wait until the intensity of his passion had passed. If he had spoken then he would have screamed at them.

There was an uncomfortable silence in the room as if Brayton were waiting. None of the others seemed to know what to say.

Dyke could manage his voice at last.

'Which of us *did* murder my wife, Brayton?'

They were startled, but Brayton most of all. The word 'murder' made him wince as if some obscenity had been shouted aloud. He looked at Dyke in dismay.

'I suppose you *do* know?' asked Dyke.

'Now look here, Mr. Farne——'

'No, look *here*, Inspector Brayton. You aren't satisfied; you're worried about my wife's death—and that's perfectly delightful of you, seeing how little you knew her—you feel there's something that hasn't been explained—though you haven't said which of us should do the explaining——'

Brayton had recovered a little from the shock of hearing the forbidden word. 'I made no accusation——'

'Not directly——'

'Not even indirectly.'

Dyke suddenly laughed. It was a loud laugh that jarred on all their nerves like the point of a knife drawn across glass.

84

'No? Then I must apologize for misunderstanding you. It seems clear enough. My wife had an accident and was drowned. But it isn't clear to you, apparently. What sort of an accident? Why did she fall? How did she fall? Where did she fall? Who was there when she fell?'

Brayton looked sulky. Beneath Dyke's carefully nursed anger an uneasy thought stirred. Perhaps he'd gone too far. It would have been better to be patient whatever the strain had cost him. But it had been growing in his mind that Brayton guessed; that he knew.

'Those are reasonable questions,' said Brayton. 'Quite reasonable.'

'Now you want to know how she got that blow on the head.'

Brayton's doubts rallied under this reminder. 'Naturally I'd be glad to be certain about it,' but he spoke warily.

Caroline did not say anything, but she caught her breath sharply. It was as good as a reproof.

'We've told you all we can,' said Dyke. 'We've told you all we know. As far as you're in the dark, we're in the dark too. The alternative is that we're all a pack of damned liars. Is that what you're trying to convey?'

'There's no need to take that tone,' said Brayton.

'No, quite—you're only doing your duty. Or overdoing it. We might all be lying. We could be. We could have killed my wife between us——'

They were all staring at him. They looked a little shocked. Very slightly their sympathies turned towards Brayton and away from him. He was going too far now.

'That's a ridiculous suggestion,' said Brayton. 'Such an idea was never near my mind.'

A sort of bravado took possession of Dyke. He had gone too far, and he was going to go even further. Better get this over and done with.

'All the others were in the saloon,' said Dyke. 'I was outside. I am the only person who could have'—he was going to say, hit my wife on the head, but the words were wrong. He could not speak them—'I am the only one who could have done anything,' he said.

Brayton, his forehead deeply creased, the eyebrows meeting, stared at him.

'I say, old man——' began Harold.

But it was between Dyke and Brayton. The others were outside, Harold's words fell off without penetrating, like pebbles on a glass pane.

'Was that what you were hinting at?'

'N-o,' said Brayton slowly. As he spoke he was thinking, considering, weighing up, one part of his mind controlling speech, the other part tearing furiously at the puzzle. 'I wasn't hinting at anything. I haven't hinted. I've merely asked questions. Doing my duty—as you said.'

The atmosphere was electric. Dyke wanting to stop now, could not. He was aware of them all watching him, distressed, yet with something that added up in the total to more than distress. Frank had finished his drink quickly and placed the glass with a sharp click on the table. Trent put down his book, Harold pushed the patience cards together and a little away from him as if he could not concentrate with them so near.

Dyke, on his slope, had started to slide and must go to the bottom.

'It's a possibility, you know,' he said to Brayton.

'I suppose it is,' agreed Brayton. Then, more slowly, 'I suppose so.'

'You could consider it.'

'I could, couldn't I?' Brayton, unsure of himself, was going cautiously. 'But I think we'll count such a—such a possibility—we can count it right out.'

Dyke knew the beginning of relief.

'I've never thought of such a thing,' said Brayton. He might have been lying, but perhaps it was the least he could say. 'The idea never occurred to me. And even if it had'—he half smiled, feeling the tension around him relax a little—'if the idea weren't too preposterous in itself, it wouldn't be much good, would it?'

'Wouldn't it?'

'Well'—Brayton made an expressive gesture—'even if you wanted to accuse yourself you wouldn't have a witness.'

He spoke pleasantly enough, but to Dyke the words jarred. Did he mean he'd be ready to consider the idea if he could have a witness? Or what would do as well, a motive? The thought scared him a little. He turned to glance at Trent, and Trent was looking at him with a curious expression in his eyes. All Trent had to do was to get up and say: Felicity was going to leave him; she was going to come away with me.

He felt his anger and hatred rise in him and had to look away. He had already said far too much.

'Inspector Brayton,' said Caroline. 'I think we have all put up with just a little more than we can endure. My brother and his wife were devoted to each other and this is terribly distressing for him——'

'I know,' said Brayton. 'I'm very sorry. But I have to find out all I can. The coroner will ask questions, you know. For that matter, so will the public. It's far better for all concerned if I have a complete story to tell. Mr. Farne only confuses the issue by getting angry with me—and by irrelevancies like pointing out that he and Mrs. Farne were alone to all intents and purposes——'

'But they weren't alone,' Alice pointed out plaintively.

Dyke saw he had done some damage; he wondered how much and wished he had kept his tongue still.

'No, not in a way. But the rest of you were concentrating on your game. You were in a lighted room and Mr. and Mrs. Farne were outside——'

'Wait a minute.' They all turned to look at Frank as he spoke for the first time. He got up as if he could speak better standing on his feet. 'You've got that wrong, Inspector.'

'What have I got wrong?' asked Brayton.

'Why, you speak as if—as if Mr. and Mrs. Farne were alone at the stern of the boat. Out of sight of the rest of us.'

'Well?'

'I wasn't playing bridge, you know. You saw to-night where I sat. From there I could see out. I couldn't see Mrs. Farne. My line of vision was—well, sort of oblique. But I could see the side of the boat as far as the stern. And Mr. Farne was in sight all the time.'

Brayton worked this out. He was back in the launch visualizing angles and lines of vision. He nodded.

'I see,' he said.

'I know,' Frank went on, 'that the whole rotten business is quite obviously an accident. But I thought I'd better say this since you've pointed out that we didn't all know what the others were doing. Because you're wrong there. We did. Mr. Farne wasn't out of my sight. I could see all of him all the time. When he was pouring Mrs. Farne's drink I suppose he was probably in sight only from the waist down. But I could see him.'

Brayton breathed deeply. 'Thanks.'

'Not at all.'

'I wish I'd known this sooner.'

'My dear man, you didn't ask.'

'I suppose I didn't.' Brayton glanced from one to another of them. 'You all gave the impression that Mr. and Mrs. Farne were—how shall I put it?—apart from the rest of you.'

What had he been thinking, Dyke wondered. After all, he was far from being a fool. If he'd known about Felicity's plan. . . . Dyke's anger was evaporating. He was still angry, but no longer in that wild unreasonable way. The only person he was still angry with was Trent. He wished he had not lost his temper; already he was searching back into his mind wondering exactly what he had said.

Brayton gave a deep, gusty sigh. 'I must be going,' he said. He made a part rueful, part apologetic grin to Dyke. 'I'm sorry I've been tiresome.'

'It's all right,' said Dyke.

'I know your wife's death was an accident. But it is such an unexplainable accident in so many ways.'

'All accidents are,' said Dyke. 'Until after they're explained.'

'Perhaps so. But I couldn't get out of my mind two possibilities. One was that your wife might have had too much to drink——'

'You can wash that out,' said Dyke.

'The other was that someone might have been on the launch, or might have got on to the launch and—well, and knocked her out.'

'Impossible.'

'All right,' said Brayton. 'I have to consider these things, though.'

Dyke nodded. Now Frank had gone back to his seat by Alice, he and Brayton might have been actors playing out a scene, the others their audience. Only nobody applauded. None of them spoke. There was one of those awkward silences when all that had to be said was said and none were quite sure what came next.

'I'll be getting along,' said Brayton.

'Have another drink before you go,' said Dyke.

Brayton was obviously going to refuse, then he thought better of it; a drink more than anything else, would restore the normal relationship between them.

'A very small one,' he said. 'Thanks.'

Dyke poured the drink and one for himself at the same time, and they drank together, and then he went to the door with Brayton to see him off.

Chapter Ten

*

WHEN Dyke came back into the hall, Frank was crossing it on his way to the stairs.

'I think I'll go up,' he said. 'I'm tired.'

'Yes, you must be,' said Dyke. 'Get some sleep. It's a damned shame dragging you into all this.'

'I'm not being dragged into anything.'

'It's all mighty unpleasant, anyhow,' said Dyke. 'And thanks—for what you said just now.'

Frank had a foot on the bottom stair; his hand was on the banister. He turned.

'That was nothing.'

'It was quite a lot,' said Dyke. 'In fact it was quite a useful lie.'

'Lie?'

'You couldn't see me at all. Even if you'd been looking, you couldn't have seen much of me, and you weren't looking. Why did you do it, Frank?'

Frank grinned. 'Well, that chap seemed to be so anxious to invent some weird explanation of Felicity's fall, I wondered where he'd get to next. So I thought it would be as well to head him off.'

'Perhaps it was,' said Dyke. 'Thanks for doing it, anyhow.'

'It was nothing at all,' said Frank. 'Good night.'

Harold and Alice were coming out of the lounge on their way to bed as Dyke went in. Trent had picked up his book again and was reading.

'Caro, you look worn out,' said Dyke. 'Why don't you go and get some sleep?'

Trent closed his book and put out a hand as if to get up.

'Don't go for a minute, Trent,' said Dyke. 'I'd like a word with you.'

He could feel his anger rising against Trent again. He wished now he had saved it all for Trent, but it was too late to bother about that. Caroline, looking from one to the other of them was uneasy and a little disappointed. She wanted to stay and hear what they had to say, but after what Dyke had told her during the afternoon this was her cue to leave them. Dyke's suggestion about getting some sleep was no less than a dismissal. Her instinct was to reach out to share anything he had a part in. But this was a situation she could not share.

'Would either of you like anything before I go?' she asked.

'Nothing for me thanks, Caroline,' said Trent.

'You ought to have something, Dyke,' she said. 'Something to make you sleep. Hot milk?'

'No thanks, Caro. Nothing at all.'

She rose reluctantly and said good night to them and went. Dyke walked slowly across to the fireplace.

Trent was lighting his pipe. 'What's the matter, Dyke?' he asked. 'Anything I can do for you?'

Dyke turned. He was pale and his hands shook a little

'Yes,' he said in an unemotional, level voice, though it was costing him an effort to remain calm. 'You can get out.'

Trent, drawing the match flame into the bowl of his pipe, threw the match on to an ashtray and took the pipe out of his mouth. 'Get out?' he repeated.

Dyke's voice lost some of its flatness. 'Yes. Go,' he said emphatically.

'But my dear chap——'

'Go,' said Dyke again. 'Clear out. Beat it. Get to hell out of here.'

91

'Good lord!' exclaimed Trent. He pushed the pipe into his pocket and stood up. 'Of course I'll go if you want me to, Dyke, but what on earth's the matter?'

'Look here,' said Dyke. 'There's no need to act the innocent. I know.'

'You *know*? What do you know? Are you crazy?'

'Probably,' said Dyke. 'It's a wonder if I'm not.'

'But what is it you say you know?'

'Ah, don't act the fool,' said Dyke in disgust. 'Don't pretend. I know about you—and Felicity.'

Trent looked at him in blank surprise.

'I think you *are* crazy,' he said. 'I haven't the faintest idea what you're talking about.'

He sounded so genuinely surprised that Dyke looked at him in doubt. Was it possible he had been mistaken? Of course, Trent would naturally pretend and deny. Trent was open enough, but for Felicity's sake, now she was dead, he would have to deny there had ever been anything between them. He'd been trying to protect her memory and his peace of mind. All his suspicions welled up again.

'That policeman's got under your skin, hasn't he?' said Trent. 'You can't think I had anything to do with Felicity's death?'

'The sooner you go, the better, Trent.'

'But it's ridiculous,' said Trent. 'What *is* it about me and Felicity?'

Dyke had gone very pale. 'You knew Felicity was leaving me, didn't you?'

'Leaving you?' Trent took a pace forward, then stopped. 'Look, Dyke, you've had a terrible blow, I know——'

'She was leaving me,' said Dyke. 'She was going away with you.'

A moment passed. 'Where did you get that yarn from?'

Dyke became wary. Trent wanted to find out how much he knew.

'Never mind where I got it from.'

'But, my dear chap, you can't come out with a preposterous accusation like this——'

'It is not preposterous. She told me herself.'

'She told you—that she was leaving you for me? I don't believe you.'

Dyke had to be fair. He wanted confirmation of what he knew was the truth. He wanted Trent to confess before he went. But he could not lie about it.

'She told me she was leaving me,' he said.

'I don't believe you. Man, you're overwrought. You're all worked up—and I don't wonder at it. But you're making a mountain of some petty molehill.'

'It's no molehill. She was leaving me. She was going away with another man.'

'Are you sure about this?' said Trent.

'Of course I'm sure. You don't think I'm making it up—or imagining it?' His anger surged up again. 'And you know damn well I'm not.'

Trent had taken his pipe out of his pocket and was lighting it again. Over the bowl he watched Dyke, and the expression in his eyes was sobering.

'Do you mean to tell me that Felicity said she was leaving you for me?'

'No,' shouted Dyke. 'No! She didn't say it was you.' He was stung into the admission and he hated making it. If he were not careful Trent would get away without admitting anything. Trent was always like this, calm, cool, hardly ever ruffled. He was too damn quiet—and deep. But he'd have to own up now—and go. 'Who else would it be?' he said angrily. 'You always were in love with her, weren't you? You'd have had her in the first place if you'd had the chance. I know you, Trent. You've waited all these years for the chance to take her from me, haven't you? And now you thought you'd got it. Only you were wrong. Felicity's dead. You didn't take her from me, after all. You've lost——'

'Dyke,' said Trent sharply. 'Lower your voice.'

Dyke stopped. He lost his erectness and seemed to droop as he walked over to the couch where Alice had been, and sat down on it dejectedly with his shoulders hunched up. His head sank forward so that his eyes no longer saw Trent, and he passed both hands wearily down the sides of his face.

'Now listen to me.' Trent's voice, though low, was decisive and commanding. 'You've been through a hell of a time in the last twenty-four hours. Are you sure what you're telling me is the truth? That Felicity was going to leave you?'

Dyke nodded. 'Go on. Keep up the act. You know nothing about it, of course. But if you want it this way you can have it. She *was* going to leave me.'

'All right. She told you that. But she did not say I was the man?'

'No,' said Dyke. 'She tried to keep you out of it. Don't worry about that. She didn't give you away.'

'She wouldn't say who the man was?'

'No, she wouldn't.'

'You just guessed it was me?'

'I know——'

'All right. You know. But——'

'If you had any sense of decency you'd have gone without any of this fuss. What's the good of arguing? I never want to see your face again——'

'Wait a minute,' said Trent. 'Take it easy. If I could do any good by going, I'd go. But we've always been friends, and I can't clear out letting you think a lie like that about me and Felicity.' Dyke was going to speak, but he put up a hand to stop him. 'Wait a minute. Let me finish. I'll take your word for it that she was going to leave you. It seems incredible, but I can see it must

94

be the truth. And if you don't know who she was going with I can see, in a way, why you thought it was me. I've always been fond of her. Perhaps when you married her I was a bit in love with her as well. But I never had a chance. I never even tried for a chance. And I certainly haven't thought of her all the years you two have been married, except as a fine and lovely woman. I've never thought of having a shot at taking her from you. I've never wanted to take her from you. And if I had wanted to, I know I couldn't have done it.'

'All right,' said Dyke wearily. 'I expected something like this. You had to protect her—if it is protecting her—or is it yourself? Finish your speech and go.'

'I'd go if I thought it would help,' said Trent. 'But I don't think it would. So I will finish, though it means I'll have to tell you something I didn't want to tell you. Has it ever struck you, Dyke, to wonder why I've never married?'

Dyke looked up. 'I've never thought about it.'

'I suppose you've had it at the back of your mind that because I was a bit in love with Felicity when you married her I've gone on nursing a hopeless passion for her——'

'I tell you I've never thought about it. Not until now.'

'And it struck you that I was very fond of her, which is the truth. I was. But I was fond of both of you——'

'That's delicately expressed,' said Dyke.

'It happens to be the truth. But to come back to what I was saying. And perhaps this will help to show you you've been barking up the wrong tree. You see, Dyke, there *is* a woman——'

Dyke looked up again. 'What the devil are you talking about?'

There was a queer, strained smile on Trent's face.

'Well, to put it plainly, I'm already in love. In fact—to keep on putting it plainly—she's my mistress——'

He nodded in answer to Dyke's incredulous stare.

'Yes, it's the truth.'

'Then why haven't you married?'

'Because she already is married. And her husband won't divorce her. If he ever did get as far as that he'd take her children away from her. And if she ran away with me he'd still take them. So for their sakes she sticks it out. And I get'—his smile became even more strained—'I get the crumbs that fall from his table.'

Dyke stood up and the two men stood facing one another.

'Is this the truth?' demanded Dyke.

'It is,' said Trent. 'I'd think of a cleverer yarn if I had to make one up.' He put his hands in his pockets and turned away.

'Is it anyone I know?' asked Dyke.

'I suppose you must have met her. It's Margaret Spencer. You know what old Spencer's like. She doesn't live with him. I have that small comfort. It's been going on for ten years. We keep hoping for something to happen—at least I do—wondering if Spencer will break his neck, or fall over a cliff or something, but he's the sort who lives to be a very trying and bad-tempered hundred. Margaret says when the children are grown-up and old enough to understand——' He shrugged his shoulders. 'What I'm afraid is that we'll have grown too old to mind very much.'

Dyke did not know what to say at first. They looked at one another in silence. Then Trent went back to his chair and began lighting his pipe again.

'I'm sorry, Trent,' said Dyke at last.

Trent sounded weary. 'It's all right.'

'I've made a damn fool of myself.'

'It's all right,' said Trent again. He waved the hand holding the pipe as if to put the whole business right out of the way. 'I suppose it was natural for you to think what you did.'

'I just couldn't think of anybody else, that was the trouble,' said Dyke unhappily. 'We've all been so close all these years. I couldn't imagine Felicity falling for anybody else. For her to love you seemed—almost natural.'

'We're a cheerful pair,' said Trent. He grinned, but wryly, as if at something that hurt. 'You know, Dyke, I still can't get it into my head what you've said.'

'I haven't altogether got it into mine yet. It was only a few days ago she told me. Like a damned nightmare it's been——'

'You're sure it *isn't* a nightmare?' said Trent. 'You know you've been through a hell of a lot——'

'I'm not imagining it if that's what you mean. It's no nightmare. I'm still sane.'

'I don't suppose you want to talk about it——'

'No, I don't. But I don't mind talking about it to you. It's a relief in a way.' He began to pace backwards and forwards across the room. 'I haven't been able to talk about it to anybody else.'

'You don't know who she was going with?'

'No. She wouldn't say. In a way it didn't seem to matter. The important thing was that she was going, not who she was going with.'

'But why?' said Trent. '*Why?*'

'That's what I'd like to know. And yet, at times, I seem to understand. For one thing, she'd never been in love.'

'But, my dear chap——'

'She'd not, Trent. It's the truth. She always liked me but that was all. She didn't love me when we married. And she never did love me. Not physically. She was fond of me. I believe that. In fact, I know she had a real affection for me. But I'd never moved her. She'd never really been awakened. Perhaps it was my own fault. I don't know. Perhaps I wasn't very clever about it. We get thinking love is something that just happens.' He paused, recalling what Caroline had said. 'And she'd got to the age when if it was ever to happen at all it had to happen damn quick. She didn't want—she didn't expect'—he paused again—'I don't think she expected anything lasting. I think she just wanted to be in love for once in her life—she felt she'd missed something——'

He stopped, halted in his pacing to face Trent. 'What's the good! I can't explain. Either you understand or you don't.'

'I do,' said Trent.

Dyke resumed his walking to and fro.

'Desire is the devil,' said Trent. 'It's all right when it works out all right. But very often it doesn't. If only we could keep our affections and our lusts separate. Or not let them affect each other. But they do. It doesn't seem very well arranged, does it? I suppose there's a purpose in it. Or isn't there? It would be a bit too tough on us to be merely haphazard.'

'I've not thought about it,' said Dyke. 'All I know is that everything seems pretty bloody.'

'It's queer,' said Trent. 'Once you want something like hell you're finished. In a way I've had more from Felicity than you have, though it was you who married her. I've liked her more than I've ever liked any woman, and I think she liked me——'

'Of course she did.'

'But we didn't want each other and that left us free,' said Trent. 'I've never wanted to cuckold you, Dyke, and I'm sure she never thought of such a thing, either. The result was near perfect. But you've had her and it's just a torment to you. You can't be happy because you possessed her. It's the same with me and Margaret. All I live for is the hours we can be together. I can go to bed with her in a secret, furtive way every now and again. We have to be careful—discreet's the word, I suppose—like always looking over your shoulder to make sure nobody's spying. It's sheer damn misery. I'm even envying old Spencer all the time because I know that she feels an affection for him, loathsome though the old devil really is.'

'You make me wonder what Felicity's unknown felt about me,' said Dyke. 'Let's drop the subject.'

'That's a good idea,' said Trent. 'There are times when I look forward to when desire won't exist in me. And that idea's not attractive, either. Only it will be a release. And you get to a point where release seems more important than anything else. I wonder if that's what suicides feel.'

'I wouldn't know.'

'Only they know, and they don't tell.'

'I think I'll go to bed. I feel completely washed out. But I don't suppose I'll sleep.'

'We'd better both go to bed,' said Trent. 'I'm not so spry myself. By the way, I suppose nobody else knows about Felicity?'

'Caro knows. I told her the bare facts, that's all. Though bare facts are about all I know myself.'

'I shouldn't think about it,' said Trent. 'Silly damn thing to say, because you won't be able to help yourself thinking about it. But it's good advice. And I wouldn't tell anybody else, either. Caroline's all right, of course. She won't talk. But for better or worse it's all over. Talking about it won't do any good. Come to think of it, it's perhaps as well that Brayton doesn't know this.'

'Yes,' agreed Dyke thoughtfully. 'That hadn't escaped me.'

'I didn't know he was such a worrying sort of chap.'

'I suppose he doesn't get many violent deaths to worry about.'

'If he knew there'd been trouble between you and Felicity he'd start making up a theory to fit it.'

'You mean he'd think I murdered her?'

Trent looked startled, almost frightened. 'Good lord, Dyke, you don't need to say things like that!'

Dyke had not meant to. He had said it before he could stop himself. He only had to be with someone like Trent, someone with whom he had been intimate for years, to grow careless. Not that it mattered saying things to Trent.

'I didn't really mean it,' he said. 'Only Brayton's attitude has got me on the raw a bit.'

'I don't wonder. But don't say that sort of thing in front of anybody else.'

'I won't. But it's over now. Unless Felicity's—lover, if he was her lover—comes into the open.'

'I should think he'll keep very much in the dark,' said Trent.

'Queer,' said Dyke. 'I shall never know who he is.'

Trent rose from his chair and tapped out his pipe in an ashtray.

'I'm for bed, Dyke. I hope you get some sleep.' He paused on his way to the door. 'You haven't any idea what you're going to do, I suppose.'

'Do?'

'I mean after it's all over. Inquest, funeral, and so on.'

'I haven't thought about it. I'll stay on here probably.'

'You ought to get Caroline to come here. You'll have to have somebody to look after you.'

'I daresay she will,' said Dyke. 'Something like that has been at the back of my mind.'

'You couldn't do better.'

'I suppose you're right,' said Dyke. He sounded lonely and unhappy. 'Yes, I suppose it's the only thing.'

'Quite a good thing,' said Trent.

After Trent had gone, Dyke felt empty of emotion. He was glad that Trent had not betrayed him, but he seemed to have no energy left for worrying over the problem. They had been friends all their lives and it would have been doubling his loss if he had lost Trent as well. But emptied of the hatred that had filled him, nothing came to take its place. He was not, for the moment, even wondering who Felicity had fallen in love with. The worst tragedies get to a point when nothing seems to matter any more.

When he went to bed he fell asleep heavily, and it was late the next morning when he awoke.

Chapter Eleven

*

HE had hardly finished breakfast when Caroline came in to tell him he was wanted on the telephone.

'It's Dr. Ryder,' she said. 'He wants to speak to you particularly.'

'Ryder?' he said. 'I thought he was on holiday.'

'Evidently he's back.'

'Evidently.' He put down with a sigh the newspaper he had been looking through. 'Ah well, I'd better see what he wants.'

'Dyke?' said the doctor's voice when he picked up the receiver.

'Good morning, Arthur,' said Dyke. 'I thought you were away.'

'I was. I only got home an hour ago. My dear chap, about Felicity, I'm most dreadfully sorry.'

'Thanks,' said Dyke. 'Thanks very much, Arthur.' So many people had said they were sorry that the words did not register any more. No doubt they were, and if anybody was Arthur Ryder would be, for he had been their friend as well as their doctor for many years. But condolences had become merely something that had to be answered suitably.

'I only saw it in the paper yesterday, Dyke. I was in Scotland, you know——'

'Fishing, I suppose. You had a good time, I hope?'

Ryder did not answer the question. 'I packed up and came home at once.'

Dyke thought a moment. The Ryders were friends, but the

friendship was not so deep that they would break off their holiday because of Felicity's death.

'D'you mean you came home because she's dead?' He was puzzled.

'Yes, of course——'

'That's awfully good of you, old man——'

Ryder's voice interrupted. 'Listen, Dyke. I can't talk to you properly on the phone. Could you come over to see me?'

'What, now?'

'Yes, this morning, if possible. I'd come out to you, but I may go back to Scotland in a day or two, and there are a few things I want to see to while I'm here.'

'I could come into town'—said Dyke doubtfully. He did not particularly want to see anybody or talk to anybody just then, but Ryder sounded urgent—'if it's important.'

'It is important.'

'The inquest is this afternoon, you know?'

'Yes, so I've heard. That's why I want to see you this morning if I can.'

'Is it about Felicity's death?'

'Yes.'

'All right,' said Dyke. He thought a moment. 'All right. About half an hour.'

'I'll be waiting for you.'

What now, he asked himself as he replaced the receiver. He stood a minute by the telephone, motionless, trying to think. He was losing that blessed indifference that had descended on him at the end of the previous night. He wanted to cling to that, but he felt tension, and that excitement so closely akin to fear rising again in him, waking his brain, quickening his pulse, so that as soon as he started to think the muscles of his stomach seemed to tighten. After to-morrow I can relax, he thought, but he wondered if that really would be so. He never seemed to relax.

He was like a man walking all the time on a tightrope, keyed up, watchful.

The doctor, whatever his other concerns, was waiting for him. He took him through the surgery into his private office.

'Sit down, Dyke,' he said, pulling forward a chair. He himself took the seat by his desk, a fact Dyke did not fail to observe. It meant that the interview was to be official. 'I don't need to say again how sorry I am——' He cleared his throat, fidgeting with the articles on his pen-tray. 'We both are. You have—our deepest sympathy and all that.'

'Thanks,' said Dyke. Ryder had said all this on the telephone. He could have offered all the sympathy he wanted to then. This was not the reason he had asked to see him. He added, 'You know what happened, of course?'

'I saw it in the paper.' Ryder looked at him quickly, then away again. 'And I've heard since I've come home—details that weren't in the newspaper account, and so on——'

Again that crinkling and tautening of the stomach. The sensation induced a quick spasm of nausea.

'What you mean,' said Dyke, after a slight pause, 'is that you've heard rumours?'

'No,' said Ryder quickly. Then, 'Oh well, yes, put it that way if you like. That's why I'm glad I came back.'

'You really did come back specially because of the accident?'

Ryder looked grave. 'I thought it best.'

Dyke's mind had moved away from Ryder's admission about rumours, but he came back to it.

'What's being said about the accident?' he asked.

He watched the other man intently, fearing the answer, yet determined not to be put off.

Ryder did not try to put him off. He looked uncomfortable, but Dyke knew he would speak the truth.

'Well—I suppose people have got an idea—she had probably drunk too much.'

'They're wrong,' said Dyke promptly. It was a relief that attention so far had not focused on the detail that only he could have caused Felicity's death—at least he was spared that—yet, much as he longed to avoid that focus, he could not bring himself to be shielded by pretending Felicity was drunk. 'You're wrong, Arthur. She wasn't tight. She was perfectly sober.'

'I'm glad you're sure of that.'

'I'm quite sure.'

Ryder got up from his chair and went a few steps toward the window. He took out a cigarette and lit it, and then, as if it were an afterthought, offered his case to Dyke. Dyke shook his head.

'It wasn't suicide,' said Ryder. 'If she'd wanted to commit suicide she wouldn't have done it like that.'

'Who said it was suicide?' demanded Dyke. He was beginning to feel angry. Was this to be another inquisition like Brayton's? 'It *could* have been just an accident.'

Ryder gave him a quick glance. 'I wasn't suggesting it was suicide, Dyke. I'm sorry, old man, we're not getting anywhere. I ought to have come to the point sooner. Only I suppose I'm dodging it.'

'Dodging what?'

'Why do you suppose I broke my holiday like this?'

'I haven't had time to think about it yet,' said Dyke. He had done nothing but think about it since he had put down the telephone, but he could hardly admit the fact. 'You said it was because of Felicity——'

'Well, here it is,' said Ryder. He came to stand facing Dyke, his cigarette between his fingers. 'About a month ago Felicity came to see me.'

Once more Dyke could feel himself shrinking inside. The least thing now set him on edge. Surely she hadn't confided her intentions to Arthur Ryder.

'As a patient,' added Ryder.

'A patient? But there wasn't a thing wrong with her.'

'No,' said Ryder reminiscently. 'No, that's what she said. She had a touch of indigestion, that's all. Or so she told me. She'd had it on and off for some time. She just came to make sure——'

'Well,' said Dyke impatiently. 'Go on.'

'I'm afraid it wasn't indigestion.'

There was a slight pause.

'What d'you mean?' demanded Dyke.

'She was seriously ill.'

'Ill?' repeated Dyke. 'Felicity? My dear chap, you must have made a mistake. She was as strong as a horse. Why, I can hardly remember her having as much as a headache——'

'Listen to me,' said Ryder. 'I'll try to tell you the whole story. Most of my patients who come to me with heart troubles are suffering from indigestion. Felicity came with a suggestion that she had indigestion—I don't know what suspicions she'd had, mind you—and it turned out to be her heart——'

'Not serious,' said Dyke.

Ryder corrected him. 'Very serious indeed. At first I tried to put her off. I told her her heart was the trouble, of course, but I said we'd have a fuller examination and she'd better bring you along and all that. I didn't want to tell her, Dyke, but you know what she was. She knew right away that something was seriously wrong, and she made me tell her the truth. And then she made me promise that I wouldn't tell you.' He shrugged his shoulders expressively. 'You can guess how much chance I had. If she'd been an ordinary patient instead of a friend I could have held her off——'

'And what was the truth?'

'The truth——' Ryder drew hard at his cigarette a few times,

then threw it down into an ashtray from which it sent up a lazy spiral of smoke. He stood watching this. 'The truth? That's harder, Dyke. There's no absolute truth in medicine. The truth, so far as I could tell her, was that her heart was in a very dangerous condition. It could let her down any time——'

'You mean she might have died suddenly?'

'It was liable to give trouble at any moment. That doesn't necessarily mean she was going to die soon. There aren't many diseases in which any doctor can predict so much with absolute certainty. But it meant, if she wanted to live, she would have to change her life completely.'

Ryder stopped, took up the still smoking cigarette and stubbed it out viciously.

'A radical change. That was her only hope. She'd always led a very active, full life, as, of course, I knew very well. And I pointed out it would have to end. No more games, no golf or tennis or anything like that. She'd have to cut out smoking and drinking completely. A great deal of rest would be necessary. A great deal——'

'Do you mean she'd have been an invalid?' asked Dyke.

Ryder's forehead wrinkled as he answered. 'For a time she would have had to give up every form of exertion. Every one. Even walking. The condition might have yielded to treatment. To some extent, anyhow. You never know with these cases. And then—well, she could have been allowed some limited activity. Not a lot, I'm afraid.'

'What you mean is she *would* have become an invalid?'

Ryder was not willing to commit himself. 'She'd have had to live her life on a different plane. I tried to explain that to her. A quieter, more subdued plane. After all, you've done a lot, Dyke. You've travelled, done things, been to places. She'd had that. It couldn't be taken from her. You've been always on the move. It's been a restless sort of life'—he qualified his words—'at least it seems so to me. But life isn't all being on the move. Plenty of people are happy living a very quiet existence——'

'I see,' said Dyke. He repeated, 'A very quiet existence.'

'To some extent the sort of life you live when you're down here. You and Felicity have always been happy over there on the river. You could have settled down there for a year or two for a start—that would have been a beginning. Until we saw how she went on.'

'Always the fear of sudden death?' suggested Dyke.

Ryder made a face. 'Always a possibility, I must admit. That is, if she took risks.'

Dyke got up and walked across the room. He went to the window so that his back was to the other man.

'Well?' he asked over his shoulder.

Ryder breathed deeply. It was almost a sigh. 'There's really not much more to say. You know what she was like. You should. She was your wife. She didn't show much. She didn't say much——'

'Did she promise to do as you advised?'

'She didn't promise anything. It must have been a hell of a shock for her. She said she wanted time to think. Something like that. And she insisted that I should not tell you until she said I could.'

'I wish I'd known,' said Dyke. He still had his back to Ryder. He wondered what difference it would have made if he had known. Would it have made any difference? He was too stunned yet to see what it all meant. 'I wish you *had* told me, Arthur.'

'I wish I could have done. But she wouldn't agree. My hands were tied.'

'Yes, I understand.'

He turned round at last. Ryder had lit another cigarette and was smoking it quickly. He did not inhale but puffed the smoke out rapidly so that he was standing with his head in a faint blue haze. They looked at one another.

'Where are we?' said Dyke, sounding a little bewildered. 'I'm lost.'

Ryder nodded. 'I know. It's the devil! On top of everything else. But this is how I see it, and it's why I felt I had to come home. There was always the danger of Felicity having a heart attack——'

'Do you mean——' Dyke searched for words. 'Do you mean she was likely to—drop dead?'

'Hardly,' said Ryder. 'A slight one at first, perhaps.'

'Yes?' said Dyke.

'That must be what happened the night—she was drowned. She was sitting there—I know the way she used to perch up on the stern—I've seemed to be seeing it in my mind's eye ever since I read she was dead. She was sitting there, had an attack, and fell backwards into the river.'

To Dyke it was as if a curtain had been ripped away. He saw many things—a jumble of pictures that sorted themselves out gradually. For the moment he forgot Felicity in her relationship to himself. All he could see was a woman with a very bad heart who sat on the stern of a launch and collapsed alone in the darkness. . . .

His voice suddenly became excited.

'Have you seen Inspector Brayton since you came home?'

Ryder shook his head. 'No.'

'Then you'd better. You'd better tell him what you've told me.'

'Yes, I've been meaning to do something like that. It struck me that he might like me to give evidence at the inquest.'

'That's right,' said Dyke. 'That clears things up. That clears things up nicely——'

He became aware that his friend was eyeing him with curiosity.

'You see, Arthur, Brayton's been a damn' nuisance ever since—ever since it happened. He wasn't satisfied. Those are his own words. He couldn't understand what happened or how it happened. He even suggested—that there'd been foul play——'

'Oh *no!*' exclaimed Ryder. 'Not our Brayton! He's usually such a sensible type.'

'He's been nagging away at one or another of us for days.' Dyke passed a hand over his forehead. 'Seems more like years. He's had an idea we were keeping something from him. On the day she—died, Felicity knocked her head against that low branch of the beech tree on the edge of the lawn. It left a bit of a bruise and *that* kept Brayton up to concert pitch.'

'But how ridiculous!'

'Perhaps so. But you'd better have a word with him as soon as you can.'

'I shall,' said Ryder. 'Mind you, Dyke, you've got to be fair. To anyone who doesn't know what I've just told you, the accident does seem a strange affair. Of course, newspapers are nothing to go by, but the paper I saw the account in had a heading "Woman Disappears From Launch," or something like that. Sensational as they could make it sound, naturally. It was the most damnable luck that none of you heard her. She must have fallen by Gather's Mill. But the public makes up its mind from the facts it gets.'

'Damn the public!' said Dyke.

'Quite. But the conclusion they'd come to is that Felicity must have been hellish tight, and the rest of you even tighter, since you didn't hear anything or do anything. We'll be able to put their minds at rest for them.'

'The state of their minds is a terrible worry to me,' said Dyke.

'Don't be bitter about them, Dyke. Everybody who knew Felicity loved her, and they like you and are sorry for you. You've nothing but sympathy. But it's only human nature to speculate over and relish anything that might be scandalous.

"Public school boy in dock" is news, you know. "Boy in dock" isn't. The higher you go, the further you fall.'

'Well,' said Dyke. 'I'd better be going.' He looked at Ryder and gave a nod. 'Thanks for everything, Arthur. I won't forget what you've done.'

'Nonsense!' said Ryder. 'I saw I could clear things up. I'd have had to clear them up eventually. The sensible time was before the inquest—at it, if necessary.'

'You're going back?'

'I'm not sure yet. Anyhow, I shall stay over the funeral.'

Dyke moved slowly towards the door.

'Have lunch with us?' Ryder invited. 'Muriel is out at the moment, but I know she'd like to see you.'

'Not now, old man, thanks all the same. I'm poor company at present, for one thing, and for another I've a lot of things to do.'

'I'll see you this afternoon then, I expect.'

'Yes, this afternoon.'

Dyke got into his car and drove away from the doctor's house with something akin to elation in his heart. Free, really free now. Nothing to worry about. What Ryder had said, what he would say, would leave him clear for ever of suspicion.

And he was just beginning to realize how much he had feared suspicion. Only one thing he lacked. There was no Felicity for him to go home to and tell of his relief.

Chapter Twelve

*

HIS relief was short-lived. It carried him through the inquest, but once that was over it died away like the effects of a drug, and his mind was tearing and worrying at his problem again. He could not get what the doctor had told him out of his mind. Felicity under sentence of death. And, in quite another way, sentence had been carried out. With him as her executioner. The horror of what he had done descended on him like a dark pall, smothering him so that he felt he could not breathe. He kept trying to decide what she had been thinking—trying to understand what had been going on in her mind since her interview with the doctor. And it was not so difficult to understand. He had possessed her all her life. She had only been able to give him affection. And, knowing she was going to die, she had decided that the little that was left of her of life was her own. Her own to do exactly what she liked with. There was someone for whom she felt the physical attraction he had never held, and she was going to take this one paltry offering of the gods before it was too late. It was not happiness she looked for. She could not ever have expected it. Only to take this one thing left before it was too late. She might have died in her lover's arms but at least they would have been the arms of a lover, not of someone she only liked.

He was under no illusion any more. He knew exactly what he had received, realized that it might be he had received more than she could ever give to anyone else, but he had not received what he had wanted because it had not been in her power to give that. They had neither of them received what they wanted.

We're all the same, he told himself. We're like children at a Christmas tree. We never want what we get. We're all exactly the same. Felicity and me and everybody else. I'd have done what she was going to do. I can't blame her. It took courage, and courage was the one thing she always had.

The thought went on pounding at his brain, advancing and receding in a series of waves. When he was with others it receded, to return as soon as he was alone.

Desire was a curse and each of them in their separate ways had lain under its bane since the day they first met.

He had expected that when the whole business was comfortably cleared away by Ryder's evidence he would be able to come out from under the cloud that had settled over him. He would be able to live decently with his sorrow. But it was not so. Fear was gone, but there was no room for kindly sorrow, so bitterly and so fully did he regret. His regret was a torment to him. He had never wished so fervently that he had not done what he had done, as now. If she could be back, if it could all be only a nightmare, if only the last few days could be wiped out he would let her go gladly to live out the last short pitiful act of her life in whatever way she chose.

I owed her that, he mourned. That little at least I owed her.

He knew he was mixed up, perverse, inconsistent. But he believed that had he known everything, he could have given her the gift of her freedom, that final toy she had wanted.

He went up to look at her, hoping the experience would crystallize his thoughts for him and give him some certainty of where he stood. But it had no effect on him whatever. This cold, beautifully-formed shell was not Felicity. The Felicity he knew was quickness and thought; a smile, a quick word, a voice, a certain movement of the head, a drifting of scent to the nostrils.

This form, pale and waxen, was empty. It meant nothing. It was no more than the beautiful gown they had dressed her in. Caroline had wanted her to wear her wedding dress, but that awful mockery he had definitely forbidden. It was all he had to be glad about.

He began to have a feeling that she was there in the room with him. Standing with him looking at the clay she had discarded. He knew so well how she would look, the tolerance, the kindly mocking of her smile. She would understand how little all this meant.

It was no superstitious fear, he felt, no ghost-at-his-elbow dread, but for a moment he felt that nearness of her, and imagined they were closer than they had ever been in their life together. He imagined her saying: Dyke, you took something I wanted from me. And he was ashamed of what he had done, not repentantly, nor horrified, only ashamed.

And then it was all gone and he was alone in a room with a body that meant nothing at all. And there were far too many hothouse flowers. Their perfume suffocated him.

He turned and went out.

On the day of the funeral the weather changed. It turned cooler, the sun did not show itself, and the sky was covered with chasing clouds like a heap of soiled, rumpled blankets. A wind came up the river and the waters seemed to flow more slowly, grey and broken. It was a day to lower spirits. From every window one could see the willows bending sadly to the wind and the aspen leaves waving their timid everlasting farewell.

The house was too full of people. He was grateful for the core of his friends, but wished the others had not come. Their solemnity was forced and weighed on him. He felt that they were watching him all the time. He could hear their thoughts creaking round him: How's he taking it? Poor old Dyke! He's bearing up well. Shocking business for poor old Dyke.

He did not go up again to see Felicity. The others went and returned, some of them weeping, or wiping their eyes furtively.

Felicity's mother arrived and grief became real. She did not cry much, but he could see how deeply her feelings went, and was angry and hurt that he had not thought of her before. He had wanted what had happened to be between Felicity and himself, but you couldn't keep death to yourself. To this woman of seventy the loss of Felicity was a finality, a loss that could never be made good.

She pressed Dyke's hand, kissed him on the cheek and murmured her sorrow for him, but he knew she was not thinking of him. A part of herself had been destroyed. The loss of her husband some years before had been a severing, but this . . . this was a part of her own life gone.

Michael, too, was taking it badly. Dinah was with him, quiet, watchful, ready to be comforting. Michael could hardly contain his grief. Dyke, detached, felt that there was a link between Felicity, her mother, and her son. They were all of each other's bodies, and he was apart from them.

For a time he felt nothing only a scarifying sense of guilt. He had thrown a stone into a pond and the ripples had spread and risen like waves, destroying more than he had wanted to destroy. He was jealous of his son's grief, and loathed himself for being the cause of that grief.

Then suddenly, when they came to the church, his mood changed. Heads lowered to hide tears, heads bowed to avoid the wind, hands raised to hats, heads pressed sideways to hear, the creaking of harness and the shuffling of feet, gravel grating underfoot, faint whispers of instructions, a sob. A surplice was pressed against a man's middle-aged body, a voice, and words caught and tossed away to the groaning elms round the little village churchyard.

I am the resurrection and the life . . .

114

The gravestones stood row on row, painfully erect or crazily bent to watch and listen, to hear the words that went flying away on the wind.

We brought nothing into this world and it is certain we can carry nothing away . . .

It doesn't mean anything, said Dyke. It doesn't mean anything at all. These are words spoken by a man who is paid to speak them, who has spoken them so many times that they come out of his lips as mechanically as a tune off a gramophone record.

Nevertheless, he felt his skin shrink, the hair prickle at the base of his scalp. . . .

He was lost in his own thoughts and did not listen. I have no business here, he told himself. I am a hypocrite. I ought to stand up and shout that I destroyed her, and that my sorrow has been nothing but a cloak for my fear of being found out, and destroyed in my turn. . . .

These are they which came out of great tribulation . . . They shall hunger no more, neither thirst any more, neither shall the sun light on them nor any heat . . . God shall wipe away all tears from their eyes.

Good-bye, Felicity, he said. You shall not hunger any more nor thirst any more. You shall not hunger for the sun, nor for the coolness of night, nor for the scent of flowers, nor the song of birds. You shall not desire, nor be perplexed, nor be angry, nor hurt. Nothing any more . . . nothing . . . nothing . . .

Man that is born of a woman hath but a short time to live and is full of misery. He cometh up and is cut down like a flower; he fleeth as it were a shadow . . .

It's not fair, he cried. It's not fair. Words: words like music, words like a trumpet from the hilltops. Nobody had any business to make magic like that of words. Words are the ordinary currency of life, the pennies and ha'pennies of everyday trafficking, and it is not fair to weave them into spells.

But he suddenly felt the tears pricking at the back of his eyelids, and his throat seemed to fill out; it was so full he could not swallow. If he swallowed he would have to sob, and he did not want to make a scene. He wanted to be inconspicuous. He hated the furtive, peering eyes, the black, the veils, the sunken heads. It meant nothing to him, nothing at all, the trappings of a convention.

Thou knowest, Lord, the very secrets of our hearts . . .

He felt Caroline at his side thrust her arm through his, and realized that he was trembling.

Then he heard soil fall hollowly on the coffin and it was all over and he had come to the end of everything, and he bowed his head so that they should not see his face, and he wept, and heard no more and saw no more as he was led blindly away.

Chapter Thirteen

*

THE curtains were drawn back, there was light in the rooms, the voices that had been lowered were raised again to a normal pitch. Even the day outside seemed to have lost some of its grim cheerlessness.

The visitors were leaving, sped by Trent and Frank, Harold and Alice—though these two had spoken of leaving in the morning—and Caroline. Always Caroline. Caroline had fitted into charge as if she had done nothing else all her life. Her quality of indispensability had been one of the standbys of conversation whenever all else had failed.

But the others went. Michael and his quiet, efficient Dinah had been among the first to leave. Old Mrs. Denham—she was not going home until the morning—had taken her heartbreak and her memories to her room. The others dissolved in ones and twos, some to catch their trains, some to their cars. Lifts were offered and accepted, good-byes spoken.

The house was empty. And how empty it was! Dyke sensed a change in it. It had never been like this before, not since the night Felicity had been drowned.

It was not the absence of her body that made any difference, but all the time, always since that awful night, he had felt her still near. Nothing had been as bad as it might have been, because he could always imagine her at his elbow, seeing things as he saw them, sympathizing, mocking a little, understanding. Perhaps that had been the secret of it. He had felt she was there and that she understood. And now she was there no more, and her understanding was gone, and he was more horribly alone than he had ever been in his life. He was totally and completely alone, and the aloneness was a torment to his spirit.

Everybody had gone at last except those few of them who had been there on that night. They were back where they started, right back at the beginning again, and Dyke could not imagine Felicity's presence in any room, he could not listen for her foot on the stairs, or her voice; he could not look up and expect to see her.

Alice said that they would probably leave after lunch.

'I wish you'd stay a few days longer,' said Dyke. He meant it. It was not so much that he wanted them there themselves, but he dreaded the time when they would all have gone.

'Can't manage it, old boy,' said Harold decisively. 'I simply must get back.'

'Why don't you go somewhere, Dyke?' suggested Alice. 'Come and stay with us for a week or two.'

Dyke shook his head. 'No thanks, Alice.'

'You ought to get away,' said Harold. 'Right away. I don't agree with Alice. It wouldn't do you much good coming to us. You need a real change. Go abroad for a year or something like that.'

'I shall stay here,' said Dyke. Strangely, it was only as he said it that he realized it was the truth. He would stay here, he would always stay here. He was chained to the place. He did not know whether he was glad or sorry. But he had to stay.

'Harold's right,' said Trent. 'You need a change, Dyke.'

'I think so too,' put in Frank.

Dyke did not answer. Only Caroline came in on his side.

'I think he's very wise to stay here.'

'You're wrong, Caroline,' said Alice. 'You should encourage him to travel for a while.' She knew Caroline's ambition to devote herself to Dyke and had little sympathy with it. Caroline was being selfish.

'Get away,' said Harold. 'Get right away for a bit. That's what I say.'

'You simply can't live by yourself, Dyke,' said Alice. 'Like a hermit.'

'He won't be by himself,' said Caroline swiftly, glancing at Dyke. 'And he won't be a hermit. I shall be here as long as he needs me.'

'Naturally,' said Alice, as if it were a foregone conclusion. 'But you should neither of you be here. You look worn-out, too, Caroline.'

'Of course I look worn-out,' snapped Caroline. 'Anybody would look worn-out after this last week. I shan't look worn-out when I've had a rest.'

'I don't like the idea of you two on your own here,' said Harold. 'Everything you look at will be a reminder.' It was as if he had said: Now the funeral is over it is time to start to forget. Already he and Alice had started to forget. He looked at Trent. 'How long are you staying, Trent?'

'I'm leaving to-morrow,' said Trent.

Dyke, who had not been particularly interested in the argument, looked up.

'To-morrow?' he said.

'Yes,' said Trent. 'I had a letter this morning'—he was looking at Dyke, and Dyke suddenly knew what he meant: Trent had been recalled to a further instalment of his intermittent and fragmentary paradise—'I didn't want to bother you at the time.'

'Are you leaving, too?' Dyke asked Frank.

'I shall have to go soon,' said Frank. 'I think perhaps I should have gone before. It's been very good of you to have me, Dyke.'

Dyke did not care who went and who stayed, but he did feel as if they were suddenly all of them deserting him. The funeral

119

was over, so he had no more to offer. Felicity was gone and they had no further interest in him. That was not the truth, but his imagination had grown peevish. While they stayed there would be times when he would not be able to think, but it looked as if they were determined that he should face things out on his own.

'So we'll be alone, you and I?' said Dyke to Caroline. 'Unless you are leaving me, too.'

Caroline almost snapped. 'Don't be ridiculous!'

'Don't talk as if we're purposely leaving you by yourself,' said Alice. 'I still think you should go away from here. You ought to shut the place up for a twelvemonth.'

'Alice is right,' said Harold. 'You'll feel better after a year——' He stopped, perhaps wondering if he'd said too much, been too blunt.

Dyke wondered at what point in the conversation Alice would mention the healing properties of time. As if she had read his mind, she did so now.

'Time is a great healer, you know, Dyke,' she said.

'So I understand,' said Dyke drily.

'If you went away for a while——' Alice went on. 'Why don't you go to South America? Caroline and you?' She glanced in the direction of Caroline to see if she had made an ally, but Caroline had not fallen for such a transparent device. 'You've been saying for the last couple of years that you want to visit South America——'

'Felicity wanted to visit South America,' said Dyke. 'I should loathe the place.'

'Well, South Africa then,' said Alice. 'You could spend the winter in South Africa and come back in the spring——'

Their voices went on and on, up and down, to and fro. A few words, a light suggestion, tossed up like a ball, caught, tossed back. Go here, go there, go anywhere. Dyke was hardly interested. They had to talk and to talk of what he should do was something to talk about. Besides, Alice, who had a natural capacity for continuing an argument, would have liked to make him take advice that was originally hers.

Then the time had passed, and one by one they drifted wearily up to bed. Only Dyke and Caroline were left.

'You mean what you say?' said Caroline. 'You really intend to stay here?'

'Yes,' said Dyke, 'I shall stay.'

'You don't want to travel?'

'No, I want to stay here.'

'Do you want me to stay too?'

He was not sure that he did. He had not thought about it. It had been one of the things they had all taken for granted. But she needed kindness as badly as he did himself. He smiled at her. 'If you don't, I shall have to get a housekeeper.'

'Don't be silly,' said Caroline. 'If we're going to stay for any length of time we shall have to have servants, of course.'

He knew how desperately she wanted to be assured of his need for her.

'I don't want you to feel you have to look after me,' he said.

She came to sit on a chair nearer him.

'I don't feel I *have* to look after you. I'd like to be with you if you want me here.'

He stretched out his hand to put it over hers reassuringly. 'Of course I want you here, Caro.'

'I mean'—she looked at him doubtfully—'if you'd rather be alone——'

'I'd hate to be alone,' he said.

'Very well. Then I shall go up to town and make arrangements. I shall have a few of my own things sent down, and then I can let the place—perhaps to the Maunds. They had it while we were at Nice, and they are very good tenants . . .'

She went on talking of what she would have to do. Without

knowing it her voice became cheerful and animated. This was the arrangement she had always wanted, sometimes consciously, sometimes unconsciously. She occupied Felicity's place. She could not understand that anyone else in Felicity's place was utterly impossible. Her voice went on and then, without meaning to, he lost track of her words.

Perhaps it was the tiny element of triumph in Caroline's voice, the triumph of one who has waited so long and at last sees things falling into the desired pattern, but as she talked his mind had wandered back to Felicity who was now so far from him. A puzzled, tortured Felicity, who saw life at an end and wanted to hold it in her own hands for a short while. Ever since Ryder had told him of her illness he had ceased to blame her for her threatened defection. Gradually he was coming to see her as the wronged one. She had given so much and received so little. Why shouldn't she have been free for the little time left to her.

Without his knowing it his feelings, since learning of her illness, had been undergoing a change. While Caroline talked, his thoughts were busy. The sensation of separation, complete and final, that had been growing gradually stronger since the funeral, gave him a feeling of despair.

He had imagined he was being so clever. Brayton had for a time appeared dangerous, but he had evaded Brayton. He had believed he had beaten Brayton. They had met in conflict and he had won. Silently and secretly he had met the whole world in conflict and had won. And now he was beginning to wish he had lost. His victory had only left him on a peak, apart from everyone, and terrifyingly lonely. All his life from here would have to be lived in that loneliness. It set him apart from his friends, from his son, from his dead wife. If Brayton had won, the image of Felicity would have been there at his elbow consoling and encouraging him. But with his victory she had vanished. He felt he could not bear it. Fear was growing in him more intense than any fear could have been if he had been discovered. His mouth was dry and his palms wet from the intensity of it.

Perhaps this is what they call the voice of conscience, he said, and inwardly tried to laugh it away.

Only it would not be laughed away.

To-morrow I shall feel different, he told himself, next week, next year. I shall forget what I did, I shall stop wanting the memory of the kindness of Felicity.

Only he did not believe that, and anyhow it was not to-morrow, nor next week, nor next year. And every second of the present was a reality, shattering his strength and his courage.

I couldn't live, he said. Even if I could get over it someday, I couldn't live so long.

And: I wish I had been found out. Brayton was a fool after all. Anybody but a fool would have found me out. I wish he had.

Caroline stopped speaking, and with the silence he became aware of her. He looked up to find her watching him strangely.

'My dear Dyke,' she said. 'You do look——'

She stopped, and seeing how she paused, not willing to say what she felt, he finished her sentence for her.

'I look awful?'

'You look ill,' she said firmly. 'And no wonder. You've gone through enough to make anyone ill. First that awful accident, then Brayton being suspicious, and then what Dr. Ryder told you. It's been one thing after another.'

'Yes,' he agreed. 'One thing after another.'

'You'll be better now,' she said. 'You must try not to think about it. The worst is over.'

The trouble was the worst was not over. He was on his peak of misery and must stay there.

'Shall I get you a drink?' she asked.

'No,' he said, then changed his mind. 'Yes, perhaps I will. Thanks, Caro.'

'It may make you sleepy,' she said. 'It's late, you know.'

'I don't want to go to bed,' he said. He had decided earlier that he would not go to bed unless he were certain he would sleep. 'You go up.'

'I don't want to go,' she said. 'Not unless you want to be by yourself.'

But he did not want to be by himself. The last thing he wanted was to be by himself. He did not really want her company, yet was grateful for it.

'I'd like you to stay with me,' he said. 'As long as you want to.'

She had brought his drink by now and had a glass of her own as well.

'I'll always want to, Dyke,' she said. She was standing over him, and for a minute they looked at one another. She meant more than the mere words could express, and there was something pitiful in the devotion in her eyes. He tried to be thankful for her love and trust. Only it's too late, he thought. We're middle-aged and there's something between us. She dreamt of a touching picture of a brother-and-sister attachment, devoted, always together. Growing old together. Oh, poor Caro, he thought, you too! You, too, must pay for what I've done.

She drew up a footstool so that she sat close to Dyke's chair.

'Don't worry,' she said in a low, warm, comforting voice. 'Don't worry, Dyke. Things will get better. I don't want to intrude into your memories of Felicity, but you know what Alice said was true. It's a silly old saying, but time does heal, and you'll have me always to help you and look after you. We get on together, we always have done. We can do things together and go to places together, can't we? We've got the same tastes; we like the same things . . .'

Poor Caro, she was in her heaven not knowing anything of his hell! There was something maternal in her voice as she talked. That's how it had always been. The two had always been close together, and her greatest desire had been to mother him. As children they had been inseparable; it was always Caro and Dyke; only marriage had forced her away from him; and now the end of marriage was bringing them back to the old relationship. Something queer about it all, he thought. She'd been a pretty, feminine child, and then become spinsterish. Now she seemed feminine again. The psychologists would make hay over it, and yet it's perfectly innocent . . . always was . . .

He finished the whisky in his glass, and putting it down lit a cigarette.

'You know,' she said, 'the others may have been right'—he looked down to see her turning to him—'it might be well to get away for a while.'

He felt himself harden, a kind of stiffening of his will against hers.

'No,' he said. 'I shall stay here.'

'Of course,' she said. 'For a time. But we could go abroad later. Perhaps at the end of the summer. A month or two? In the sun? Cannes, perhaps——'

He shook his head, but before he could speak she had gone on.

'—or some quiet place. One of the villages, where we shouldn't meet people?'

'I shall stay here,' he said again.

He heard her sigh and wanted to soften his refusal. 'I don't want to go anywhere at present, Caro——'

'No, I know. Not now. Not for a long time.'

It was on his tongue to say: Not for ever, but he forebore. She would have expected a reason and he could not offer any reason. He did not really know of any reason. There was some inner compulsion that made him believe he could never leave this place again, but he could not explain it, even to himself.

He did know that he had lost Felicity completely and he could not bear to cut himself off from this only link with her.

Caroline's voice was soothing. 'It's all right, Dyke. You don't have to go. You don't have to go anywhere. I don't specially want to go anywhere. I only suggested it because I thought it might do you good, but as long as you'd sooner stay here, I would, too.' Her dreams ran ahead of her tongue and she spoke incautiously. 'We'll be perfectly happy here.'

He could not help it. The word escaped him.

'*Happy!*'

'Why, Dyke!' She looked at him swiftly and saw the anguish in his face. 'I'm sorry, dear. Not yet, of course. Not now. I don't mean now. I don't mean until—I don't mean—not for a long time. But you will be happy again some day.'

'I shall never be happy again,' he said roughly.

'You mustn't talk like that——'

But saying it had helped him to understand. She believed life held a promise for her. And he knew it was a mockery. He could not go on with it, Caro wanting to be everything to him, Caro looking after him. Caro trying to make him comfortable. Caro trying to make him happy. And he with his secret knowledge of what he had done. Caro always watching him, waiting for him to be contented, waiting for him to smile, waiting for a sign that the desired idyllic relationship was realized. It would be more than he could stand.

'It's no go, Caro,' he said.

She was staring at him and he bent his head and put his hands over his face. He was aware of her getting up from her stool and moving away from him.

'Don't worry, Dyke,' she said. 'I understand——'

She was still in her make-believe world. And he had to get her out of it. He wondered if he could. He wondered if he dared.

'It's no good,' he said. 'It won't work. It'—he took his hands from his face, looking at her wildly—'it's just no good.'

'You feel like this now, Dyke, but presently——'

'I shall always feel like this. Always. My poor Caro——' For a moment he was overwhelmed with pity for what he had to do to her. 'My poor Caro——'

'I'm all right,' she said. 'Don't mind me, Dyke——'

'But I do mind you, my dear. I mind for you very much——'

She stood near the mantelpiece, looking at him.

'Don't you think we should go to bed? You're overwrought.'

'No,' he said. 'You don't understand. I wish I didn't have to, but—there's something I want to tell you. Or I don't want to, but I shall have to. Only I'm not sure if you'll be able to stand it——'

She smiled a little. 'It can't be so very terrible.'

'It is terrible,' he said. 'It's very terrible indeed.'

'Dyke, dear, you are exhausted. All this has been too much for you. In the morning——'

'Not in the morning,' he said. 'Now. Unless—' he was not sure whether he grasped at this in fear or in hope—'unless you'd sooner I didn't tell you.'

'Of course I want you to tell me,' she said. 'If it's anything that concerns you I want to know. Is it about Felicity——?'

'Partly,' he said.

'You're still worrying because she was going to leave you.'

He gave a short laugh. 'As a matter of fact, I'd practically forgotten that she meant to leave me. That doesn't count any more. I wish she had left me. If she could be alive again she could leave me whenever she wanted——'

He got up and walked over to where she stood. 'Sit down, Caro.'

'It's all right. I'm tired of sitting down.'

'Do as I ask.'

She went to one of the fireside chairs. 'Now what is it, Dyke?' she demanded when she was seated.

'I don't know if I can find the words to tell you,' he said.

But once he had started the words came easily enough.

And as he told her, a strange thing happened. Once again he was conscious of Felicity. It was nothing ghostly, nothing spiritual, only again she was at his elbow, sympathetic, aware of his difficulty, smiling a little, mocking a little. She was there as she had been there soon after her death. When he had finished she was gone, but for a short time, while he talked, he was nearly happy again.

Chapter Fourteen

*

FOR what seemed an age they looked at one another in silence.

'I don't believe it,' she burst out at last.

'Oh, it's the truth.'

'No,' said Caroline. Her voice was strong, matter-of-fact, competent. 'I've told you before, Dyke, it's all been too much for you. You've let it get you down——'

She was beginning to rise, but with a swift gesture he stopped her.

'Stay where you are.'

She sank back slowly. 'It's nonsense, Dyke. It's the effect of worrying about Brayton's attitude. That on top of everything else. I don't wonder——'

'But you don't believe me?'

'No, I certainly don't.'

'My imagination, eh?'

She was not at all comfortable, but was determined to stand no more nonsense.

'My dear Dyke, it *is* your imagination. You've always passed for a strong man, but the truth is you have the imagination of a poet.'

He was shaking his head.

'Yes. You have. You always have had. Because you were physically strong, nobody ever gave you credit for the sort of mind you had.'

'Listen, Caro——'

'Listen to me, Dyke. Do you remember when we were children, you and I tried to persuade mother we'd seen fairies by the garden pool?'

In spite of everything he smiled faintly. 'So we did, Caro. Fancy you remembering. I haven't thought about it for years. But we made that up between us. We arranged to tell the others——'

'Wait a minute. I was going to remind you. Yes, we made up the story and fixed all the details. It started off as a sort of joke. And what happened?'

'Why, I believe mother was half persuaded we had seen them. Wasn't there some chap she was going to ask to come down——'

'We persuaded mother. And after that?'

'Was there anything after that? She didn't write. Or he didn't come.'

'There was something else. You began to believe you had seen them.'

'Oh nonsense! I didn't really——'

'You did, Dyke. You started to tell me they were really there.'

'I was teasing you——'

'No, you weren't. You'd said so often they were there that you persuaded yourself.'

'I don't remember. Anyhow——'

'Do you remember coming into my room one night and making me get out of bed and come to the window with you to watch. We could see the pool from my window and it was moonlight, and you were so sure that I was beginning to wonder myself. And we sat there watching and watching, and persuading ourselves that there was something moving about under the willows.'

'Didn't we fall asleep in the end?'

'Yes. And Harold woke up and saw you weren't in your bed and called mother and she came and found us.'

'I believe that was the end of the fairy hunt, wasn't it?'

'Yes, that was the end of it,' said Caroline. 'And the sooner you realize that this fairy tale——'

'This isn't a fairy tale,' said Dyke, coming back abruptly to the present.

'Felicity's death has been a terrible shock to you,' said Caroline severely. 'Dyke, the sooner you realize what a strain all this has been to you, the better for all of us. Brayton's persistence worried you a lot——'

'I thought I had a good reason to be worried. I thought he was going to find out what I'd done. And now I wish he had——'

'And then Arthur Ryder telling you how ill Felicity was——'

'Yes, it was that which put the finishing touch,' said Dyke. 'Perhaps if it hadn't been for that——'

'My dear, you've had one shock after another. Nobody can stand that sort of thing indefinitely.'

'Caro,' said Dyke. 'You've got all this wrong. What I've told you is the truth. I murdered Felicity.' He saw the expression on her face. 'All right, I killed her. Put it that way if it sounds any better. It wasn't planned or anything of that sort. I didn't mean to do it. I don't think I even wanted to do it. But I suddenly saw how it could be done, and because she was going to leave me I did it.'

'Nonsense!' said Caroline. 'You're imagining this.'

'It's not imagination,' said Dyke. 'I swear to you, Caro, that I killed her.'

For a moment there was no word spoken. As they looked at each other their wills clashed, neither would give way.

'I can't believe it,' said Caroline at last. 'If I could I would, Dyke, because you want me to, but I can't.'

'You don't want to,' said Dyke. Some subtle sense warned him that Caroline had closed her mind to any possibility of what he said being the truth.

'I can't.'

'I'm off my head, then?'

'You're not normal,' said Caroline. 'You've been through so much that you're imagining things. Dangerous things. There might be awful consequences if you said what you've said to me to the wrong person?'

'I don't care who I say them to,' said Dyke. Caroline's attitude had made him careless. He had begun by wanting to confide in her. But if she would not believe him he must tell somebody who would. 'I don't care who knows. I'll soon find somebody who will believe, if you won't.'

'You mustn't say such things.'

'I could tell Brayton. He'd believe me. He'd sift and sift and he'd soon know it's the truth. Somebody's got to believe. Somebody's got to know the truth. I can't go on like this much longer. I can't keep it locked up inside myself——'

His voice had been rising, and then as he saw the horror on her face he stopped.

'*Dyke!*' she exclaimed.

He became almost sulky. 'I'm sorry, Caro, but that's how it is. I've been playing the hypocrite all the week and I'm not going to do it any more. It's been a bit of a relief to tell you—although you don't believe. It'll be a lot more relief when I've got it off my chest and done with.'

'You're saying awful things. You don't know what you're saying. If you were to—to go making confessions, perhaps somebody would believe you. And what about the others then?'

'The others? What others?'

'All of us. Me and Harold and Alice. And Michael. And Mrs. Denham.'

'Yes,' he said, suddenly thoughtful. 'That's the devil of it.' He voiced what he had been thinking. 'Murder isn't something you can keep to yourself.'

'We should all be dragged in.'

'I suppose—in a way, yes.'

'Please, Dyke! Go to bed now. Have a sleep. Rest. Come away from here with me for a while.'

'No,' he said fiercely.

'Just for a while. Give yourself a chance to get over this——'

'I can't. There's nothing to get over.'

'Listen.' She became persuasive. 'Listen, Dyke. Do this for me. Don't say any more about it now. Don't tell anybody else what you've said to me. Come away with me for a holiday. A few months——' She saw no sign of yielding in him. 'A month, if you like. Then if you still insist that what you've told me is the truth, I'll believe you.'

He stared at her. She was waiting for his answer.

'Yes?' he said. 'And what then?'

'What then?'

'Yes. What happens after that? Are we going to do something about it? Or nothing?'

'We can—there's plenty of time to discuss that.'

'It won't do, Caro. All you are suggesting is that a month or two away from here will cure me of my hallucination. Isn't that it?'

'You could give yourself a chance,' she said vehemently. 'At least you could give yourself a chance. You could do that much for me.'

He shook his head. 'It wouldn't work. It wouldn't do any good. It might if it were an hallucination. Only it isn't.'

She was going to reply, but he stopped her.

'The truth is, Caro, you won't believe because you don't want to believe——'

'It's not that——'

'It is that. And somewhere inside yourself you know it is. If you were to believe me it would cut right across your plans——'

'Dyke, I haven't any plans——'

'I mean the plans you've been making subconsciously ever since Felicity was drowned. Coming to live with me and looking after me. You've built up a picture of us together for the rest of our lives. Once I'd got over Felicity's death we could be happy together. You're willing to devote yourself to my comfort. I'd be damned lucky. We'd become a devoted brother and sister— just like when we were kids—before there was any Felicity. And what I've told you makes it impossible if it's the truth.'

He had spoken swiftly, the words tumbling out, and only now he saw how he had hurt her. He wished for a moment that he had not spoken.

'I'm sorry, Caro,' he said. 'My dear, I'm terribly sorry. I'd like it to be. If it could be that way I'd like it more than anything.'

She was biting at her lip in an effort to appear calm.

'I'm only trying to show you that it's no good. Felicity's death is between us. I could have gone on—and on—and on. At least, I suppose I could. But not pretending to you that everything's lovely. It isn't lovely. It's damned awful.'

It was a minute before she could speak without her voice shaking.

'But you won't even try, Dyke. You won't do what I ask. You don't give things a chance.'

'Your chance is based on the surmise that my story isn't true. It would be no good.'

She would not give in. 'Suppose you put yourself in my place. I suffer the most appalling strain, one shock after another. Then I come to you and confess I've done something terrible. Wouldn't you wonder if what I'd been through had been too much for me and I was imagining things?'

He thought a minute.

'You would, Dyke,' she said. 'Anybody with the least imagination would.'

'Well—perhaps,' he admitted.

'Then can't you admit the possibility that *you* have imagined things?'

He had imagined so much lately, from the suspicions of Brayton to the presence of Felicity at his elbow, that he saw the reasonableness of what she said. He tried to twist the position in his mind. I didn't kill Felicity, he thought. She never was going to leave me. I had a fit of jealousy and thought she might, or she could, but she never meant to. She said it to make me angry, to make me jealous. Or I misunderstood her. And if she was going to leave me I did not kill her. I could not have killed her. She died and I saw how I could have been the cause and I was half crazy and then presently I was believing I'd done it. But I didn't. I'm just a bit off balance for the moment, that's all. In a few weeks, a few months, I'll be better again. . . .

It was all quite plausible. It was a very reasonable line to take. He had always been imaginative and it was the fairies of his childhood at the bottom of the garden all over again. You started out by thinking a thing was possible, and after a time you were telling yourself it actually happened. . . .

Yes, it was very plausible.

But he shook his head. 'I'm sorry, Caro.'

She had been watching him intently as if she would force her will on him. Now her mouth set in a hard line.

'You're hopeless,' she said.

'I know what I did. No amount of pipe dreams will alter the fact.'

She made one last attempt. 'All right. You killed Felicity. You say you did, so you must have done. What then? What are you going to do?' Publish your guilt? Would that help anybody? Would it do anything except bring a lot of suffering to a lot of people you like? You killed her. All right, you had a reason for killing her. Now forget it. Put it out of your mind. You start again from here. In a year's time it won't matter——'

'It will always matter,' he said. 'Always. It's mattered since I did it, more and more. It'll grow worse, not better. We wouldn't stand a chance of any sort of life. You'd look at me and see me miserable, and you'd say: That's what it's like to be a murderer——'

She nearly lost control. Her voice went up dangerously. 'Do you think I care what you did? Or what you are? You aren't a murderer. You're a fool and you're being hysterical about a dead woman——'

She saw how he stared and woke to the fact that she was shouting, and her voice fell immediately.

'You didn't kill Felicity,' she said sulkily. 'It's ridiculous.'

He shrugged his shoulders and turned away from her.

'We'd better go to bed,' she said. 'I'm worn out and you must be, too.'

'I wouldn't mind going to bed, but I don't think I can sleep.'

She stood up 'I've some sleeping tablets upstairs. Will you take some if I get them for you?'

'Not much good,' he said.

'Of course they're good. I wouldn't suggest them if they weren't good. They were prescribed for me after my operation, but I got better and didn't use them all. Will you take them?'

'I'll try them, if you like,' he said dully.

'Then pour yourself out some more whisky. You can swallow them with that.'

He had hardly poured the whisky before she was back. In the palm of her hand she held out two small white tablets.

'Now, swallow those.'

He obeyed mechanically, chasing them down with the whisky. He was a small boy taking medicine again under his mother's

136

watchful eye. Caroline's expression softened as she watched him. She took his glass from him and her voice became kinder.

'Better get upstairs, Dyke. They work quite quickly.'

'I don't want to go to bed,' he said. 'I'll sit in a chair.'

'You'll not sit in a chair. You'll go to bed. I've made up the bed in my room for you. Your pyjamas are there and I've put the lights on.'

'I'm not going to turn you out.'

'You're not turning me out. I'll have your room for the present. I think that would be better.'

He wanted to protest, but he felt heavy and slow and had not the energy to argue any more.

'Go on,' said Caroline. 'I'll see to everything here. I'll look in to see you're safe in bed. Don't worry about anything.'

He went up very slowly. The light from Caroline's room shone across the landing and he went in. He did not remember undressing or putting on pyjamas or getting into bed, but he must have done all these things because presently Caroline was moving about the room. He was not asleep, he did not think he would ever sleep again, but he was very weary and it was too much effort to open his eyes and watch Caroline. It was too much effort even to think any more.

He knew she was straightening the bedclothes round him; he could hear her moving about the room.

He lay there in the darkness knowing he would not be able to sleep, but it was a relief not to think about anything. He was in emptiness, in a vacuum, he did not exist. There was no self, no Felicity, no Caroline. It was like being in a drum. In a big empty drum on which a demon drummer tapped out a steady beat. The tapping became louder, changed to a hollow banging, which fitted in with the thumping of his heart, and the noise became louder and louder, filling his ears so that he heard nothing, knew nothing except that hollow, rhythmical *bang . . . bang . . . bang . . .*

Caroline stood at the side of the bed looking down on him, and she wanted to cry. Asleep he looked natural, younger, just Dyke again. That awful confession . . . was it possible? No, it couldn't be true, she mustn't let herself even think it. The figment of an overwrought mind . . . imagination. If once she started to doubt. . . . Dyke a murderer? Impossible. The alternative? Madness? No, don't call it that. Say—a breakdown. Temporary. But at the worst . . . oh yes, madness rather than the other thing.

She felt alone and frightened. She wanted someone to turn to. She wanted to talk to someone who was bound to think as she thought. Harold ought to know. He'd have to know sooner or later. It concerned him—and Alice—and their children. It concerned so many of them. They were like mountaineers on a dangerous slope . . . roped together. And one of them in danger . . . slipping. . . .

Dyke moved uneasily and moaned. She went quickly to the light switch, turned off the light and went out of the room.

Chapter Fifteen

*

WHEN he awoke, the sunlight was streaming into the room. He realized that someone had shaken him by the shoulder and when he turned his head he saw that it was Felicity's mother. She held a cup of tea in her hand. He sat up in bed quickly and was rewarded by a sharp stab of pain at the back of his head. He looked at Caroline's clock on the mantelpiece and saw to his surprise that it was ten o'clock. Even as he was staring at it the clock broke into a silvery chime. He turned to look at Mrs. Denham.

'Good heavens, it's late,' he said. 'You wanted to catch the early train. I'm dreadfully sorry, Gran.' He had called her Gran ever since Michael had been able to manage the title, before which he had called her nothing at all in a nervously polite way. 'Surely we didn't all over-sleep——'

'It's all right,' said Mrs. Denham. 'Drink this.'

She was holding out the tea and he took the cup from her.

'I expect you want a cigarette,' she said, and fetched a box that was on Caroline's dressing-table and found matches for him. He took a cigarette and lit it and drank the tea.

'I really am sorry——' he began again, but she cut short his apologies.

She was standing near the side of the bed looking down at him, and when he looked back at her he was amazed. Really, she was a remarkable old woman. Yesterday he imagined her life was at an end, yet this morning she was upright and seemed as well as he'd ever seen her. There was a firmness about her, a stand-no-nonsense sort of look that he had seen on her face before and did not care for much. They had always agreed rather well; in fact, he was very fond of her, but he preferred not to be in her company when she was in one of her speaking-her-mind moods. She'll live to be a hundred, he thought, and memories returned, clouding the pleasant sunshine that came in from outside, and he wondered why people who seemed to have so little to live for went on living, while those for whom life held so much had to die—like Felicity . . .

'You've missed your train,' he said, half stating a fact, half in question.

'There are plenty more trains. If you've got to miss anything, trains are about the best things to start on.'

He recognized the tone of voice. In happier circumstances he would have smiled.

He had finished his tea and leaned over to put the cup on the table at the head of the bed. His cigarette was unfinished, though, and he went on smoking.

She was still standing there.

'I think I'll get up now,' he hinted.

She did not move. 'I want to talk to you, Dyke,' she said.

He wondered what it could be. Felicity? Money? His own plans? Or hers? But she would not have altered her arrangements in order to discuss any of those.

'Privately?' he asked.

'It had better be private, I think.'

There was something grim about her. A forbidding attitude that led him to expect trouble, but he was completely unprepared for what she did say.

'Caroline has some ridiculous story about you claiming to have killed Felicity.'

'Damn!' He flung the bedclothes back and swung his legs

round so that he was sitting on the edge of the bed. He sat there staring at her, his pyjamas rumpled, his hair a tangle. 'What the devil's she been saying. What possessed her——'

'Calm yourself, Dyke.' The old lady was very calm herself. 'Caroline did not tell me anything—at least, not until I made her. I overheard her talking to your brother and his wife. A sort of council of war, I should think. Caroline was very distressed—as she might well be. She apparently thinks that Felicity's death has —well, preyed on your mind. You told her you pushed Felicity off the launch.'

Dyke stood up. He took a few steps away from Mrs. Denham, running his fingers through his hair.

'Oh hell! Why couldn't she keep her mouth shut?'

'Dyke, look at me.'

He turned to her. This was something he had not counted on and he felt lost. He liked her. But since the damage was done he had to face it. Though what he should say . . .

'Dyke, it is a preposterous story.'

He wanted time to think. 'Is it?'

'Of course it is. You weren't drunk when you came to bed, were you?'

'No,' he said. 'Oh, I don't know. I might have been.'

'It is a preposterous story,' she said again. 'I know how upset you are at the loss of Felicity. But even that——'

'*You* don't think I'm mad, do you Gran?'

'I don't know what to think. I'm very upset. Your brother and sister believe you are. But you've always been sane enough.'

He had been trying to think of some way in which he could temporize, some way he could put her off. When he had opened his eyes, the night before seemed far off and unreal, but as he became more fully awake the reality returned and his unhappiness came back to him. Also, he was a little angry. Caroline had brought in Alice and Harold without so much as a word to him.

And she'd told Gran. Of course, Gran wouldn't have given her much chance once she'd had a starting point. But his exasperation made him reckless.

'Caroline also said that Felicity intended leaving you?'

'Yes,' said Dyke. 'That's the truth.'

'The truth! Impossible. It is a lie. I will never believe it.'

'I assure you——'

'I don't want your assurance. I think it is a shocking thing to say about a woman who is dead.' For a moment Mrs. Denham's lip quivered. 'Felicity was a good wife to you——'

Dyke wanted to be gentle. He was going to hurt somebody whom he did not want to hurt.

'I know, but——'

'She was very fond of you.'

He looked at her unhappily. 'Yes, Gran, she was very fond of me, I know But being fond isn't everything. Felicity didn't love me. The truth is—I don't know whether you knew this or not—the truth is she never did love me. Being fond isn't being in love——'

Colour had risen in the old lady's cheeks. She looked very pink and very indignant. 'I don't know what on earth you mean. Felicity was always very happy. I should have known if she hadn't been. Mothers always know. And remember, she was nearly forty——'

'Does desire stop at forty?' he asked.

For a moment she did not answer. But he saw how her colour deepened. 'I think that is a disgusting way to talk.'

Dyke made a vague, despairing gesture with his hand. 'I'm very sorry.'

'Are you telling me that she was going to leave you for another man?'

'Yes,' he said. 'She'd fallen in love.'

'Who is the man?'

'I don't know.'

'Do you mean you don't know, or you don't want to tell me?'

'I mean I don't know.'

'Did anyone else know of this plan of hers to leave you?'

'Not so far as I'm aware.'

'I see. Dyke, you should be ashamed. You stand there and calmly tell me that Felicity, who had always been a good wife and mother, suddenly decided to run away from you for no better reason than—than some disgusting animal has for prowling about in the night. And nobody else knows of this decision. And you don't know who the man is.'

'I'm sorry,' he said. 'I suppose it sounds a bit mad to you——'

The word was not well chosen.

'Mad!' she exclaimed. 'Mad! It is either mad or wicked. I am beginning to think that Caroline is right. Dyke, it is time to take hold of yourself. I know what you've suffered. I tell you very seriously, you should not say the things you have said. You should not even think them. You loved Felicity. Do you realize how you are besmirching her memory——'

'I am not besmirching her memory,' he said, and his voice rose. Exasperation made him brutal. 'I can understand how she felt if you can't. I don't know who she was leaving me for, nor when she was going. But she meant to. She thought she was going to die, and I expect that made her reckless. She still liked me, but there was somebody who could give her what I couldn't, and that was too strong for any ordinary affection to hold in check. And even to think of it drove me crazy. And then when we were on the launch I pushed her off in a fit of madness——'

He had used the word again, and again it stopped him. He lowered his voice, and said what he had said to Caroline. 'I didn't mean to do it, and I didn't want to do it. It was—it was a sudden impulse—of anger—of misery. I couldn't have her and nobody else should. That was madness, if you like. Yes, I was mad, then——'

The look in her eyes stopped him. They had always been good friends, but for this moment the primeval instinct of the parent against the mate rose uppermost in her and she hated him. It was not mere loathing, but something more: an active militant hatred that rose now from its smothering trappings of milleniums of civilization and stared nakedly at him. He was abashed, almost frightened.

'I'd give anything not to have to tell you this. It's—it's terrible.'

She fought to control herself. 'Yes, Dyke—it is terrible.' Her voice was very quiet. 'I'm Felicity's mother. I brought her into the world. I watched her grow up—my baby—then a girl—a young woman—becoming a mother herself. I thought some day she might cry a little over my grave—and instead I've known the bitterness of weeping over hers. I was glad when she married you. I thought you'd be a good husband to her. I believe you have been. Can you imagine what I'm feeling now?'

'Yes,' he said. 'I know. I'm sorry, Gran.' It seemed a very inadequate description of his feelings, but he repeated, 'I'm sorry.'

'If I believed what you've said it would be—it would be unbearable. I don't know what I should do.'

He made a quiet gesture with his hands. Almost of renunciation. 'It is the truth.'

'It is not the truth and you are not to say it is the truth. Felicity behaving like a—like a street-woman, and you like—a common murderer. If you believe that, I am sorry for you.'

'I'm afraid it's the same with you as it is with Caroline. You won't believe because you don't want to believe.'

She went on as if she had not heard him. 'What I advise is that you take a complete rest. You should go away from here and not come back until you have quite recovered——'

'Did Caro ask you to say that?'

She flushed. 'I know Caroline thinks it to be the wisest course, and I agree with her. She would go with you. You might even consider selling this place. It may not be good for you to live here again.'

'Gran,' he said earnestly. 'Try to believe I'm telling you the truth.'

'You frighten me, Dyke,' she said. 'I can sympathize with you in the way you're feeling. But you won't let your friends help you——'

'There's no way anybody can help.'

'You could go away. Have a complete change, a rest——'

'What good would that do?'

'It might restore you to sanity.'

'I'm sane enough,' he said unhappily.

'Even if you believe what you've told me what can you do? You ought to *want* to get away——'

'I can't,' he said.

'It's—it's dangerous. Suppose in an unguarded moment you tell your story to the wrong person?'

'I don't feel any more it matters who knows.'

'What do you want to do? Start people talking? Gossip? Suppose the police get to hear what you have been saying? You might even be arrested.'

'That would be a relief in a way——'

She was very angry; very upright and tightlipped.

'If you *dare* to allow such a thing to happen—if you dare'—for a minute she could not go on—'I warn you I shall fight you with all my might. You shall not bring disgrace on Felicity—saying things about her——'

'But I'm not——'

'Making a scandal. Making people think she was a woman of low character. And disgracing yourself—and all your friends. You're not on a desert island. Everybody would be dragged in.

145

You shan't do it, Dyke. You shan't! If you're miserable, be miserable by yourself, at least. We won't let you ruin all our lives.'

'I don't know what I'm going to do,' he said. 'I haven't made any plans——'

'*Plans!* I should think not! Well, I'm going, Dyke, but I've warned you. You had better make up your mind to be sensible.' She turned at the door for a parting shot. 'I'm not sure you oughtn't to be certified.'

A car drove away as he was dressing and he guessed that one of them was driving her either to the station or up to town. He had been angry with Caroline at first for betraying his confidence, but his anger had evaporated now. Caroline's defection was merely a measure of the fact that she did not intend to believe what he had told her. A pity, in a way, because if she had believed it would have remained a secret between the two of them. As it was, he didn't care much who knew. Did they really think his story was all imagination? Or were they afraid to think anything else?

He smiled wryly over a thought that occurred to him. Gran hadn't mentioned her allowance. She had had one for years, ostensibly from Felicity, but of course it was he who had paid it. And he told her yesterday, as delicately as he could, that it would go on. Presumably she would accept it whether she thought him mad or not. She'd be a fool if she didn't, seeing that she had about fifty pounds a year apart from it.

He could have imagined what Felicity would have said to all this. She had hated humbug and pretence and she would have been on his side. Suddenly he felt she was on his side, and he paused in the act of knotting his tie at the comfortable feeling that for a moment she had returned to him.

Chapter Sixteen

★

HE saw Caroline as soon as he got down stairs. She was superficially no different, and greeted him with a forced cheerfulness, but he could see by her eyes that she had been crying. He said nothing about Mrs. Denham.

'I hope you've had a good sleep, Dyke,' she said. 'Shall I get you some breakfast? Mrs. Cole is going to be very busy this morning.'

'I don't want much,' he said. 'Some toast and coffee.'

'I'll fetch it at once.'

Nothing was said while he ate. He propped up a paper against the coffee-pot and made a pretence of reading. Caroline left him, came back to the room and went out again.

'The house is very quiet,' he said when she returned for the second time. 'Where's everybody?'

'Trent's gone up to town,' she said. 'He left early. He looked in but you were sleeping and he wouldn't wake you. He said he'd be back any day.'

'Where are the others?'

'Alice is in the garden. I believe Harold is writing letters in his room. Frank has run Mrs. Denham home in his car. He's coming back. As a matter of fact I was hoping he wouldn't.'

'I'm glad he is.'

She had not mentioned their conversation of the night before, but it was easy to see the way her thoughts ran.

She spoke sharply. 'We can do without strangers in the house at present.'

'Frank isn't a stranger. He's a friend——'

'I know, but——'

'A very close friend. I'm glad to have him here.'

Caroline sighed. 'Of course, Dyke.'

He detected in her voice a new tone; it was slight enough, but it hinted that he was an invalid who must be humoured. He was part amused, part angry.

He finished the last of his coffee, lit a cigarette and took his paper to one of the window seats. Caroline put his breakfast things on the tray and while she was doing this Mrs. Cole came in to fetch them.

Entrenched behind his paper he smoked and waited. Caroline, too, was waiting, waiting for what he would say, waiting to defend herself against his anger. But he was determined to say nothing. She should open the offensive.

He caught a glimpse of her as he turned a page. She was sitting at a small table writing what might have been a shopping list.

Footsteps could be heard coming down the stairs, and a moment later Harold came into the room. Like Caroline had been when Dyke came down, he was not quite natural. He was just a little too breezily cheerful.

'Hullo, Dyke!' he said. 'Have a decent night?'

'Yes, thanks,' said Dyke shortly. 'I slept, anyhow.'

'Good man!' Harold was as approving as he would have been of the cricketer who had scored the few runs needed to win the game. 'Nothing like a good sleep to put you on your feet again.'

To Caroline this sparring was the last straw. She turned in her chair.

'Dyke, I think I'd better tell you now. I telephoned Michael this morning and asked him to come down.'

'Whatever for?' demanded Dyke.

'Because I think it is only right that he should be here. You are—ill, and he ought to know about it. I asked him to come alone.'

'He'll come all right,' said Dyke. 'And if you told him what you've apparently told everybody else in the house, he'll certainly come alone.'

'I have not told everybody else in the house. I told Harold and Alice. I'd rather not have done, but the responsibility of being the only one to know was too great for me. I wouldn't have told Mrs. Denham, but she overheard us talking and insisted on knowing.'

Harold, jingling money and keys in his trouser pockets had strolled across to the window.

'Determined old devil!' he said. His voice was still far too friendly. 'Didn't think she had it in her.'

'That sort of thing makes you curious,' said Dyke. He saw Harold's eyebrows curved up in inquiry. 'The fact that your son-in-law may be a murderer.'

'Look here, old man,' said Harold. 'Don't say things like that, will you, please? I know you've been having a hell of a time and all that——'

'Do you also subscribe to the unbalanced mind theory, Harold?'

'My dear chap, you've had a devil of a swipe——'

'Isn't Alice coming in to join in the fray?' asked Dyke.

Harold rose to the attack. 'I'm sure she'll be glad to.' He was looking out of the window as he spoke. 'As a matter of fact she's coming towards the house.' He turned to Dyke. 'Look here, Dyke, before she comes—while there are only the three of us here'—his voice was frankly incredulous—'Caro and I *know* you can't have done this—what you told her you've done. We understand. You've always been an imaginative beggar and you've worked yourself up into a state over Felicity's death——'

'In other words, I'm off my head.'

Harold waved through the window to his wife and called out, 'We're all in here.' Then he turned back to Dyke.

'Be reasonable, old man——'

'I can't be reasonable *and* insane.'

'All right, then.' The temper he had so carefully kept bottled-up showed itself. 'I think you must be off your head—temporarily. And the sooner you pull yourself together——'

Dyke was the calmest of the three of them, strangely, for a turmoil was surging inside him. They were childish fools and he longed to knock their heads together: Caroline scared but determined, Harold so angry that he had gone pink. He looked at Alice as she came into the room. 'And what's *your* opinion about me, Alice? Do you say I'm mad, too?'

Alice was pale and her mouth was set in an unpleasant line. Alice was at times so complaisant as to be almost colourless, but when the mood suited her she could be extremely stubborn.

'Good morning, Dyke,' she said. 'I hope you are feeling better.'

'Thank you,' he said. 'Actually I feel like hell, apart from the fact that I'm braced up for what seems to be promising a fight with the lot of you.'

'Don't talk rubbish!' she snapped.

'I asked you if you also think I'm mad.'

'I think you're wicked.' Her voice, carefully under control, came through lips that had lost all colour. She wore lipstick, badly applied, and inside its radiance the flesh had an anæmic tint.

'Wicked?' queried Dyke. 'Perhaps—if we're thinking in the same way.'

'Wicked,' repeated Alice. 'And cruel.'

Dyke gave Caroline a look which said: This is your doing. Though he had to admit to himself that once she had unburdened herself to Harold, Alice was bound to be caught up.

'All right,' he said. 'Cruel, too, if you like. But not to any of you.'

'Don't you see what you are doing?' said Alice. She was breathing quickly now and her upper lip trembled a little as if at any minute she might burst into tears. 'Are you blind as well as mad——'

Dyke suddenly shouted. 'Don't keep saying I'm mad. You'd all of you be damn' careful not to say it if you believed it. It's just a way of covering up something you don't like.'

'Did you expect us to like it?' asked Alice.

He was calm again. He was being unreasonable. Of course they couldn't like it, but all his attention was focused inwardly on himself—on himself and Felicity.

Caroline walked across the room to shut the door. 'It might be a good idea if you lowered your voices. Both Mrs. Cole and Judy are in the house and they hear perfectly well.'

'Let them hear,' said Dyke childishly.

Alice had picked up a cigarette and was lighting it. Her fingers were shaking so much that she could hardly hold the match still enough.

'Alice,' said Harold in a concerned voice. 'You'd better keep out of this. You can't help and you're only upsetting yourself.'

She paid no attention to him. The cigarette was well alight. She came nearer to Dyke.

'You told Caroline you killed Felicity?'

He was back at the heart of it again. He nodded, unable for the minute to speak.

'Then why,' demanded Alice in a cold, furious voice, '*why* didn't you keep it to yourself?'

He looked up at her. 'I didn't tell you. I told Caroline. She knows why. She should have kept it private.'

Caroline defended herself, 'If you had done it, I would have done——'

'Why tell anybody? Why tell any of us? Did you want to boast of it? Did you want sympathy? Did you *expect* sympathy——?'

Harold tried a placating 'Alice——' but she did not appear even to hear him.

'What can we, any of us, do about it? Can we help you? Is that what you want?'

'I don't want anything,' said Dyke. 'Don't be a fool, Alice.'

'Who are you going to tell next!' said Alice.

'I'd better tell somebody who'll believe me.'

'Yes, go round telling everybody. You'll find somebody to sympathize sooner or later. They'll enjoy it.'

Harold looked scared. 'Be quiet, Alice. You're not doing any good——'

'Actually, I don't know what we're arguing about,' said Dyke. 'It's my business, anyhow.'

'Look here, old man,' said Harold. 'Whatever you say, we know you didn't do what you say——'

'Then what are you worrying about? Don't you believe it, Alice?'

She was looking at him angrily. 'Perhaps you did. You say so——'

'Alice!' gasped Caroline.

She turned on Caroline. 'Well, how do we know? He does say so, doesn't he?'

Harold, too, was growing angry. 'It doesn't matter what he says. We know damn' well it's nothing but the strain of Felicity's death. How could he have done such a thing?'

'Quite easily,' sulked Alice. 'I don't care what he did. What I do care is that he should keep his mouth shut about it. He's no business to tell, no *business*——'

'You're honest, anyhow,' said Dyke. 'Only, as I've told you, it's my own affair what I do or what I say.'

'It's not your own affair. You ought to be locked up. Why should you be allowed to ruin people's lives——?'

'The life I've ruined is my own——'

'Your own! What about all the rest of us? If you can persuade people you murdered Felicity we are the ones who'll suffer. You can't keep a thing like that to yourself. What you've done affects us all.'

Dyke was growing exasperated. 'I don't want any of you in this——'

'But we've got to be in it, whether we want to be or not. Suppose they hang you——'

'Alice——' began Caroline in a loud, commanding voice.

'I'm going to say it——'

'I forbid you——'

Alice was vixenish as she turned on Caroline. 'You can't forbid anything. I shall say what I want to say——'

'Damn it,' said Harold. 'It's not as if he did it——'

'Yes, he did. Or he says he did, and that's as bad. And if he did do it——'

'He did not——' interrupted Caroline.

'If he did do it,' repeated Alice, 'they'll hang him. And if he did it he deserves to hang. But what about *us?*'

Dyke smiled a little. 'Spare me some pity.'

'If there were only you and me in the world you could have all my pity, Dyke. But there's no pity to spare. If you were hanged——'

'This is ridiculous,' said Harold.

'It's cruel,' said Caroline.

'Don't be silly,' said Alice. 'What would the rest of our lives be worth? Harold with a brother who was hanged for wife-murder. And our children. They might as well go to the ends of the earth. They'd become the nephew and niece of the man who was hanged. No career for Basil—and what man would even look at Elizabeth after that? Can't you see, Dyke, can't you *see*?'

'I'm sorry about Basil and Elizabeth,' said Dyke quietly. 'I see what you mean. But then I wasn't thinking of my nephew and niece.'

'Anybody would think old Dyke had been tried and condemned to death,' said Harold uneasily.

'It could happen,' said Alice.

'I'm sorry,' said Dyke, sighing. 'I'm sorry for all of you. Things are rather complicated, aren't they? But when—I killed Felicity I really wasn't thinking of any of you. It seems you can't do anything without dragging everyone in. I didn't want to. I—didn't think about it.' He looked at his brother. 'Rather spoils things for you, too, I'm afraid. There was a hint about the next honours list, wasn't there? I suppose that falls through, too, once I'm known for what I am. It's rather a pity——'

Alice came back to the fray. 'We weren't thinking about it.'

'I expect you've *thought* about it,' said Dyke quietly. 'What you mean is you wouldn't throw that argument into the scales against me.'

'If you think a tuppeny baronetcy counts at a time like this——' said Harold.

Dyke's voice was humorously tolerant. 'You've a perfect right to take what you've paid for——'

Harold, touched on a sore spot, flared in anger. 'I did not pay——'

'Harold's honour has nothing to do with this,' said Alice.

'Except that he's hardly likely to get it if they hang me.'

Caroline took control. 'You've all said enough. You've said too much. It's selfish and cruel. Dyke is ill. Very ill. And you two, instead of helping, are making things worse. You're only thinking of what you'll lose.'

Alice said frankly, 'I'm thinking of the ruin he can make of our lives. But I'm thinking first of all of my children——'

'It wouldn't hurt to think of Dyke for a change.'

'I'm thinking of my children,' said Alice obstinately. 'You aren't a mother, Caroline. It's all Dyke, Dyke, with you. Well, Basil and Elizabeth mean even more to me.'

'Dyke's sick——' said Harold.

'I may be sick. I'm also sane——'

'All right,' said Harold. 'You're sane. But you thought Felicity was going to leave you and that unbalanced you——'

'I *thought* she was going to leave me? She *was* going to.'

'Who else knew?'

'The man she was going with, I suppose.'

'Who else?'

'Nobody, so far as I know.'

'And who was the man?'

'I don't know.'

Harold sniffed. 'A queer elopement.'

'You mean you don't believe it?'

'Of course I don't. I don't mean she didn't say something that started you off on the idea. Or something that's made you think—since she died—that you thought it. But we've been down here together, how long?—best part of a month. And none of us has guessed it. We didn't find her any different——'

Dyke spoke sadly. 'How many of you guessed she was under sentence of death?'

His question put Harold out of his stride. 'That's—that's quite another matter. Find the man Felicity was going to run away with and then I might believe your story. I might. But you don't know. You haven't even guessed.'

'I——' Dyke remembered his suspicions of Trent but realized that that was no help.

'Ah,' said Harold. 'You think you do know.'

155

'No,' said Dyke. 'I don't.'

'You did then?'

Dyke did not know whether to tell or not. But Harold was suspicious. Silence would confirm their ideas about him.

'I—I did think—just for a while—I had an idea it was Trent.'

'Trent!' exclaimed Alice. Harold was ·staring at him in astonishment.

'But—what on earth made you think that?' asked Harold.

Sudden anger turned him against all of them. Why couldn't they just believe what he told them instead of badgering him like this.

'Mind you own damned business!' he shouted.

'Dyke,' said Caroline quietly. 'You'd better tell us—since you've told us so much.'

'Have you tackled Trent about this?' asked Harold.

'Yes,' said Dyke.

'*Since* Felicity—died?'

'Yes.'

'And—you don't think any longer it was he, do you?'

'No. It wasn't Trent.'

'It wasn't anybody,' said Harold. 'It's something you made up——'

'I did not make it up.'

'You imagined it.'

'I did not imagine it.'

Harold sighed. 'All right. You didn't. Thank goodness a jury might believe you did.'

'Harold, you are not to say such things,' said Caroline. 'There is no question of a jury ever hearing about this.'

But Harold's kindly patience was worn out. 'If my dear brother persists that he killed Felicity, sooner or later he'll tell the wrong person. And then there will be a·jury. And either a hanging to follow—or Broadmoor. Or some other lunatic asylum.'

Caroline could hardly restrain herself. 'There will be none of these things. Never, never! You are not to suggest them. You are not even to think them. Dyke is ill. If he would come away with me he would get well——'

Dyke, looking at her, was suddenly sorry for her. They all had so much. Whatever he did, whatever the results for them, they still had so much. Whatever Basil and Elizabeth lost they would cling to their parents—they lacked Michael's egoistic self-completeness. Everybody had something—except Caroline. She had lived on the fringes of his life for so long and had seen herself whirled into the centre of it—only to be snatched out, further away than ever. For a moment he wondered if he could pretend that what they said was the truth, go away with Caroline and pretend to forget; let her think he really had been mad.

He put his hands over his eyes. *Was* he mad? Could he possibly have imagined the torture that had twisted his mind for days? Was his mind warped by the sorrow of Felicity's death?

But he knew it was no use. Not even to save Caroline could he pretend to himself. He did not know what he was going to do now. He did not much care what happened, but not for anything would he go back into that lonely hell, nursing the secret of his crime, apart from them all, deserted even by the memory of Felicity. He had to go forward, not necessarily to confession and exposure; he did not know about that; but whatever it was and led to he must go forward. He could even imagine Felicity encouraging him. He could almost hear her voice: Go on, Dyke, hold your ground. The impression was so strong that his ears seemed to catch the inflection of her voice: Hold on, Dyke. Don't give in to them.

And he wouldn't.

He heard the door close, and looked up. Alice had gone. Then he sensed something. No words had been spoken, but Harold and Caroline had become confederates. They had, by exchange of looks or signs, allied themselves against him.

'I'm sorry,' he said heavily. 'I suppose, in her own way, Alice was right. All this *is* the very devil for you. I'm sorry. But I did do it. Felicity was going to leave me and I did kill her.'

For the faintest perceptible moment Harold's eyes met Caroline's, and the exchange of glances set the seal on their compact.

'All right, old man,' said Harold. 'I give in. If you say so, it must be so.'

Dyke looked at him sharply. 'You believe me?'

'I don't want to believe you, Dyke.' Harold's voice held all the insincerity of the false comforter who tells the dying man he will live. 'I don't want to. But I do. You've convinced me.'

Dyke turned to Caroline. 'What do you say to that.'

'I say the same as Harold,' she said sadly. 'I believe what you say.'

He knew they were lying. He knew that though, while they had protested, they had felt doubts in their minds, they had now cast the doubts behind them. They had determined not to believe him, and they never would believe him. They were as separated from him as if he were dead.

Chapter Seventeen

*

HE stood up. Both Caroline and Harold were looking at him and he carefully avoided meeting their eyes. For a time he had a sickening feeling of being watched. He was being watched, would always in future be watched. He was like an animal in a cage. Whichever way he turned their eyes would be looking, calculating his next move, ready to forestall him, ready to cut off his escape.

'What are you going to do about it?' asked Harold.

'I don't know.' He suddenly decided to play their game, and grinned impishly at Harold. 'I'm sorry about the baronetcy, old chap.'

'I don't know it would have been a baronetcy,' said Harold. 'Anyhow, don't worry about that. That's the least of our worries.'

'And about Basil and Elizabeth?'

'They'll get through,' said Harold. 'If you'll take my advice you'll go easy for a bit. Don't do anything rash. Take your time. Things will sort themselves out.'

He was talking like a fool, but luckily did not realize the fact.

'I think I'll go for a bit of a walk,' said Dyke.

'You won't go far, will you?' said Caroline.

'No. I shan't go far. Along the river bank, perhaps. Or down to the village.'

'I'll come with you, if you like,' said Harold.

'I'd rather be on my own if you don't mind.'

'Just as you like.'

'Don't be late for lunch,' said Caroline. 'Michael will be here for lunch, you know. And that reminds me, I must go and see about it.'

'I'll be somewhere about,' said Dyke.

He could feel their eyes on him as he went from the room. And again there was the awful feeling of being under supervision.

He went slowly down the garden to the river. He went on to the landing-stage and stared down at the launch. It rocked a little in the slight swell, swaying gently from side to side, as if it beckoned him, coaxing him on board. But he went no further. He stood looking. There he had stood that night and there Felicity had been sitting. All the others had been in the saloon. If only they had not been so intent on their cards they would have seen him, and the necessity for all this silly pretence would have been avoided.

It was a strange position in which he found himself now. They would all pretend to believe anything he cared to say, all the while being sure in their own minds that he was slightly crazy. Unless it was Alice. Alice had more sense than she had ever been given credit for. But she would play their game. She had her eyes fixed on her own interests, but they could explain the rules to her carefully and she would do as they told her.

What he had said to Harold had been the truth. He did *not* know what he was going to do next. Last night he had confessed to Caroline because the strain of pretending had grown too great, and because he could not bear to see her building up that impossible future. But Caroline had not believed, or had not been willing to believe. Things could not stay like this. Somebody must know.

It had begun, this necessity to share his secret, with the desolation that had fallen on him when he felt Felicity was really gone. With a sense of her presence about the place it had not been so bad. And yet, perhaps, it had started further back than that—

when he had understood why she had planned to leave him. After that, his pity had been so great he did not mind much who knew what he had done, nor what the consequences were.

The one consolation was that he had, in a way, done Felicity a good turn. He had found a way out for her.

If only Trent had stayed. The others were useless now. They had made their choice and were against him. Trent or Frank might understand. Not Frank, perhaps. It would not be fair to bring him into it. Frank was a friend, but there are limits to what you can ask of friendship. And wasn't there something about being an accessory after the fact? And, besides, Frank might not understand. He was so much younger than the rest of them.

No, Trent seemed his only hope. And he did not know where to get hold of him. He remembered now how, at various times during the last few years, Trent had left them suddenly. Sometimes he had been away a few days, sometimes a few weeks. There had been an occasion once when none of them had seen him for over a month. They had not thought much of it at the time, but now it seemed important to be in touch with him.

How could he reach Trent? He had left no address and one could hardly go to the Spencer's home and ask where he was. There was his club. He might have left a forwarding address there. It was worth trying.

Dyke turned away from the river. He would go down to the village and send Trent a telegram to his club. He might not be pleased at being brought back, but it need not be for long. He had to talk it over with someone who would not treat him as a lunatic, that was all.

When he returned from the village he went back into the garden. He found a seat out of sight of the house, and lit a pipe. He would have liked to take the launch out, but he did not think he could do that ever again. And he could not sell it, either. He would have to keep it there, rotting away at its moorings.

He was sitting on a seat against the bole of one of the big trees, out of sight of the house. The morning had been misty and cool, but the sun was coming out and it grew warmer. He felt sleepy and fell into a light doze.

It was there that Michael found him.

As soon as he saw Michael he knew he had lost him for ever. Felicity's death, that might have brought them closer, was now between them as impassable as a river. Michael was polite, even respectful, but only from policy. Dyke felt anger and fear and something like revulsion emanating from his son as he joined him on the seat. He wondered how much Caroline had said to him. At least she must have schooled him carefully, for his voice and actions were well controlled.

'Good morning, Father.' Michael sat down, arranged the creases in his trousers carefully and crossed his legs. Then he busied himself lighting a cigarette.

'Oh, you've arrived, Michael? Your Aunt Caroline said you were coming. By yourself?'

'Yes, I'm by myself.'

They both spoke quickly, afraid of the clash that was coming. All over again, thought Dyke: I did it. You didn't. I did. No, you're mad, I mean, ill. . . . Do you believe me? Don't you believe me?

'How are you, Father?' asked Michael. 'Aunt Caroline said you've been—been feeling rotten——'

'How much did your aunt tell you?'

Michael studied the tip of his cigarette, watched the swinging toe of his shoe with the intentness of a naturalist seeing a new species for the first time.

'Well, actually, she said quite a lot. It's—it's a bit incredible—I mean——'

'And of course she warned you that whatever I said you must pretend to believe me——'

'She said—oh, not quite like that—she said——'

'Michael,' said Dyke. 'Let's leave off this silly sparring. I know what she's told you. And you know I know. It's all—it's a dreadful thing for a man to have to tell his son, but the sooner it's said the better. I killed your mother. I killed her by pushing her off the launch. The circumstances were such that none of the others heard anything or noticed anything. It's not much fun telling you this, but the plain fact is I'm a murderer.'

He went on. 'The wretched part is that I didn't want to do it.' He came back to his one defence, the only excuse he had to offer. 'I didn't mean to do it, or plan it or anything of that sort. It was a horrible impulse. I was very upset at the time. She was going to leave me. She was going away with another man——'

'But that's impossible,' Michael burst out. He was suddenly moved, a little disgusted, ashamed as only children can be when they realize that their parents are subject to impulses they almost believe are peculiar to themselves, and, anyhow, peculiar to their own generation.

There was not much point in going on. There could never be any sympathy between them again. But he felt that, in fairness, he must complete his story.

'It is the truth, Michael, I assure you. Your mother and I—it is very difficult to explain—she did not feel for me—she was not in love with me—not in the way women are in love with men. There was a very close companionship between us, but we were —sexually incompatible. That's the only way I can put it——'

Michael was hating every moment. 'Are you bound to tell me this——?'

'I shall tell you. You need not listen. You can go away if you like, but I shall finish what I have to say.'

'It's—it's not the sort of thing——'

'It has to be said. I'm not enjoying it any more than you are.'

Michael's cigarette scorched his fingers warningly. He dropped the end and put his foot on it and ground it into the gravel. He remained like that, his hands hanging loosely between his knees, staring at the ground.

'Your mother was ill,' said Dyke. 'But you already know. I believe that—with the fear of death over her—she felt—a small part of her life was her own—to do what she liked with. I don't know what happened—I don't quite understand—but I think she felt she was offered something life had cheated her of—and she felt she was free to take it. I don't for a minute believe she expected to be happy—but when you are afraid you are going to die—I suppose it depends how you are made—another woman might find joy in renouncing what she wanted. I find it difficult to tell you. Inside myself I understand how she felt—but putting it into words——'

'It's—beastly,' said Michael.

'Yes, you think so. I can tell that. It isn't beastly at all—not when you understand. *Tout comprendre, tout pardonner*, you know. But you *must* understand first. You can't take that saying lightly or glibly . . .'

After a time Michael spoke again. He said, in effect, what Alice had said. 'But *why* couldn't you have kept this to yourself? Surely it's your private affair.'

'I'm afraid it isn't.'

'You could—have left us out.'

'I thought I could. And then I found I couldn't. I don't think it's any good trying to explain.'

'No, I don't think it is,' said Michael, his voice rising to a swift shrill anger. 'It doesn't do much good, does it? It only makes the whole damn' lot of us as miserable as sin. It—it can play hell with all our lives——'

'At first Caroline would not believe me,' said Dyke. 'She thought I was—strung up after the loss of your mother; imagining things. Actually, I suppose she thought I was off my head.'

'Does she believe you now?'

Michael had suddenly looked up to watch him, and Dyke took it as a warning. He must be careful what he said. Whatever he told Michael would be repeated to the others.

'Oh yes,' he said. 'She believes me now. She and Harold and Alice. She brought them into this while she thought me crazy. Yes, they know now.'

There was silence between them for a while. It was significant to Dyke that Michael made no comment. Did he believe what he had been told? He might, for, like Alice, he could be sharp enough when his own interests were at stake.

'Well,' he said at last. 'Haven't you anything to say?'

'What do you expect me to say?' said Michael. He was rather pale, and looked dark under the eyes, and Dyke realized with pain that the boy had been suffering. He had mourned for his mother—now this. 'What *can* I say? It's—it's pretty awful for all of us, isn't it?'

'Yes, it's awful,' agreed Dyke. He added quietly, 'It's awful for me, too, you know.'

'Yes,' said Michael. 'But you——' He stopped and Dyke guessed that he had been going to say that what he had done was his own fault. It was true, too, but it did not help to have the fact pointed out. Michael's sudden silence was revealing, though. He was afraid. Or he wanted something. Or both.

'You tell me,' Michael went on miserably, 'that my mother was—no better than—a common whore.'

He had not understood. Of course he could hardly have been expected to understand.

'I didn't tell you that, Michael.'

'That's what it boils down to.'

Dyke sighed. 'It may seem so now. In twenty years' time you'll think differently.'

'We can't live twenty years ahead,' said Michael fiercely. 'We've got to live in the present. Of all the damn silly things that silly old man Johnson said, about the silliest was about it not mattering a hundred years from now. A hundred years' time! We've got to live in the present.'

'Perhaps you're right,' sighed Dyke.

'Aunt Caroline thinks you made a mistake about mother,' said Michael. He was eyeing his father slyly. So that's how it goes, thought Dyke. He, too, will take the easy way. I'm mad and I imagined it all.

'Yes, I know.'

'She thinks you made a mistake. That mother didn't mean what you thought she meant——'

Dyke was moved to a deep pity. He wished his son could be a child again, to be soothed and comforted by lies and half-truths. Well, if he could get rid of his misery that way, let him. Why not?

'Don't you think she might be right, Father? After all, married people don't always—don't always agree, do they? And they can misunderstand each other. Mother wasn't the sort——'

He stopped. Dyke said nothing. Michael must provide his own soporifics. He could not lie, even to smooth his way for him. And there was no knowing how this was going to end.

Something of the same thought might have been in Michael's mind.

'What are you going to do?' he asked.

Dyke shook his head. 'I don't know.'

Suddenly there was a pleading note in Michael's voice. 'Father, couldn't you do—nothing?'

'I don't know what I shall do,' said Dyke.

'If this—if it gets out'—Michael sucked in his breath swiftly— 'if anyone finds out——'

'Yes?' asked Dyke.

'If they do, it means—it means ruin for all of us.'

'Does it?'

'Of course it does. We—we'd never be able to look anybody in the face again——'

'But you've done nothing——'

'Father, please. Don't let it get out——'

'What's worrying you? Your young woman?'

Michael spoke swiftly. 'Dinah's people were against her marrying me, anyhow. If they found out about this—she'd probably give in to them. It's been hard enough to get her to go against their wishes as much as she has done. If it got out—if people were saying you were a murderer—and mother—a bad lot—I'd lose her. I know I would. And I couldn't stand it. I couldn't——'

He was working himself up into a passion. Soon he would lose control.

'Calm yourself,' said Dyke.

Michael spoke in a low voice, but very earnestly. 'I'd kill myself if that happened.'

'Don't say things like that.'

'I mean it.'

'Michael, are you blackmailing me into—into forgetting what's happened?'

'You can call it what you like. If my engagement is broken off I'd sooner be dead.'

Dyke looked hard at his son. 'Did your aunt tell you to say this to me?'

'No, she didn't. Nobody did. She only said——'

He broke off. Dyke turned away. *She only said* . . . She said all she could think of; she just did not happen to think of that. But Michael had betrayed the fact that they had been discussing how to keep him quiet.

'Listen, Father. Whatever you did, you've got to keep other people from knowing. That's only fair to the rest of us. You can't drag us all in, me and Aunt Caroline, Uncle Harold and Aunt Alice, and Basil and Elizabeth. We'll all have mud slung at us.'

'What about me?'

'Yes, and you, too.'

'You're willing to forgive me for being responsible for your mother's death?'

Michael did not answer.

'Unless, of course, you don't believe I was responsible?'

Caroline had carefully schooled Michael. Whatever he did he must not show his real feelings. He spoke sulkily:

'If you say you are—I suppose you are.'

'And you're all willing to forgive and forget?' Dyke sat up, his voice becoming stronger. 'What a noble lot you are! Anything, as long as nothing is found out. My dear boy, don't you see that that's what matters to all of you? Caroline wanted to become my housekeeper and companion; Harold wants his name in the honours list; Alice wants a career for Basil and a good marriage for Elizabeth. All your grandmother is worried about is the good name of her child. And you—I suppose you want your Dinah. I'm not blaming you, but I do wonder if she's worth what you're willing to pay. Everything can be conveniently forgotten. Nothing matters so long as you all get what you want. Your mother is dead, but that doesn't matter. I'm a murderer, but that doesn't matter, either. Go to your Dinah, Michael, and tell her what I've told you. If she loves you, she'll stick to you. If she throws you over, you're better without her. You don't think so now, but some day you'll know that's the truth. If she'd let you down now, she'll let you down anyhow, sooner or later.

'As for me, I've told you already, I don't know what I'm going to do.' His voice was suddenly hard. 'But whatever I do, it won't be just to please any of you.'

'You've a responsibility to us,' said Michael. He spoke intensely, not looking at Dyke. 'What you did concerns us all. You should have thought of that——'

'I didn't think of anything,' said Dyke. 'If my actions have become your concern, it's no choice of mine. The fact is you none of you care a damn about your mother or me, or about what happens to me—except Caro, perhaps—only how it affects yourselves. If any of you had given me a thought, I might return the compliment. As it is, you'll have to put up with what comes.'

Michael was hesitant—as if his thoughts had not kept pace with what his father was saying.

'Well, at least—you might promise to consult us before you take any step——'

'I've not thought of any step to take,' said Dyke. 'But I make no promises of any kind. Not that there's much I *can* do——'

The gong for luncheon sounded from the house, a trembling wave of sound that floated down to them, then stopped abruptly.

Michael stood up. He looked miserable, as if he had failed in something he had set out to do.

'We'd better go in.'

'You go,' said Dyke. 'I don't want anything to eat. I shall stay here.'

'Aunt Caroline——'

Dyke smiled. 'You'll be able to discuss me more freely in my absence. Go on,' he said more kindly. 'I expect you're hungry after your journey down.'

Michael managed a smile himself. 'I can't say our talk has improved my appetite. You won't come, then?'

'No. Leave me,' said Dyke. 'I'll see you later. What time are you going back?'

'I don't think I shall go back to-day,' said Michael as he went up the path.

So that was it. It seemed years since Michael had stayed longer than a few hours. But now it was in his own interest to stay, so he would stay. Dyke was sorry for him, but contempt was blended with pity. Of course it was bad for him. It was bad for all of them. But all could they think of was that if anybody outside the family found out that he had killed Felicity they would have to share the disgrace. So he must be mad. It was a convenient explanation as long as they could believe it, and apparently they had made up their minds to do so.

Michael had put their case: You've a responsibility to all of us. Dyke was moved to compassion for them. What a hell of a mess to find themselves mixed up in; but with the compassion was exasperation at their attitude. Nobody must know. Whatever happened, nobody must ever know. Felicity didn't matter any more. He didn't matter. Save us from the contempt of our friends was their cry. He would have to do something. If he did not do something soon he would be blackmailed by pity into silence for ever. From now on he would have to go carefully. They were all against him. Whatever he did must be done in secret . . . *whatever he did* . . . what could he do? Perhaps I *am* a bit mad, he said. Only it is not the madness they are thinking of.

He sat on, thinking; worrying at his problem like a dog continues to worry at something it has already torn to shreds. An hour passed. The sun came out and it became warm, and he dozed to awake to a moment's blessed forgetfulness before misery descended on him again.

There was a way out: to see Brayton and talk to him, but he shrank from the finality of it. Once he had done that . . . The others came out, went back into the house, but none of them ventured near him. He heard their voices calling to each other, but there was an unnatural, studied carelessness about the way they called. They were more with him than if they had been sitting round him in a ring, watching him and trying to see how his mind worked.

Caroline—or one of them—had said: Keep out of his way for a while. Leave him alone. Perhaps when he's had time to think it over . . .

Chapter Eighteen

*

HE went indoors for some tea.

'You must be hungry,' Caroline said. 'Shall I get you something?'

'I'm not hungry. I'll have a sandwich. Nothing more.'

He had forced his way back on them and they waited to see if he would tell them anything, but he did not. He took his tea almost in silence, holding the cup in his hand by the window, eating the sandwiches that Caroline brought him; agreed with Harold about the warmness of the afternoon. Michael read an old *Punch* with absorbed interest. Only Alice was still sullenly angry. She did not say anything, but he felt her anger like a raised fist poised to strike him.

'More tea?' asked Caroline when he brought his empty cup back to the tray.

'No more, thanks,' he said. 'I think I shall run into town.'

He might have announced a decision to do something evil. They all stared at him, Michael putting down his paper with an abruptness that betrayed the shallowness of his interest.

'What for?' asked Harold.

He looked at Harold in surprise. 'No reason why I shouldn't, is there?'

'Good lord, no!' Harold laughed feebly. 'Of course not.'

'Are you sure you're fit to go to town?' asked Alice.

'Alice!' said Caroline warningly.

'I wouldn't mind going myself,' said Harold. 'There are one or two things I want.' He looked at his watch. 'If we can catch the shops.'

'Of course we can. You come, Harold. You can drive. I don't feel a bit like driving.'

Their relief was almost tangible. As if they had all sighed in chorus.

'Yes, I'll drive, if you like,' said Harold. 'I'll get the car out, shall I?'

'Do. I'll get my hat.'

They did not talk on the way.

'Where d'you want to go?' asked Harold as soon as they arrived. 'We could go together.'

'You'd better park the car,' said Dyke. 'I'll go on to Wool-worths——'

'That's where I'm going,' said Harold. 'I'll join you there, shall I?'

'Right. They won't be open much longer. But I can get all I want there. Then we can have a drink somewhere.'

'Yes, I could do with a drink, too. We'd better not stay too late, though. Frank should be back soon.'

'Frank will be all right,' said Dyke. 'Come to that, if we go to the Crown he might stop, coming through. He nearly always does.'

Harold stopped the car and Dyke got out.

'See you in a minute,' he said.

Harold waved and drove on. Dyke stood there watching the car as it went down the street. As soon as it went round the corner he turned and walked quickly in the opposite direction. A few minutes later he was in the police station.

A constable took him into a hygienically comfortless room where a sergeant was writing at a desk. He knew the sergeant and the sergeant knew him. He stood up.

'Good evening, Mr. Farne. What can I do for you, sir?'

Dyke felt as if he had been running. He could hear his heart thumping and he felt breathless.

'I want to see Inspector Brayton,' he said.

'I'm very sorry, sir,' said the sergeant. 'The Inspector isn't here.'

Dyke realized he might have expected as much. His way was never to be smooth any more.

'I suppose you can get hold of him?'

'We-ll.' The sergeant pulled a long face. 'He's gone home, you see, sir. He's had a very busy day. And I know he's got an appointment this evening. Is it anything I can do?'

'I'm sorry, Holt,' said Dyke. 'I'm afraid it isn't. And it's most important. I must have a word with the Inspector himself.' He could see how the sergeant was inclined to temporize. 'It really is urgent.'

'I know he was going out,' said the sergeant slowly.

'I'd like you to try to get hold of him before he goes out, then,' said Dyke. He knew that the Inspector's home was not fifteen minutes away by car.

'Would you like one of the men to run you out to his place?'

'No,' said Dyke. 'Better here. Much better if he sees me here. I shan't keep him long. I tell you, Holt, it's important.' He was beginning to panic. The decision to come had been made suddenly and he was afraid of being afraid. If he didn't see Brayton pretty soon . . .

Sergeant Holt had picked up the telephone unhappily. He got the number, and then stood with the receiver to his ear, waiting.

'Yes,' he said, and seemed to spring to attention. 'That you, sir? . . . Holt speaking . . .'

Dyke had walked across to a notice-board and was studying a dismally-coloured portrait of the Colorado beetle, but he could hear Holt's end of the conversation and Brayton's voice, an unintelligible, irritated squawk.

'Mr. Farne, sir . . . Mr. Dyke Farne. . . . He wants to see you urgently. . . . He says it's very important. . . . I offered to send him over in the car, but . . .'

The sergeant was listening to a long monologue. . . . 'I'll ask him, sir.' He looked at Dyke, fingers spread over the mouth-piece. 'The Inspector says what is the business, Mr. Farne?'

Dyke hesitated, then discarded caution. He would burn his boats. 'You can say it's in connection with my wife's death.'

The sergeant, after the least perceptible stare, returned his attention to the telephone.

'It's to do with Mrs. Farne's death, sir. . . . Yes, I know, sir . . .' Again Brayton's voice could be heard. He seemed to be going on and on, and once or twice the sergeant winced as if a shot had gone home. At last he put the receiver down.

'He'll be here in about twenty minutes, Mr. Farne. He's in the middle of changing. Would you like to come back?'

'I'll wait,' said Dyke. 'It's not worth going out and coming back again.'

'Very good, sir.' There was a hard, obviously uncomfortable bench against a wall, but the sergeant brought out a padded arm-chair and put it at some distance from the desk. 'Would you like to see the evening paper?'

'Thank you,' said Dyke. He sat down and took the paper and opened it. The sergeant went back to his writing. The curious glance he gave his visitor was quite involuntary.

Dyke looked up and down the columns of the paper, reading the headlines but not aware of anything. What he had feared was happening. He was beginning to be sorry that he had come. Why exactly had he come? He was not sure. He thought back to the afternoon. He had felt walled-in by the unbelief of all his family. He had realized then that the one person he could be sure of taking him seriously was Brayton. He was afraid to confess to Brayton and yet if he did not do it soon he knew he would never do it at all. They would bludgeon him into silence with their protests. And then he would have to go all his life with the knowledge of what he had done locked up inside himself. And he knew now that he would not be able to stand it. He would break under the strain. It would end up by his believing that he really was mad. He had more than once considered the possibility seriously. Frank might believe him, but they would take good care he did not get a word alone with Frank. And, anyhow, it was hardly fair to him. Trent, perhaps, but then he did not know how to get in touch with Trent. He might not see him for a week, for a month, perhaps. And by that time anything might have happened. It would almost certainly be too late.

But the prospect of confessing to Brayton was frightening him. If he didn't come soon he'd find himself unable to do it. He would make some feeble excuse and go away—and then Brayton too would begin to think he was cracking up.

Suppose he made a confidant of the sergeant? Before it was too late. He looked over his paper. The sergeant was filling up what was apparently a form with an interminable set of questions. He held his head poised a little on one side, and when he wrote he gnawed at his underlip. Once he put his tongue out and curled it in sympathy with the careful movements of his pen.

Suppose he said to the sergeant: Look here, Holt, I really came in here to tell the Inspector I murdered my wife!

No, it wouldn't do. Holt would only be like the others. He'd think him mad. He'd say: Yes, Mr. Farne, of course . . . and he'd go to telephone Caroline privately and he'd say to the constable outside: That bloke in there, he's gone off his rocker, poor devil . . .

A car pulled up in the street and after a brief pause Brayton came in.

He nodded to the sergeant, and then to Dyke.

'Evening, Mr. Farne.'

175

'Good evening, Inspector.' Even now he was not sure he could go through with it. In fact he didn't believe he could.

'Sergeant Holt informed me you wanted to see me urgently.' Brayton was wearing a dinner suit, a reminder that he was in a hurry and must not be delayed. He walked across the room, opened a door and held it back. 'Will you come in here, please?'

Brayton's own office was just as cheerless, if more unobtrusively so, than the outer one. He had switched on the light, and closed the door behind Dyke. He walked across the room to his desk, but he neither sat down nor invited his visitor to do so.

'Now, Mr. Farne?'

Dyke took a deep breath. It was no good beating about the bush. Blurt it out or nothing. 'I came to tell you that you were right all the time.' Brayton was staring. 'I—I did kill my wife.'

Brayton did not answer. He went on staring. Then suddenly he came out of his trance. He drew a chair forward for Dyke and then went to sit down behind his desk.

'Would you be good enough to repeat that, Mr. Farne?'

Having said it once it was not so difficult after all.

'I murdered my wife.'

Brayton hitched his chair forward a little. 'You said something about me being right?'

A feeling of indignation swept through Dyke. Brayton and his damned suspicions! For a moment he had that hunted, persecuted feeling again.

'Well, you were suspicious of me, weren't you? And how right you were.'

'*I* was suspicious of *you?*'

'It was obvious enough.'

'That you killed Mrs. Farne?'

'What else?'

'My dear sir'—Brayton seemed not to know what to say next —'such an idea never entered my head.'

Dyke remembered that to the Inspector the business was over and done with. The verdict at the inquest had sealed the whole thing off comfortably. Packed away and finished with.

'There's no need to be polite about it——'

'Polite!' Brayton laughed. 'I'm not trying to be polite. I'm just telling you a fact. I did not at any time connect you with your wife's death.' He added, 'Nor do I now.'

Dyke's face must have betrayed his disbelief, for Brayton, leaning slightly forward, accenting his words with his hand, went on.

'I did think there was something damned fishy about it——'

'Exactly,' said Dyke.

'I thought the lot of you might have been too drunk to know what did happen. I was suspicious about that mark on your wife's head. I certainly didn't believe your sister's account of how she got it——'

'It was the truth——'

'Yes, I realize it now. But it came in too neatly to sound right at the time. I wondered'—his stare at Dyke had become an un-friendly stare—'there's no real reason why I should tell you everything I think, but as a matter of fact I thought there might have been horseplay of some sort. There might have been some-body else involved. Your wife mightn't even have been on the launch at all. How did I know what you were keeping from me?'

'But that's childish——'

Brayton was nettled. 'Childish or not, I had to consider every-thing. I know you Farnes. Clannish. That's what you are, clan-nish. If you had anything to hide from the simple-minded flatfoot you'd all play ball together. I was looking out for that.' He had become more heated than he meant to, and he waved his hand in a gesture of dismissal. 'But that was before the inquest. Doctor Ryder's evidence made everything clear. I'd been suspicious without any reason. I'm sorry about it. If you want an apology, unofficially, you can have it now. Your wife was a nice woman. I liked her. Nobody's more sorry than I am about what's happened. It's damned bad luck.' He had calmed down. 'We're all sorry for you, Mr. Farne. You've got everybody's sympathy. I know that's not much consolation at the moment. But it helps——'

'All right,' said Dyke. 'But you don't understand what I'm getting at. I killed my wife.'

'I heard you say that before,' said Brayton. 'You're not trying to be funny, are you?'

'It's not exactly anything to be funny about.'

'You're right there. I heard what you said first time. But I can guess you're feeling a bit wound up.'

'It's not a case of being wound up, Brayton. I'm a murderer.'

Brayton stirred. Almost imperceptibly, he smiled. Then the smile was gone and he sighed. He gave a furtive glance at his wrist watch and almost seemed to shake his head.

'You want to tell me about it?'

'I don't want to. I will, though.'

Brayton settled back in his chair patiently. 'Go ahead.'

Dyke had not expected to be taken seriously at once. But Brayton's attitude irritated him. He expected to be listened to, and he expected Brayton to sit up and take notice when he realized he was being told the truth. Brayton's attention was really little more than perfunctory. And he had not missed the quick sideways look at the watch. He felt angry and it was no help to realise he did not quite know where to start. He had not thought out how he should tell his story—if he had thought as much as that his courage would have failed him; he might never have come at all—and he realized he did not want to tell all. As long as Brayton knew he had killed Felicity, that was all that he needed to know. He did not want to admit that she was going to leave him. In the end he might have to tell that too, but if he could, he wanted to leave it out. Once they knew that they'd start thinking things about her—making up more than existed. He no longer cared what happened to himself, but he wanted to protect her.

Brayton was sitting there waiting.

'Most of what you know is the truth,' said Dyke. 'The others were playing bridge in the saloon. My wife was sitting curled up in the stern. I was pouring drinks.' For a moment he was back there. It was as real as if it were happening all over again. He stood up restlessly, took a few steps away from his chair, then turned to look at Brayton. 'I poured my wife's drink. We were just passing the mill. Everything seemed to come into my mind at the same moment. There was the noise of the water, and I suddenly realized that she couldn't cry out—or not much—with her throat full of the neat spirit—and the way she sat with her head thrown back, perched there—balanced—so I stepped forward and pushed her . . .'

Brayton didn't speak.

Dyke passed a hand over his head in a bewildered fashion. 'It happened—exactly as I'd imagined it would. And then I went back to the saloon. All the rest—well, I think you know all there is to know.'

He had been moving restlessly while he spoke. Now he looked at Brayton, and Brayton held his gaze. When he spoke it was one word.

'Why?'

'Why—what d'you mean——?'

'Why did you do it?'

Dyke's eyes wandered away uneasily. He had had nothing planned, nothing thought out. Only the driving need to escape from all the others and get rid of his lonely guilt.

'I was angry with her.'

'What were you angry about?'

Again Dyke's eyes wandered round as if seeking a way out. If he had had some convenient lie handy—though he knew that a lie was not possible. He had passed the stage where a lie could be of use.

Brayton repeated his question. 'Why were you angry with Mrs. Farne?'

Dyke shook his head. 'I'd rather not say.'

'But, my dear chap——' Brayton shrugged his shoulders.

'I don't see it affects the issue.'

'A motive always affects the issue—especially when a murder is in question.'

'Motive?' Dyke spoke dully, as if Brayton were going too fast and he could not keep up with him.

'A murder implies a motive, naturally. If there is not a strong motive . . .'

Dyke felt himself trapped. Sooner or later he would have to explain. It might as well be now.

'Very well,' he said. 'She was going to leave me.'

'Indeed.' Brayton's eyebrows went up. He sat forward again. 'I wish you'd sit down, Mr. Farne.'

Dyke stared at him a minute then sank back into his chair.

'That's better. Would you mind making things a little clearer? Do you mean you had quarrelled?'

'No, it wasn't like that. We didn't quarrel——'

'Then——' Brayton looked in enquiry.

'Oh damn it!' exploded Dyke. 'She was going to leave me for another man.'

'I—see. You mean she'd been unfaithful to you?'

'No, she had not been unfaithful.' Dyke was flaring up but, with an effort, calmed himself. 'At least, not then. That is to say—she would have been, naturally—she—she just told me she was going to leave me—for somebody else.'

'She told you, then, the night of the—of the tragedy?'

'No, a couple of days earlier.'

Brayton was speaking a little more sharply. 'I suppose you'd been discussing a divorce?'

'No, we hadn't——'

'No? I should have thought—still . . . Tell me, who was the other man?'

'I don't know,' said Dyke.

'You—don't know?'

'No.'

'H'm. So you don't know if it was one of your friends. Or somebody you'd never met——?'

'I've no idea.'

'Isn't that rather strange?'

'It may seem strange to you. Actually it isn't strange at all. It—it was more important to me that she was going to leave me than who she was going with.'

'You weren't worried about who she was going with, then?'

'Yes, I was. Of course I was.' Dyke was growing angry again. Why wouldn't Brayton understand? 'But the other was more important.'

'I see. So you murdered her.'

'I destroyed her,' said Dyke miserably. 'I mean it wasn't a murder in the sense that I'd thought about it or planned it or anything of that sort. I suppose I was angry with her and then that opportunity offered itself——'

'Quite. A pity you didn't tell me all this in the first place.'

'I suppose it is. I don't think I quite understood what I'd done. I was afraid of you finding out, of course. I suppose being afraid of that stopped me thinking of anything else. But I've realized that being found out isn't what matters most.'

Felicity was at his elbow sympathizing with him over Brayton's obtuseness, as she would have done over, say, a gardener who wouldn't do things his way. He felt suddenly more cheerful. There was a great weight gone from his mind.

'And exactly what,' Brayton was asking, 'do you think is going to happen now?'

'I don't care much what happens,' said Dyke. He found it possible to smile at Brayton. 'I don't think anything matters much after the awful, desolate loneliness——'

Brayton, though the smile had not escaped him, did not seem to be listening.

'I suppose you realize that the evidence that was given at the inquest tends to cut across all you've said now?'

'But as long as I admit——'

'Your admission isn't much help. The law can't punish a man for a murder unless it can prove he committed it. And on the other hand a murderer can't convict himself unless he can bring reasonable proof. What proof have you? You were angry with her because she was going to leave you. Did anybody else know she was leaving you?'

'No,' said Dyke.

'There you are, then. *You* say she was going to leave you for some other chap, but you don't even know who he was——'

'You don't believe me——'

'Oh, I believe you, Mr. Farne,' said Brayton cheerfully. He spoke as one speaks to a naughty child. 'I believe you. But is there any jury, anywhere, in its reasonable senses, that would? That's the point, you know. It's not what I believe. It's quite possible your wife did fall in love with somebody else. They get funny ideas about that age, I know. Most of 'em go for film stars in a big way—from a distance, luckily. So no harm's done. That's what film stars are for——'

'Look here,' snapped Dyke. 'Are you making fun of me?'

Brayton pressed the thumb and forefinger of his right hand into his eyes for a moment. 'Personally, I thought it was rather bright,' he said. 'Explains a lot of things—things covered by the word vicarious.' He put his hand down, opened his eyes and stared hard at Dyke. 'Mr. Farne, do you know that nobody ever dies in questionable circumstances—*ever*,' he repeated, 'but what some bright person comes in and confesses that he killed that person.'

'That's nothing to do with this——'

'It's got a lot to do with it. You don't know—we were very careful not to tell you, because we didn't want to distress you— that we've already had one confession from a man who said he'd murdered Mrs. Farne——'

Dyke sat up, electrified. 'You've—*what?*'

Brayton nodded. 'It's the truth, I assure you. Chap in town here. You may know of him. William Bruce—the people call him Silly Billy—always hanging round one of the inn yards— generally the Bull—minds horses on market days, looks after parked cars—or pretends to. Yes, he came and said he'd swum out to the launch, stretched out an arm and pulled your wife off—oh well, it's not very pleasant——'

'But that's crazy——'

'Yes,' agreed Brayton. 'Particularly as Billy can't swim, and also was in the tap of the Bull the whole of the night Mrs. Farne died.'

'But look here, you aren't comparing what I've told you with what some lunatic——'

'Mr. Farne,' said Brayton quietly. 'I've told you about Billy. That's an extreme case. But I assure you the police get confessions just as ridiculous from people who seem sane in every way.'

'Yes, I've heard something like that. But——'

'Death worries people. It worries some more than others. And as for an unexpected violent death——' he paused. 'I don't know what it is exactly. You need a psychologist on this job. But an accident can get you down. You can get thinking and thinking, and imagining and imagining till you don't know what's real and what's imagination. I can understand how your wife's death has preyed on your mind——'

'Now listen to me, Brayton——'

'No, you listen to me. It would serve you right, you know, if I took you at your word and put in a report about this conversation, and let things take their course. But I'm not going to. I'm going to use my discretion. That's one thing about having reached the giddy height of inspector—one is allowed to possess a little discretion——' He was on the point of laughing, but the expression on Dyke's face discouraged him—'I'm going to say nothing about what you've told me——'

'If you're too wooden-headed to listen, I can go higher——'

Brayton was very far from laughing. 'Perhaps I ought to say I'm going to say nothing—*officially*.' For an instant he looked angry. 'Man, d'you want to get yourself certified? Listen to me and take my advice. Don't say anything about this to anybody. Keep it to yourself and have a good rest, and then in a month's time—or three months' time—as long as you like—come back here and we'll talk it over——'

'Look here,' said Dyke, 'don't try to treat me like a child. I know what you mean.'

Brayton did not speak.

'And you're wrong—*Wrong*. I'm telling you the truth——'

'Who else have you told before you came to me?' He saw the expression on Dyke's face and nodded as if it confirmed a suspicion. 'You've told somebody, I suppose?'

'I told my sister,' said Dyke briefly. He paused. 'She told my brother and his wife—and my son.'

'Yes?' Brayton waited.

'Oh yes, you've guessed it, all right,' said Dyke sadly. 'Of course I'm mad. I'm making it up. I'm—I'm breaking down under the strain of my wife's death. I suppose it's what I ought to have expected. Especially since they don't fancy the unpleasantness if the truth comes out——'

Brayton was making every effort to be gentle. 'Quite a reasonable attitude, don't you think——'

'But can't you see, they aren't thinking of me—or of Felicity—nothing matters now only to hush it up, keep it quiet——'

'I still think it's reasonable,' said Brayton. 'Selfish, perhaps, but natural. Nobody in their right senses'—he paused, but he had said it and had to go on—'would want to find themselves in the centre of a murder trial. *You* feel you've got to get it off your mind. But look at it from their point of view instead. Keep quiet for their sakes.'

Dyke shook his head. 'It won't do, Brayton. I can see you're like the rest of them. You think I'm daft, too.'

'Over this one point I do,' said Brayton. 'I can say that frankly, because in other respects I expect you're as sane as I am.'

'Self-interest isn't making up *your* mind for you?'

'Why should it?'

'You wouldn't look too clever if I were telling the truth.'

Brayton thought a minute. 'I'd hate to look a fool,' he admitted. 'And perhaps I should—if your yarn were anything but a bee in your bonnet. But I'll tell you plainly: if I thought you were telling me the truth I'd put you under arrest right away.'

'I am telling the truth,' said Dyke. 'I'm not enjoying telling it, but it's the truth. The way everybody thinks I'm crazy is enough to make me crazy. I keep wondering myself if I *am*.'

'Then the sooner you give in to the idea the better for everybody. Man, it's a nightmare you've had. You got this idea into your head about your wife going to leave you——'

Dyke was shaking his head.

'Listen,' said Brayton. 'You *couldn't* have done it. It's

impossible.' He saw Dyke was not moved. 'Don't you remember what Mr. Calvert said? Don't you remember him telling me he could see you all the time——?'

'Oh that,' said Dyke. 'He couldn't see me at all. He said that to help me out.'

'I went to the launch and tried it. He could have seen you.'

'He wasn't watching me. I tell you he said that because he thought you might suspect me. He told me afterwards.'

For the first time Brayton's confidence was slightly shaken. 'He told you that? When?'

'After you'd gone.'

'Oh, nonsense! You're making this up. Did he think you—murdered Mrs. Farne?'

'No. But he saw how it was possible. He was just racing you to get there first.'

'I wasn't even aiming in that direction.'

'He was heading you off, anyhow. You can ask him.'

'It wouldn't prove a thing if I did.'

'At least it would prove it possible I'm telling you the truth.'

Brayton looked at his watch and gave a grunt of annoyance. 'Where is he?' he asked in an irritated voice. 'Where is he? Is he in town now?'

Dyke remembered that he did not know where Frank was. But he might be back at the Lodge.

'He took my mother-in-law home this morning. He hadn't come back when I left——'

Brayton was thoroughly disgruntled. 'Look here. I'm supposed to go out this evening, and I'm late already. This is absolutely a waste of time——'

'He's probably there by now. Let me use your phone and I'll see——'

'There's no point in it at all. None at all——'

'He could be here in a quarter of an hour.'

Brayton bit his lip in annoyance. 'But what good will it do—' he pushed the telephone across the desk. 'Oh, all right. If he's there and can come at once, I'll hear what he has to say. Not that it'll prove anything—if he *does* corroborate your story—except that he's a liar——'

Dyke, who was paying no attention, had picked up the receiver and was waiting for his number. He sat tensed for a minute, and then spoke eagerly.

'That you, Caroline? Dyke speaking. Has Frank come back? . . . Never mind where I am . . . of course I'm all right. I want to speak to Frank. At once. It's urgent . . .'

He turned to nod to Brayton, but did not say anything.

'Frank? . . . I say, could you come here at once . . . I'm at the police station with Inspector Brayton. . . . It's important. Can you come now? . . . By yourself? . . . Right away . . . Thanks . . .'

He put the receiver down. 'He's coming,' he said to Brayton. 'Hadn't even put his car away.'

'There's no real point in it, you know——'

'If he wasn't watching me—as he said he was—at least I *could* have done what I say.'

'You're *too* determined to be guilty, that's what's wrong with you,' said Brayton. 'I wish you'd be sensible.'

'And I wish you wouldn't be so stubborn.'

Brayton made a gesture that seemed to indicate the hopelessness of arguing with someone who was off his head. If Dyke had been a person of less importance he would have probably thrown him out by now. He got up and went towards the outer office.

'Excuse me,' he said.

Dyke lit a cigarette and paced up and down restlessly. He could not bear to be still. The situation was developing into a nightmarish sort of farce. Were they all right, after all? *Could* he be a bit off his head about this? It was impossible. He couldn't have imagined it. And yet, everybody was against him, everybody said he was crazy. He knew he was not, but then the madman was always the one sane person in a mad world. He tried to remember exactly what had passed between him and Felicity, but it was difficult to recall anything with clarity. It was like trying to look at a scene through gauze. Nothing would stay in focus. Even the words spoken would not come back clearly.

He finished his cigarette and was smoking a second when Brayton returned. He went back to his desk, looked with irritation at Dyke's pacing, seemed to be going to say something about it, and then, perhaps realizing the futility of protest, took a clipped bundle of papers and began flicking them over as if looking for something.

There were voices in the outer office. The door opened and then the sergeant's voice:

'Mr. Calvert, sir.'

Frank came in, giving a quick look, first at Dyke, then at Brayton, then back to Dyke.

Dyke had stopped walking.

'Frank! Good man!'

'Hello, Dyke! Good evening, Inspector.'

'Good evening,' said Brayton.

'Listen, Frank,' said Dyke. 'I want you——'

'Wait a minute.' Brayton spoke authoritatively and held up a hand for silence. 'I'll handle this, Mr. Farne, if you please.'

'Yes, but——'

'*If* you please, sir.'

'What's up?' asked Frank. He seemed young as he stood there, a little bewildered, looking from one to the other of them. In contrast with the other two—Brayton, tired and irritable; Dyke lined with worry, grey, with dark shadows under his eyes—

Frank's freshness was almost boyish. His hair was ruffled a little and the colour in his cheeks was high.

'I shan't keep you long,' said Brayton. 'But there's a question I'd like you to answer.'

'Of course,' said Frank. 'Anything I can do.'

Dyke began. 'Brayton, you *must* make it clear——'

Brayton was not a man who relied on anger as part of his equipment, but he had little patience left. 'And, I'll repeat, Mr. Farne, you must let me do this in my own way.'

'There's nothing wrong, is there?' asked Frank.

Dyke drove his hands deep in his pockets and turned away.

'You remember when I was investigating Mrs. Farne's death?' said Brayton.

Frank nodded. 'Yes.'

'You volunteered a statement——?'

'Did I?' said Frank.

'You told me that'—Brayton paused to think—'you said that all the time Mr. Farne was outside the saloon you could see him.'

'Yes.'

Dyke turned sharply as if he would speak, but he caught Brayton's eye and restrained himself.

'I want to know if that was the truth.'

Frank raised his eyebrows. 'Of course it was.'

'Frank——' began Dyke desperately, but Brayton broke in.

'Be quiet!' he ordered. He turned again to Frank. 'I want to know the truth this time. The *truth*.'

'It is the truth.'

'If you tell anything but the truth you're doing Mr. Farne a great deal of harm. Don't say something because you think it will help him——'

'Tell him the truth,' said Dyke quickly.

Brayton gave him an angry glance.

'I have told the truth.'

'Where were you sitting?'

'Directly facing the door of the saloon.'

Again Dyke broke in. 'You weren't. You were at one side.'

Brayton ignored the interruption. 'Could you see Mr. Farne?'

'Yes, clearly.'

'All the time after he'd poured the drinks until he came into the saloon?'

'All the time.' Frank wore a slightly surprised air. 'What *is* all this?'

Dyke could not be restrained any longer. 'Look here——' He turned on Brayton when he would have silenced him. 'No, it's no good, I must speak.' He turned to Frank. 'Tell the Inspector the truth, man. I want you to——'

Frank's bewilderment seemed to increase. 'But that's what I have done——'

'Tell him that you couldn't see me at all. That I wasn't in your line of vision. That you only said I was in case he was suspecting me——'

'Suspecting you? Of what?'

'Of murdering Felicity.'

'My dear chap!' Bewilderment gave place to shock.

'Do you still hold to your statement?' demanded Brayton.

'I most certainly do.'

Dyke pushed his hand through his hair. He seemed to slump, his shoulders were rounded. He was looking at neither of the others. Unobserved, they exchanged a quick glance, enquiry in Frank's eyes. Brayton shook his head gravely. Then he spoke:

'I think that will do. Mr. Farne had better go home——'

Some of Dyke's spirit returned. 'I don't know what this is, a conspiracy——'

Brayton went across to him. They were both tall, but Dyke seemed slim beside the other's bulk. Brayton put both hands on Dyke's shoulders. Very gently he rocked him to and fro.

'Listen. Will you take my advice? As a friend, not as a policeman. Go home and rest. Even better, get away from here for a while. Try not to think about what's happened. And *don't* talk about it. You can get better if you give yourself a chance——'

There was no response in Dyke's eyes. Brayton's hands dropped. He turned away to his desk.

'Good night,' he said pointedly.

'Good night,' Inspector, said Frank. He put a hand through Dyke's arm and spoke in the cheerful voice reserved for chronic invalids. 'Come on, old man.'

Chapter Nineteen

★

THEY stood a moment on the pavement outside the police station, neither of them speaking. Frank's car was drawn up at the kerb.

'We may as well go home,' said Dyke. There seemed to be no spirit left in him.

'We'll have a drink first,' said Frank. He had opened the door of the car and held it back. 'Hop in.'

Nothing was said as Frank drove through the streets. He pulled up at the Golden Fleece, an inn in a quiet street, and one Dyke hardly knew. Frank seemed to know it, however, for he led the way, not to one of the bars, but down a long, dimly-lit passage at the end of which he opened the door into a small room.

'Quiet here,' he explained. 'What are you going to have?' A girl had come up the passage after them, and stood in the door-way. 'Double whisky?'

'Anything,' said Dyke. 'I don't care.'

'Two double whiskies,' Frank said to the girl. He came back into the room. 'We'll be left to ourselves in here. Matter of fact, I asked that we shouldn't be disturbed because we had some business to discuss.'

'I think you've done me a bad turn, Frank,' said Dyke. 'You think you were helping me, but I wanted you to tell Brayton the truth. Unless I *am* off my head——'

'You're all right,' said Frank reassuringly. 'Sane as anybody. Don't let that worry you.'

'I suppose as soon as you arrived they got at you,' said Dyke. 'I don't know what they told you, but I can guess——'

There were footsteps in the passage.

'Hold it!' warned Frank. He went to the door, collected the tray with the drinks, paid the girl, then, after placing the tray on the table, shut the door.

He took up one of the glasses, splashed a little soda in it, and, without speaking, drank most of what was in the glass.

'I want to talk to you, Dyke,' he said. His voice had a business-like ring. All the sentimental friendliness with which he had coaxed him out of Brayton's office had vanished. Dyke was not paying particular attention. He was mixing his own drink.

'You let me down,' he said in a tired voice.

'I did exactly what I meant to do.'

'I suppose Caroline warned you——'

'Wait a minute. Caroline's nothing to do with this. I got back soon after you and Harold came to town. I sensed something wrong straight away——'

'Didn't they tell you——?'

'All Caroline told me was that you were obviously heading for a breakdown——'

'You shouldn't have taken any notice.'

'I didn't. She also, without in any way becoming less than the perfect hostess, managed to get the idea across that a house whose master is going off his rocker is better without guests——'

Dyke looked up in annoyance. 'You mean she hinted you oughtn't to stay——?'

'She didn't hint. Caroline doesn't descend to hints. She just gave me the idea—like I told you.'

'She'd no business to. I told her plainly——'

'Anyhow, I'm not coming back. I've got my things in the car. But I want to talk to you before I go.'

'But you must come back, Frank. I insist.'

Frank's smile, for the first time, was anything but friendly. 'You won't. Not when I've finished. Let me get on. Harold arrived with the news that he'd lost you. Or you'd given him the slip. The result was a very thinly concealed panic. You might have been a lunatic at large.'

'Broadly speaking, that's the idea. Or they pretend to think it is.'

'Your voice on the telephone,' said Frank mockingly, 'was the cause of such gusts of relief they nearly blew the roof off. I told them where you were and that you wanted me. That scared them again and Caroline tried to make me understand that discretion is about the greatest of the underrated virtues, and I said good-bye. Harold followed in your car to take you home.'

'Harold?' said Dyke. 'Where is he?'

'Biting his nails in the Lion, I expect. That's where I parked him. I promised to deliver you safely to him there. Which is why we're having this chat here.'

Dyke was growing puzzled at Frank's attitude. It was flippant yet at the same time bitter. 'Look here, what *is* all this about?'

Frank's question came with a suddenness that startled Dyke. 'Just tell me one thing. Did you kill Felicity?'

'Yes,' said Dyke.

'I suppose'—Frank took a deep breath—'you pushed her off the stern or something like that—took her unawares?'

Dyke was not sure whether Frank believed him, or if it was part of the conspiracy they had all joined in against him.

He nodded. 'Yes,' he said again.

'Why?'

'I don't suppose you'll believe me, Frank——'

'Never mind what I'll believe. Just answer me.'

'She was going to leave me—going with another man——'

'Do you know who he was?'

'No. They all think that's ridiculous, but——'

Frank tapped his chest. 'Of course it isn't ridiculous. I was the man, Dyke.'

Dyke was so astonished that for a moment he could not speak. 'Don't be a damn' fool!' he said at last.

'It's the truth.'

Dyke rose to his feet. He looked grim. 'I suppose this is all part of some plan to really send me off my head. I suppose you're joining with the others——'

Frank was equally grim. 'Felicity promised to come away with me. I'm the man she was leaving you for.'

Dyke suddenly saw that he meant what he said. For an instant he raised his hands in a gesture so threatening that Frank stepped back a pace. They remained like that a moment.

'Relax,' said Frank. 'There's a lot to say and not much time to say it in.'

Dyke finished the whisky in his glass and put the glass back again on the table with a bang.

'You——' he began, but seemed to choke on the word. 'She couldn't have loved *you*.'

'Whether she did or not, she'd have come away with me.'

Dyke scoffed. '*You*—ten years younger than she was?'

'I expect that was to my advantage. If I'd been her age she'd have laughed at me.'

'But you? You couldn't love a woman ten years older than yourself.'

'No?' said Frank quietly. 'Well, whether I could or I couldn't, I did. Age didn't come into it.'

'I—I can't believe it.'

'I'll tell you, if you want to know,' said Frank. 'I'm sorry about this part of it. It's nothing to be proud of. I'm not proud of it. In fact I used to be ashamed. I wished it hadn't happened. But it did. Soon after we met I fell in love with Felicity. You know how it was with me at that time. I'd had to give Honor her divorce and I was sick about it. I swore I'd not be bitten again. And I'd have been on the watch not to fall in love with a woman my own age. I suppose Felicity being older—that made it different—I can't explain——' He burst out, 'Oh hell, why should I explain? How can I? What's the good of trying to turn myself inside out? I fell in love with your wife. I didn't want to and I felt a swine about it, but I did.'

Dyke had become calm. In some strange way he was now much more in command of the situation than Frank was.

'Go on,' he said.

'There's not much to tell,' said Frank. 'Or not much I want to tell.' He added, after the slightest hesitation: 'I was never her lover.'

'You needn't have told me that,' said Dyke.

'I'm telling you on her account, not yours.'

'If you had been, I think I'd have known—whether I was told or not.'

'I told Felicity I loved her and I asked her to leave you.' Frank was speaking slowly, not looking at Dyke, choosing his words carefully. 'She wouldn't. She—I'm not sure if she loved me—not at first, anyhow—she did in a way, I think. Then suddenly she changed. She said she'd come——'

'This was—not very long ago?'

'Since we all came down to the Lodge.' He looked up at Dyke guardedly. 'I suppose it must have been after the doctor told her she was so ill. I suppose—I haven't seemed to be able to think clearly about it—I think she must have—sort have decided to take a chance—perhaps on getting something from me that she had never found with you. She was—a bit strange about it——'

'In what way?'

'I don't know how much she told you. She wasn't going to ask you for a divorce. If you divorced her, that was all about it, but I had a feeling that in some queer way she wanted to hold on to you——' He thought a moment then added, without appearing to notice the irony of what he said—'as if you were a sort of lifeline.'

'I wasn't *that*,' muttered Dyke, almost to himself.

The remark reminded Frank. While he talked he had grown quieter, as if his companion had been some third person unconnected with what had happened. When he remembered, his voice rose a little. There was a hint of savagery.

'You murdered her,' he said. 'So that she shouldn't come with me?'

'I destroyed her——'

'You needn't choose your words so nicely——'

'I'm not splitting hairs, if that's what you mean. There's no more excuse for what I did than for any other—murder, if you chose that word. I didn't plan it, I hadn't even thought about it. I just put out my hand and destroyed, on a sudden impulse, like a child destroys——'

'And now,' said Frank, '*now* you're going to damn' well suffer for it.'

Dyke smiled grimly. 'My dear chap, don't you realize that I'd take any punishment handed out to me—gladly. But nobody will believe I did it. I tell them'—he spread his hands in despair—'and they all think I've gone mad. And you haven't helped. If you'd told Brayton the truth——'

'What I did, I did on purpose,' said Frank. He sounded triumphant. 'How do you think I felt the night Felicity was drowned? I loved her, but I couldn't show it. Any of the rest of you could have bellowed your heads off if you'd wanted to. I'd only lost a friend—or the wife of a friend. I'd no rights, no business to be there except on sufferance. I wanted to jump in the river after her, but I couldn't show my feelings. I did what I was told. Sit in the bow and waggle that blasted light under your orders. And she was there—somewhere down under that water——' He seemed to choke, then recovered himself. 'The person I loved most in the world. Oh, it was very terrible for you, Dyke. Dyke, the bereaved husband. Can you imagine what it was like for me?'

Dyke said nothing. He was not looking at Frank any longer.

'I didn't realize at first that something was wrong—something more than a mere accident. And then I began to see Brayton was worried, I could see that—oh, he thought we'd been tight and fooling about, or something of the sort, but I didn't realize that at the time—I kept on wondering why he was so worried. And then you, Dyke. You were frightened, frightened as hell. You were frightened you'd be found out. Once anybody knew, it was plain. You were on edge all the time. I kept thinking about it and thinking about what had happened. I knew Felicity had told you she was going away. And you might have decided she shouldn't. It didn't need a brain the size of Brayton's to realize if Felicity hadn't fallen into the water by accident it must have been because of something you did. You could have pushed her in. She'd have called out. But perhaps not if she'd been drinking at the time—and with the noise of that damned mill . . .'

Dyke was standing with his back to Frank. He spoke over his shoulder. 'You've worked it all out very cleverly.' Then he turned suddenly. 'But *why* did you tell Brayton that wretched lie which made it seem impossible that I could have done it?'

Frank put his hands on the table and leaned forward so that his face came nearer to Dyke's. 'Because, my dear Dyke, I knew you'd weaken sooner or later. I know you. You're too introspective to make a good murderer. You'd start thinking. Your beautiful conscience would begin whipping you up—and from what I know of you you're the sort to take your shirt off so the lashes hurt more. You weren't the type to wash your hands and say, Let's make a clean start from here.'

'There's one factor you haven't taken into account,' said Dyke quietly.

'There's enough.'

'I loved Felicity,' said Dyke. 'I'd loved her for years, ever since I've known her.'

Frank's voice dropped. 'You don't need to remind me. I hated you for that often enough.'

'And I was going to lose her.'

'Were you bound to destroy what you couldn't have?'

'Men often do,' said Dyke wearily. 'If they don't think carefully, that's exactly what they do.'

' "All men kill the thing they love," ' quoted Frank. Then he repeated the final lines of the stanza:

> ' "The kindest use a knife because
> The dead so soon grow cold." '

He spoke in sudden anger. 'You're not pretending there's any truth in such gibberish. A whining pose!'

'Leave Wilde out of it,' said Dyke. 'I destroyed what I loved. Never mind about reasons. What I'd like to know is your reason for not giving me away.'

'Haven't you seen that yet? It's simple enough. I've hated you too much, Dyke, just to hope you'd be punished. You'll do your own punishing. You'll do it a lot better than anyone else could. I never saw just how it would work out, but it's better than I ever guessed it could be. You've got the rest of your life to live with the memory of what you did hanging over you. And you can't do anything about it. If you say you killed Felicity, people will think you're mad. They'll never believe you. Never.'

He was breathing quickly. His voice was triumphant.

'You've a nice mind, Frank. Is it really going to be as bad as that?'

'If I know you, it's going to be worse—worse even than you

think. I've got to live with the thought of losing what I so nearly won. That's bad enough. But I wouldn't change with you, Dyke. I wouldn't change. In a way we've each made our own hell. But you've made one you can never get out of as long as you live.'

Dyke said nothing. He walked across to the window and looked out, but it was dark and he could see very little. There was some sort of back garden with a line of washing showing up in a series of grey blurs. Here and there lights shone in rooms, tiny stars that twinkled through uncurtained windows, or shrouded pale rectangles. A feeling of deep depression settled on his mind There was a kind of loneliness about the quiet town that made him realize his isolation.

Behind him the door slammed. When he looked round, the room was empty.

He turned away from the window, uncertain what to do next. Then the door opened again and the girl who had served them put her head in.

'Did you want anything else, sir?'

Dyke looked at the glasses on the tray.

'No,' he said absently. 'No, nothing, thank you.'

She swept up the tray and was gone, leaving the door open.

He remembered Harold waiting anxiously at the Lion. He'd better get along there.

Chapter Twenty

★

HAROLD was obviously so relieved to see him that he asked no questions. He apologized hesitantly for going home without Dyke. He had looked everywhere and failed to find him and had been sure he had gone home some other way. Then Frank had had his message and, of course, he'd come back, since Frank had decided to leave that night and they didn't want to give Frank the trouble of running him back. Every now and then Harold would pause expectantly to give Dyke a chance to talk if he wanted to. But Dyke hardly answered at all.

Not a word was said about the visit to the police station. Harold, whether under instruction, or of his own accord, was going to leave the questioning to Caroline and Alice.

They were plainly curious, but it was a cautious, veiled curiosity. Everybody was like that now. Pains must be taken to make it all appear perfectly normal. A carefully fabricated web of pretence had been drawn over the most ordinary event, so that every question or the simplest statement had to be peered into to see what hidden meaning lay beneath.

All the same, they knew something. They were hugging it to themselves, but at the same time wanting amplification. He felt it but was too tired and hungry to care much what it was.

Alice, with a controlled anger under her self-possession, was the most impatient.

He was having some sandwiches and a bottle of beer. He did

not want dinner, he explained, and they, of course, had had theirs —a very poor dinner, he guessed. Caroline waited on him.

'Inspector Brayton rang up a while ago,' she said, when he pushed the tray aside, refusing more sandwiches.

Dyke guessed then. Brayton had been warning them, joining forces with them.

'I suppose he told you I'd been to see him?'

'Yes—he did say——'

'It's all right, Caroline. He's on your side. He thinks I'm as dotty as you do.'

'We don't think you dotty, Father,' said Michael.

'For goodness sake, Michael, don't sound so damned polite. You've been indifferent enough for ages and it sounds forced. I can hear your words creak.'

Michael retired, beaten, to the book he was pretending to read.

'Dyke, my dear,' said Caroline reproachfully. 'You needn't have done that.'

'Done what?'

'Gone to Inspector Brayton.'

'No,' he said. 'I suppose not. But I felt—oh well, it wasn't much good, anyhow. I suppose he told you I'm mad.'

'He didn't say anything of the sort. He said you were ill—and he said you ought to see a doctor.'

'Not much point in that,' said Dyke.

'I telephoned Arthur Ryder to ask him to run over to-morrow.'

'You shouldn't have bothered. There's nothing he can do for me. I'm perfectly well.'

Alice could not control herself any longer. 'You are not perfectly well——'

Dyke looked at her blandly. 'My dear Alice, I thought you all agreed with me earlier in the day that I am not off my head, and that I did—all I say I did——'

'Suppose we do?' Alice stood up. The knitting she had had in her lap fell to the floor, but she did not notice it. 'Suppose we do. Do you imagine we want to go on thinking about it and talking about it? You did a wicked thing, Dyke. I can hardly forgive you.' He knew she was referring not to Felicity but to his visit to the police station. 'A wicked, cruel, selfish thing. Surely decent people should keep their—their family troubles to themselves.' She noticed the knitting and began to pick it up, but the ball of wool rolled away playfully and she had to follow it half-way across the room. 'You might have caused untold trouble by going to the Inspector like that without consulting anybody. It's lucky for us that Mr. Brayton is such an understanding man——'

Michael got up, thrust his book into a shelf and went towards the door. 'I think I'll go to bed. Good night, everybody.'

'You might consider your own son if you don't trouble what happens to anybody else,' said Alice, when he had gone.

'Very well, Alice,' said Dyke. 'Don't say any more. I'll try to behave myself better in future. I suppose it does seem unkind to involve you all. I don't want to involve you, you know. I'm not doing it on purpose. What happened was really between Felicity and me.'

'It's a pity you couldn't have kept it to Felicity and you.'

'I would have done if I could.'

'You could,' said Alice angrily. 'You could. You could have kept it to yourself. You needn't have told anybody. Why should we all suffer for what you have done?'

The vehemence of her attack amazed him. At first he could not reply.

He said at last: 'You really do believe me, don't you, Alice?'

Both Caroline and Harold were uncomfortable. He caught the quick exchange of glances between them. Alice was breaking down their confidence. They, at least, whatever they professed in order to quieten him, had made up their minds that they would sooner believe him insane than a murderer.

Alice had not yet replied to him. She realized that her anger had carried her further than she wanted to go. Privately, she too was clinging to the respectable dogma that he had had hallucinations. She looked at Harold uneasily, but Harold was too unhappy to make any comment. In any case, he was too much under her domination to be able to make a useful one. Caroline was not, though.

'I think, Alice, if we can't say anything to help Dyke, it would be better to say nothing at all.'

'That's quite true,' said Harold weakly.

Alice gathered together her knitting and her book. 'I shall go to bed,' she said. 'Are you coming, Harold?'

He stood up. 'Yes, I think I'll come. I'm tired.'

Alice went to stand in front of Dyke.

'Dyke, I'm sorry! I didn't mean to go for you like that.'

He smiled at her. 'It's all right.'

'Only, Dyke—please don't—don't let us all down. We're sorry; we're terribly sorry, but'—she sounded as if she were going to cry—'you know, it's awful for us as well as for you—awful——'

She really did catch her breath in a sob then, but before Dyke could reply she had gone out of the room. Harold said good night and followed her.

Caroline and Dyke sat in silence for a while. She spoke first.

'You saw Frank?'

'Yes,' he said. 'I saw him.'

She was uneasy about Frank's departure. 'I hope you don't mind that he's gone. He said—oh, something about he really ought not to stay any longer'—she waited to see if Dyke would speak, but he did not—'I didn't try to keep him. I thought just at present—while you—feel like you do——'

'It's all right,' said Dyke. 'We're better without him.'

She brightened. 'We are. We really are, aren't we?'

Strangely, he had hardly given Frank a thought once he had gone. They had been fond of him, he had become almost one of the family, but now that was over, and they would never see him again. It did not matter. It didn't even matter much that he had nearly become Felicity's lover. He was a link in a chain of causes that led up to an effect. The causes were no longer of any importance.

Caroline broke into his reverie. 'Arthur said he'd run over in the morning.'

'Arthur?'

'Arthur Ryder.'

'Oh,' said Dyke. Then, with more spirit: 'What's the use, Caro? What's the use?'

'You will see him, won't you?'

'There's no point in it. I'm perfectly well.'

'To please me, Dyke.' She almost pleaded. 'It's ridiculous to say you're perfectly well. How can you be after all you've been through?'

'I'll see him if you like. But he may have returned to Scotland.'

'No, he hasn't. I told you. I spoke to him on the phone. Oh, that reminds me, Trent rang up while you were out.'

'Trent? What did he want?'

'He's coming back to-morrow.'

Dyke had wanted Trent, now the news only annoyed him. What was the good? Trent would take up his stand with the others. It would only be one more against him.

'I wish you'd put him off, Caro.'

'But I thought you'd want him.' She spoke with the eagerness of one seeing a strong ally in sight. If anybody could help, Trent would. 'Besides,' she said, 'Trent! How could I put him off? He never has been yet. He's one of us.'

'Oh, it's all right.'

He was thinking of Arthur Ryder. Perhaps Arthur would understand. He was rather glad now he was coming.

'I think I'll go up,' he said. 'I believe I shall sleep.'

Caroline wanted to say something to him. Bnt she did not know how to say it. He could see the entreaty in her eyes.

'Suppose—if Arthur Ryder said you were ill—very run-down or something—if he suggested you ought to take a rest——'

He shook his head at her. 'It's no good, Caro. I don't feel I can leave here at present.'

She stood up. 'But *why?*'

'I don't know, I can't, that's all.' She was standing there, biting her lip, angry with him, yet eating her heart out with sorrow. 'It's no good, Caro. You're still banking on the fact that I might be unbalanced——'

'Oh no,' she said. 'As long as you're sure——'

'Drop that silly pretence,' he said. 'Humouring me—is that what you call it? Drop it. If you believe I'm mad, say so. Don't pretend. Only let yourself think. You're just fighting against believing I killed Felicity. You heard Alice. She knows. In her heart she knows all right.'

'I don't care about Alice,' said Caroline fiercely. 'I don't care what she thinks or what she says. You didn't kill Felicity. You think you did, but you didn't. It's—it's an illness—saying that. I won't believe. Never. Never.'

He looked at her, shaking his head. Poor Caro! In a way she was worse off than any of them. Because he wanted to be kind he kissed her and she clung to him and he could feel the tears on her face.

'Good night, Caro,' he said.

Chapter Twenty-one

*

THE doctor sat with Dyke in the little-used room that was called his study. Ryder was talking about fishing. He talked about fishing in such a determined way that he might have been trying to hide the fact that he was a doctor. Dyke was only moderately interested in fishing at the best of times, and at the moment completely uninterested, so his share in the conversation was not very helpful, and after a while even Ryder, whose one hobby was fishing, began to find the going heavy. Dyke waited patiently for him to come to the point where, having put the patient at his ease, he could begin to work.

'It wouldn't do you any harm to get away with a rod yourself, old chap,' said Ryder at last. 'This last week has been a strain for you. You want to relax.'

Dyke did wonder if it would be worth while breaking through all this sparring, but it was too much of an effort to make. He felt dull and heavy.

'I'm all right,' he said. 'A bit tired, that's all.'

'I'm not so sure you are all right. Caroline's worried about you, you know.'

'Yes. I do know.'

'She feels you need a rest. A complete change and rest.'

'D'you want to examine me?' asked Dyke.

'D'you want me to?'

'Not particularly. You can if you like.'

'I don't think there's much wrong with you physically.'

'There's not.'

'Not physically,' repeated Ryder. 'Look here, why not do as I say and get in a spot of fishing? You ought to try that bit of water I use. It's about the best——'

'I don't care for Scotland,' said Dyke. 'I like to be in the sun——'

'There you are, then. Go south, somewhere. Somewhere where there is sun——'

'I don't feel like going away at the moment.'

Sweet reasonableness bringing no result, Ryder's air became more professional. 'I want to give you some advice, Dyke.'

'As a friend or as a doctor?'

'Both. What I should say to you as either is the same. Physically you are, I agree, at the moment, sound enough. Mentally, I'm not so sure. What has happened has preyed on your mind—naturally——'

'You mean I'm insane—or likely to be.'

'I didn't say anything of the sort,' said Ryder sharply. 'I certainly think your mind isn't stable at the moment. There's nothing wrong—now, but you're running a risk.'

'Why don't we stop wandering round the subject,' said Dyke. 'I know Caro and Harold have been talking to you, and you know I know. They don't or won't believe I killed Felicity——'

'Don't talk rubbish, man!'

'It happens to be the truth, Arthur.'

'And I happen to know it is not the truth. You've been so worried and upset at losing Felicity that you've let it prey on your mind. I know exactly how she died——'

'You think——' began Dyke.

'I know,' insisted Ryder. 'My dear chap, do you think I'd take this attitude if I were not sure And I know what's happened to you since. You've turned a dream into a reality. You've imagined something that might have happened—are you listening, Dyke?'

'Yes, I'm listening.'

'Then try to understand me. You're an educated man. You *can* understand if you try. I'm not an alienist, but it really doesn't take more than a bit of common sense. Something happened between Felicity and you.'

'They've told you the whole story, of course.'

'Never mind the whole story. Whatever it was, it left you unhappy and resentful.'

'She was going to leave me.'

'All right, if you want it that way, she was going to leave you. But don't forget I was Felicity's doctor. *She* wasn't exactly her normal self. She couldn't have been—in the circumstances. She said something that made you think she was going to leave you, didn't she?'

'Why ask me? You know.'

'But don't you see, man. She didn't mean what you thought she meant. She thought she was going to die and she was trying to warn you.'

Dyke began to laugh quietly.

'What's the matter?'

'Nothing,' said Dyke. 'Only it's queer the way the pieces fit together to make quite a different picture from the real one.'

'I wish you'd try to follow my reasoning.'

'Go on. I'm listening.'

'Whatever she said, I don't suppose it was what you've since come to believe she said. And I want you to pay attention to this. You thought she was intending to clear out. You didn't get her real meaning at all. And—I don't know what went on between you, of course—but you were filled with resentment. And it occurred to you, consciously or subconsciously, that you could stop her going by killing her. Since you're a civilized person I don't suppose the thought was ever formulated. But in your subconscious it was probably pretty strong.'

'I begin to see your drift,' said Dyke. 'You're going to say that a part of me wanted to murder Felicity.'

'Something of the sort. We're all a bit queer underneath—part of the time. It's nothing to worry about. We're civilized and restrained. The man who turns to look at a pair of pretty legs doesn't necessarily want to go to bed with the owner, though subconsciously the idea isn't unattractive.'

'The subconscious would like to grab her up and get on with it?'

'The subconscious, Dyke, is uninhibited.'

'Aren't we getting away from the point a bit,' said Dyke.

'Not at all. I'm suggesting that the subconscious part of you was very angry with Felicity, having misunderstood her, and was quite willing to destroy her rather than lose her. After all, it's any man's normal instinct towards the woman he loves: If I can't have her, neither shall anyone else. Then Felicity actually did lose her life. That was a shocking blow to you, but added to it was the—how shall I put it—the remorse felt by the subconscious murderous part of you. You've brooded too much, thought too much, and the result'—Ryder shrugged his shoulders—'the sub-conscious has got the upper hand and persuaded you you really did commit the murder.'

He stopped. Dyke sat thinking.

'You've got it nicely worked out,' he said.

'That's how I see it, Dyke. Honestly. The mind can play funny tricks. I should know that. You know it yourself. Be reasonable, man, admit that what I say may be the truth. Give yourself a chance. Whatever you've decided in your own mind, you must see that there isn't a shred of evidence that you even *could* have killed Felicity.'

'Oh, I should say there's a shred,' said Dyke. 'You know, Arthur, all this would be funny if it weren't so damned horrible.'

'I'll tell you something else,' said Ryder. 'I had a word with Brayton before coming over.'

Dyke looked at him quickly. 'My word, we are going into it thoroughly.'

'Well, Caroline told me that you'd been talking to Brayton.'

'Was that how she put it?'

'It was a damn silly thing to do, you know. It might—it might have caused a lot of unpleasantness. Luckily, Brayton's a sensible sort of chap. He understood.'

'You mean he agreed with you that I must be dotty.'

'He knows as well as I do that you couldn't have killed Felicity. And he has proof that you couldn't have done.'

'Has he? He didn't mention the fact.'

'Didn't Frank tell him in your presence——?'

'Oh *that!*' Dyke wondered if he ought to explain. But making these explanations was like running his head against a brick wall. And the process was actually giving him a headache. He would not be believed. The idea of Felicity and Frank—anyhow, he did not want to talk to anyone about Felicity and Frank. It wasn't fair to Felicity, either.

'Yes, that,' repeated Ryder. 'It's proof, Dyke. Proof that you're imagining things. Can't you *see*, man——'

They were both sitting in chair near the window. Dyke got up.

'All right, Arthur, have it your own way. I'm off my head. What then?'

Ryder saw that all he had said had had no effect.

'I suppose I'm harmless?' said Dyke. 'I don't need a keeper, do I? All you can do is leave the patient alone and hope he'll get over it. There are bigger fools at large, I suppose. Or would you like to lock me up?'

'Don't talk like an ass!' snapped Ryder.

'After all, if you're going to lock up some of the lunatics, you ought to get the lot under lock and key. The ones who say the

world is flat, and the chaps who say Bacon wrote Shakespeare—
or didn't write Shakespeare, according to how you look at it.'

Ryder stood up. He went to one side of the window so that he
faced Dyke. He was very serious.

'Would you be willing to go into a nursing home?'

'Would I—*what!* Like hell! No, certainly not.'

'Now, don't go off the deep end. You put the idea in my mind
yourself.'

'Then you get it out,' said Dyke grimly. 'Quick.'

'There's no need to get hot under the collar.'

'I shall get very hot under the collar if you suggest locking me
up in an asylum—private or otherwise.'

'I said nursing home——'

'You might just as well have said looney-bin. That's vulgar,
but it means what it says.'

'I was thinking of somewhere absolutely private. As free as a
very exclusive hotel——'

'No, thank you!'

'You'd be at liberty to come and go as you wished——'

'In that case there's no reason for going in the first place. Did
Caro put you up to this?'

'For heaven's sake, Dyke, relax. Nobody put me up to it.' He
was grim himself now. 'But I'll tell you frankly, an illusion like
you've got doesn't stay static. It gets better or it gets worse. And
if it gets worse . . .'

'There's nothing to get better or worse——'

'I want you to listen to me, Dyke. I'm speaking as your doctor
and I'm speaking very seriously. You keep saying that we think
you've gone off your head. We don't think anything of the sort.
What I do think myself is that you've got a definite hallucination.
If it's any comfort to you to know it, you're not the first case I've
come across since I've been practising. Though you are about the
most obstinate. Otherwise you're sane and normal enough. And

because you are, I'm able to talk to you like this. You can't go on having this hallucination. You've got to be cured of it. If you don't, you'll almost certainly get worse. You'll start hearing Felicity's voice. Or seeing her. Imagining things about her.'

'And what then?'

'And then, my boy, you'll *have* to have treatment—whether you want it or not.'

Dyke smiled. 'You're not threatening me with—how is it politely put—restraint?'

'I'm not threatening you with anything. I'm warning you to get a grip on yourself. In time.'

'Thanks,' said Dyke. 'That all?'

'That's all,' said Ryder. He took a step away from the window. 'I suppose I'd better go. I don't seem to have done much good. Of all the stubborn, obstinate——'

Dyke laughed. 'I'm sorry, Arthur. I appreciate that you're trying to help me.'

'Look,' said Ryder. 'Do one thing.'

'What's that?'

'Do it to please me, to please Caroline, for the sake of your friends——'

'It sounds formidable.'

'It's not formidable at all. Will you see an alienist? This sort of thing isn't in my line, really. I've had too many sick bodies to mend to have had much time for sick minds. But I know Sir James Jacobsen and he's a first-class man——'

'There's no point in it, Arthur, no point at all——'

'Damn it, man, it can't do any harm.'

'It would mean I'd have to go up to London, and I don't want to. I don't want to go away from here at all at present.'

'You needn't go away from here. I'll get him to come down. I know him quite well, as it happens, and I'm sure he'd come.'

'Trouble for nothing. Let him stick to those he can help.'

'Dyke, you're purposely being obstinate now. You could agree to see Sir James—for all our sakes.'

Dyke did not want to see anybody. There was no reason for seeing anybody. He knew he had killed Felicity and it served no useful purpose talking to people who only wanted to persuade him he had not done so. But he was beginning to feel sorry for all the others, for Harold and Alice, for Caroline and Michael and Trent, even for Ryder who was genuinely upset at his failure to make any impression. If it would make them any happier to have him talk to this chap, why not do it? Please them and do no harm to anybody. He'd have to be careful, of course. He was tired now of trying to make people see what he had done. It was better to keep his knowledge to himself. He would grow crafty in time.

Crafty? That was how mad people got.

He laughed.

Ryder was watching him with anxiety.

'I don't see what's funny.'

'All right,' said Dyke. 'Bring your Sir James. If it will please any of you it'll do that much good anyhow. I don't seem to have pleased anybody much lately.'

'You will? Good man.' Ryder plainly was very pleased; perhaps relieved as well.

'When shall I expect the great man?'

'I'll get on the phone to him as soon as I go home. I expect he'll come quite soon. Perhaps to-morrow, but I'll let you know. I'll ring up as soon as I've made arrangements with him.'

'All right,' said Dyke. 'I won't come out with you, if you don't mind. I want to stay in here a bit. And it'll give Caro a chance to ask you if I'm any better. Don't be too professional with her. Tell her you have every hope. And that I've agreed to see the great mind-specialist, Sir James what's-it . . .'

When Ryder had gone he went back to the window. Michael

was sitting on the seat by the path that led to the landing-stage. He was reading a book. They had all become rather devoted to literature lately. Everywhere he went or looked, one of them seemed to be deeply engrossed in a book. Were they beginning to keep an eye on him already? He saw Michael look up towards the house and he stepped back quickly, then sat down in a chair. He did not want to be observed, he did not like the feeling that they were looking at him all the time, then pretending not to when he glanced their way.

He was thinking over what Ryder had said. After all, it was very reasonable. He might even have managed to think there was something in it but for what had happened last night. Frank had very effectually closed the door of his hell on him. And yet— was it such a hell? What did Arthur say: You'll start hearing Felicity's voice. Or seeing her. And *that* was madness, was it? Not that he could *see* her. Not yet. He'd be very glad to. Even if it meant he was mad. But it was not difficult at all to imagine her voice. He could imagine it quite plainly. And the things she'd say. *Poor Dyke! They do torment you. How foolish people can be! But you don't want to take any notice of them. . . .* Yes, he could imagine her speaking, easily, hear every lilt and inflection, and the little intimate laugh. . . . *It's pretty foul having to keep things to yourself. I had to keep it to myself when Arthur said I was going to die. . . .* He had only to close his eyes to hear her, hear the actual voice, the words he knew she'd say. . . . *And I couldn't sleep at first and I used to want to wake you up and tell you.* It was as if she talked to him to keep his mind away from his worries. *I used to stretch out my hand in the dark wanting to put it on yours and say: Dyke, wake up. I want to tell you something . . .*

Chapter Twenty-two

*

IN the afternoon Dyke did an unexpected thing, as unexpected to himself as it must have been to the others. He took the launch out.

He had walked to the landing-stage, more from a desire to be out of their sight than from inclination, and had stood there looking down into the launch. It had not been moved since the night he had taken Brayton on the river. He had mentioned casually that it ought to be put into the boathouse if none of them were going to use it, and Harold had said he would see to it, but he had not done so.

On an impulse Dyke jumped on board, started the motor and cast off. The next moment he was in midstream.

His action, he imagined, caused some alarm. As he turned for a run upstream he could see Michael in the garden, not reading now, but his book hanging loosely in his hand, shading his eyes with the other. Presumably he had called out, for first Caroline and then Harold and Alice came on to the verandah, and they stood looking, all with hands raised to shade their eyes.

Dyke smiled as he opened out the engine. He felt as if he had been triumphant in doing something he should not have done. They were all uncomfortable at the notion that he could get away from them and there was nothing they could do about it. If they had seen him coming aboard they might have offered to accompany him, but he had gone too far for them to offer casually, and to suggest themselves less than casually would have betrayed their anxiety.

At the first bend he turned and came slowly downstream. He had had a mischievous impulse to clear out for a few hours but decided against it. There was no reason to be wilfully unkind.

They were still on the verandah when he came back, all except Michael, who was now on the landing-stage. He called out:

'I say, father, if you're going for a run, I'd rather like to come.'

Dyke did not alter his course. 'I'm not going anywhere,' he replied. The launch was going slowly, the motor quiet, and he hardly had to raise his voice. 'I only wanted to try the engine. I may fish a bit now I'm out.'

He said it on impulse, but he remembered that there was some fishing tackle in one of the lockers. He hardly ever did fish, but sometimes when they had all been staying at the Lodge and he had wanted to be by himself he had taken out a rod and line and sat brooding over it for an hour or two. It had seemed to him a pleasant way for a man to spend an afternoon when he did not want company, and it had come to be taken for granted that when he fished he did not want company.

A little way below the house he brought the launch closer to the bank, shut off the engine and threw the anchor out. As he went to look for the tackle he could see that only Caroline was left on the verandah, and then she went in, too. Michael was walking slowly up the garden again.

The afternoon sun was warm on his back and he felt strangely at peace. He had thought he could never use the launch again, but no unhappy thoughts worried him as he sat on the wide gunwale above the long seats, staring at the little red-and-green float that curtsied to the flowing stream. He had put some bait on the hook as a matter of course, but he hoped he was not going to catch anything. He did not want to catch anything, only to be alone and to rest. Ryder's visit that morning had worried him a little, and he was not sure that he had done wisely in agreeing to see Sir James. After all, their attitude was perfectly reasonable; if it had not been for Frank he might have let himself be persuaded that they were right and that the whole business was nothing but a horrible nightmare.

He must have dozed, for all of a sudden he heard the splash of oars quite close at hand and when he looked up he saw Trent rowing down in the dinghy. His first impulse was to pull up the anchor quickly, start the motor and clear off, but he knew he could not do that without appearing to be as strange as they thought he was. He did not want Trent, he did not want any-body. He wanted to be by himself. Now the same old argument would start up again: You couldn't have done it . . . you've imagined it . . . the strain of losing Felicity . . . go away . . . take a rest . . . clear out for a while . . .

He remembered he had accused Trent of being in love with Felicity, and suddenly that made everything worse. Trent would be even more sure and more tiresome than any of them. . . . Oh damn!

Trent clambered aboard, trailed the dinghy's painter round and tied up under the stern. Then he came to squat close to Dyke.

'Hullo, Dyke,' he said.

'Hullo,' said Dyke.

'I came as soon as I got your wire,' said Trent. 'Motored over.'

Dyke turned to glance at him. 'Where were you?'

'Norfolk,' said Trent. He took out a pipe and pouch and filled his pipe slowly. 'Can't stay very long. I'm going back to-night. But your wire sounded urgent. So here I am.'

He lit his pipe, and some flies that had been circling round his head soared upwards from the little cloud of smoke.

'I'm sorry I fetched you back,' said Dyke. 'I really am. I thought—I thought I needed you and now I find I don't. I was in a bit of a panic at the time——'

'It's all right,' said Trent. 'If you don't need me, you don't. Good job, I suppose. The drive did me good and it's nice to see you, anyhow. How are you?'

'Fine,' said Dyke.

'Good.'

Dyke looked up towards the house but there was nobody in sight. Even Michael had gone in. Presumably they had all gone to pray in their own ways that Trent would bring him to a better frame of mind. Sort of keeping their fingers crossed.

'I suppose you've seen Caro?' asked Dyke.

'Talked to her, you mean. And Harold—and Alice. I should say so. Or rather they talked to me. What the hell have you been up to?'

'Why ask me?' said Dyke stiffly, 'if they told you. Didn't they inform you I'm off my rocker? Got an hallucination I killed Felicity.'

'Dyke, don't be a damn fool!'

Dyke looked at him. Trent reclined on one elbow, his pipe clenched between his teeth. They eyed one another steadily.

'What *did* happen?' asked Trent.

'Look, Trent, if you've come to tell me to be a good boy and stop being silly, you can go back to them——'

'Never mind about the others, or what they said. Apparently you know what they said. I want the truth.'

'The trouble is nobody recognizes the truth when they get it——'

'Dyke—let's have it.'

'All right, then—in four words. I did kill Felicity.'

Trent whistled.

'And that's all there is to tell. And don't start on all the reasons why I couldn't have done, because I've heard them all. And don't pretend to believe, because they've tried that too, and it's worse.'

'Are you sure you—killed her?'

'I'm quite sure. I'm not making it up. I'm not mad—though I might quite easily go mad if my dear family don't leave me alone——'

'Calm down,' said Trent. 'Of course you're not mad. I suppose they're all afraid you did do it—in fact, Alice—well, anyhow they're doing their best to work up a defence mechanism against the idea.'

Dyke was not sure of Trent. He suspected a new angle of approach. They'd been working out a fresh plan which Trent, with sweet reasonableness would put into effect.

'I've told you all there is to tell,' he said. 'I felt sort of—desperate at first, and that's when I wired for you. But since there's nothing you can do about it, I don't know why I bothered you in the first place.'

'I wish you'd drop this pose,' said Trent. 'I haven't come all this way to repeat Harold's platitudes. Nor to sit and watch you pretend to fish. If you want to shut me out, that's your own affair. Personally, I think you'd do better to open up and have a cry on my shoulder.'

'I don't trust you,' said Dyke.

'You should know if you can trust me by now,' said Trent 'But please yourself. You seem to have the idea I think you crazy. I don't—but the others do.'

'I murdered Felicity,' said Dyke sullenly. 'Do you understand that?'

'I believe you,' said Trent. 'I don't understand it. Not really. Caroline explained it, Harold explained it, Alice explained it. Michael is too sensitive on the point to want to discuss it as a possibility. But I still don't understand. You're not the sort to kill a woman because she was going to leave you.'

'You can do anything,' said Dyke, 'as long as you haven't thought about it, and as long as you don't think about it. Anything.'

'Try and be a bit clearer,' said Trent.

'Haven't you ever done an action on impulse? Slashed off the head of a flower, put your foot on some inoffensive creature, and then thought afterwards: what on earth did I want to do that for?'

'Ye-es. I can see what you mean.'

'That's how I killed Felicity. I saw in one instant how she could be destroyed, and in the same instant it appeared to be the answer to my misery over her leaving me. And I acted—and it was done.'

'So that's how it was.' Trent's pipe had gone out and he poked about in the bowl with a charred matchstick. 'You haven't found out who the man was, I suppose?'

'Yes, I have. I haven't told any of the others because they've stopped believing there was anyone. It was Frank.'

Briefly he told of Frank's perjury. Trent nodded from time to time.

'Yes,' he said, when Dyke had finished. 'Yes, I can see it now. He'd fallen in love with Felicity all right. I'd have guessed that if I'd thought about it, but I fancied it must be somebody we didn't know, somebody we hadn't met. But I remember I've sometimes seen him looking at her, watching her. I didn't realize—I wouldn't be surprised if Caroline saw it—also without recognizing it for what it was—she wasn't always so keen on Frank, you know.'

'That's quite true,' agreed Dyke.

'A kind of—instinctive dislike.'

They fell into silence, broken only by the water lapping gently against the sides of the launch. A little breeze, dark like a cloud, rippled up the river and was gone. The float bobbed up and down, sank beneath the surface and then came up again.

'You'll be catching a fish if you aren't careful,' said Trent. He shifted himself to find a more comfortable pose. 'You know, Dyke, that young man weighed you up pretty well. You'd be happier paying for your sins—whatever they did to you—with the slate wiped clean, than living always with the horror of what you did. If anything could send you off your rocker, that could. I suppose he got it worked out. He must have come to hate you like hell. You need absolution. And we haven't got the religion that offers us absolution, and we haven't got the faith to accept it if we had. What the devil are you going to do? Are you sure Caroline's solution isn't the right one?'

'Which solution?'

'Get away from it. Forget.'

'I can't get away from it and I can't forget. Wherever I went I feel I'd carry my horrors with me.' He paused. 'There's a quotation I've just thought of: *If I take the wings of the morning and dwell in the uttermost parts of the sea, even there thy right hand shall hold me*. You know what I mean. There's no escape. I've got a feeling—I suppose in a way I am a bit crazy—not like the others imagine, but in a way they haven't thought of. You mentioned absolution. Well, I've got a sort of idea, not a crystallized, clear-cut idea, but something vague at the back of my mind, that only Felicity can help me. And while I'm here I feel I'm in touch with her. I can hear her speak'—he looked at Trent and smiled at the grave expression on his face—'oh, not her voice. I haven't had any visions yet, but I imagine it. I know what she'd say and then imagine her saying it. See what I mean?'

Trent nodded. 'Watch yourself, Dyke! You're sane enough now, but you could easily be heading for a breakdown. You're in danger.'

'I'm safe enough——'

'Don't be too sure. If you're not seeing things yet, you're quite willing to see them. That's not so good. The point is that when you killed Felicity you did something to yourself at the same time. Murder isn't private. Even when it isn't found out, it isn't private. Everybody gets involved. Everybody has a share in it and gets involved——'

222

'I know,' said Dyke. 'I've learned something this last week. Those who destroy others, destroy themselves. It's the same right through life. The destroyer suffers as much as the destroyed. That goes for everything, and for everybody who kills. Whether he kills animals or his fellow creatures. When a man has got to the point where he can destroy anything without compassion, some of the virtue has gone out of him. When he can do it as a matter of course, a lot of virtue has gone out of him. He's a different person. Often quite a nice person, but different. He's gone backwards. He's lost something.'

'Tell me, Dyke, why have you been so anxious to own up?'

Dyke stared into the water, his forehead wrinkled. 'I don't know. Call it conscience, if you like. Or the utter domination of guilt. Compassion for Felicity'—he glanced swiftly at Trent—'which I suppose I didn't feel completely until I found out how ill she'd been. And there was Caro, and her plans. I suppose she hadn't been so happy since we were kids. I don't mean she was glad Felicity was dead, but Felicity being dead did seem to leave things clear for her.'

Trent nodded. 'Caroline's always been a lot too fond of you. A pity. If she'd found a man she could have made a fool of herself over, she'd have got free. But you've remained the most important thing in her life.'

'It's not my fault.'

'No, I know.'

Dyke brooded before going on. 'I couldn't face the sort of life Caro was building up for us. She didn't realize—still doesn't—but it would have been a failure. It would have been founded on a lie—with what I'd done always seething away deep underneath. Like a house over a bed of molten lava. I'd never have been free. I felt if I could only own up—face up to what I'd done——'

'I suppose it comes back to what we call conscience——'

'Perhaps so. But they'd none of them believe me. I *had* to make somebody understand. I didn't *want* to go to Brayton. I just had to speak to somebody who'd take notice, and I thought he would.' He pressed a hand over his forehead. 'You can't think what a relief it is to talk to you, Trent.'

'Yes,' said Trent. 'I think it's as well I came.'

'I didn't feel like this at first. I felt—oh, a mixture of elation and absolute funk. Funk when I thought I'd be found out, elation at my cleverness when I thought I wouldn't be.'

'Perhaps you're lucky. Some people stay like that all their lives. Those who cheat either feel proud of themselves or suffer from conscience. You've got to be damned insensitive to stay permanently in the first category, I think. You can't cheat and remain the same.'

'You're a wise old bird, aren't you, Trent?'

'Am I? I don't know about that. I've often been a miserable old bird.'

'You've helped a lot.'

'I'm glad,' said Trent. 'I'm sorry I've got to go back. Sorry I've got to leave you, I mean.'

'It's all right.'

'What comes next? What are you going to do?'

Dyke shrugged his shoulders. 'Nothing. What can I do? I expect Harold and Alice will leave soon. And Michael. I hope so. They're watching me all the time.' His voice rose irritably. 'I hate them watching me. And that reminds me. I promised Arthur Ryder I'd see a pal of his. Or rather he's coming down here to see me. Sir James Jacobsen. Mind specialist, I believe. Though what good that's expected to do, I don't know.'

He felt rather than saw Trent's immobility and turned to look at him.

'What's the matter?'

'Nothing,' said Trent. 'Nothing.'

'You look as if there were.'

'Oh well—I don't altogether like that.'

'Like what?'

'You seeing Sir James. Mind you, he's a clever devil. No doubt about it. I've heard of him. But the clever ones often haven't any common sense at all.' He became suddenly very earnest. 'Listen, Dyke, be careful what you say to that bird.'

'There's something on your mind, isn't there?'

'I suppose there is, really. Ryder's had a go at you, hasn't he?'

'Yes. Had it all worked out. Quite reasonably, too.'

'Any mention of a nursing home?'

'Yes,' said Dyke.

'I thought so.'

'I stamped on it hard.'

Trent drew down the corners of his mouth suddenly as if he had tasted something unpleasant.

'Say what you're thinking,' said Dyke.

'I'm thinking if you're not careful you'll find yourself trapped. I *thought* Alice said a bit too much, but Harold butted in and managed to shut her up. If Ryder says you're mad and Sir James backs him up——'

'Then I am mad? Is that it?'

'Legally, yes.' Trent put a restraining hand on Dyke's arm. 'Now don't go off the deep end.'

'I'm not going to.'

'If you're mad you can be put under restraint.'

'Lunatic asylum?'

'Private mental home in your case.'

'Worse, if anything.'

'Could be. Not likely, though.'

'They wouldn't dare!'

'Look at it from their point of view,' said Trent. 'Having made up their minds you've imagined it, they must stop this disgraceful story becoming public whatever happens. They don't know who

225

you'll tell next. Perhaps somebody who would believe you. They're scared as hell.'

'So they'll lock me up?'

'I don't know. They're afraid, and people do damn funny things when they're afraid. Heroes turn into cowards, and cowards into heroes——'

'They'll lock me up!' said Dyke again. 'They will, like hell!' He had gone white, and the veins on his temples swelled out. 'Not on your life, Trent.'

'Calm yourself,' said Trent. 'You're doing no good working yourself up. I don't know exactly how the law works in a case like this, but it takes time. In a case of urgency it can work pretty fast. But since you're not a danger to yourself or anybody else they can hardly claim urgency. I know two medical certificates are the important things—and a claim from your next-of-kin.'

Dyke was calmer, but he was still angry. 'Blast them!'

'Everybody that matters is convinced you're dotty,' said Trent. 'Your own relations, the police, your doctor. Sir James will clinch it, I suppose. There's only one thing to do, Dyke.'

'What's that?'

'Pretend you're better. What they'd call better. You've got to pretend you *didn't* kill Felicity.'

'No, I'm damned if I will.'

'My dear chap, don't you see you've got to be careful——?'

'I'll not pretend and lie and scheme any more, Trent——'

'All right,' said Trent. 'All right. Sit still. You're rocking the boat. Take it easy. Look here, I don't think I'll go back to-night. I'll phone Margery——'

'You'll do nothing of the sort. I'm not having you do that for me——'

Trent sighed. 'It's all right——'

'It's not all right. Don't worry about me.'

'I'd rather stay,' said Trent uneasily.

'And I'd rather you didn't. They aren't going to put me in a strait-waistcoat, or anything like that. You said yourself it takes time. Anyhow, you're on my side.'

'Talk sense. Where does that get us? You admit you killed Felicity. They say you couldn't have done and therefore you must be mad. I say I believe you. That's a lot of good, isn't it? Who'll believe *me*? And if I could persuade anybody to believe me you'd face a charge of murder. How d'you think I'd enjoy that? Quite honestly, Dyke, I'd sooner know you were comfortably alive, even in a nursing home, than stand outside a prison one miserable morning to read the notice that they'd hanged you.'

'I seem to have done a lot more than kill Felicity,' said Dyke.

'Yes, you have. I told you, Dyke, murder isn't private.'

They were hailed from the garden. Michael was standing about half-way down it, his hands cupped to his mouth.

'Would you two like some tea?'

'Yes, please,' Trent called back.

'Are you coming in, Father? I'll bring a tray down, if you like, if one of you will bring the dinghy over.'

'That would be best,' said Dyke.

'No,' said Trent. 'Let's go up to the house.' He called to Michael: 'We're coming in. We'll be there in five minutes.'

Michael turned back.

'I'd rather go in,' said Trent. 'They can't keep asking you if you still believe you're a murderer. Just behave normally.'

Dyke was reeling in his line. 'I've got a few things I'd like to say——'

'I know. Forget them. Don't be an awkward cuss. They aren't enjoying this any more than you are. Give 'em a break.'

Dyke stowed away the fishing tackle and went to start the motor. His eyes met Trent's.

'I'm worried,' said Trent. 'Naturally, you're on edge——'

'It'll be all right,' said Dyke. 'Don't worry. Don't spoil your few days.'

'I'll come down as soon as Margery goes back to town.'

'Right-ho.' The launch was moving now, turning in a wide arc to run into the landing-stage. 'Thanks for coming.'

'It's funny,' he said, as they tied up. 'I thought I'd never be able to go out in her again.' He stood a moment looking down into the launch. 'But I didn't mind at all.'

'Things often aren't as bad as you expected,' said Trent.

Chapter Twenty-three

*

IN the morning Dyke took the launch out again. Again he
tried a run up and down and then settled to his fishing. As on
the previous day, he anchored in full sight of the house. The day
was fine, the sun warm, and light danced on the water. Now and
then a boat passed, a breeze ruffled the leaves on the trees, but he
was not particularly aware of his surroundings.

When he returned after lunch he took up a new position on the
far side of the river. He had chosen this spot carefully before he
settled down in the morning. From it he had a clear view of the
end of the house and would be able to see when a car arrived.
Ryder telephoned earlier to say that Sir James would be arriving
at about half-past six. Dyke had decided that Sir James's arrival
would be the signal for him to go for a few hours' run down the
river.

He made up his mind not to meet the specialist. In the first
place he had intended to stop his coming at all, but he knew that
that would start a flood of protest and argument which he did
not feel equal to facing.

In spite of his reassurances to Trent about being all right, he
was nervous. If he allowed himself to be examined by the
famous specialist he would be lost. The man would have made
up his mind before the meeting, and sooner or later they would
have him under some sort of restraint. That would be the final
indignity. His pulse beat rapidly at the thought; there was an
angry, sick feeling in the pit of his stomach.

He had only to get out of the way. Keep the great man waiting. Not turn up at all. The fellow would soon get sick of that. Nothing do those who have made a success in life value more than their time. He would refuse to be bothered any more.

There were flaws in his argument, he knew. Sir James might be a patient man. This running away might convince him of the importance of seeing him. He might not mind waiting; he might, after his experience of unbalanced minds, have developed his own form of craftiness.

I wish I'd not agreed to see him in the first place, he said to himself. I wish I hadn't agreed. I was a fool to give in to Arthur. Giving them a leg-up. Putting myself in their hands. He kept saying in his own mind, I wish I hadn't agreed . . . over and over again . . . I wish I hadn't agreed. It's what Felicity would have said: *You were silly, I wish you hadn't agreed . . . I wish you hadn't agreed* . . . He could hear her voice saying it . . .

Perhaps I am mad by now, he thought. A bit mad. It's been enough to drive anybody off his head. Better to give in and have a rest in their nice, quiet, well-run home.

He shouted to Michael, who seemed to be never out of the garden or out of sight, to bring him some tea over on the tray. He did not want to go to the house because they would be so anxious to impress it on his memory that Sir James would be there at half-past six.

'Aunt Caroline told me to remind you that Sir James will be here at half-past six,' Michael said as he handed up the tray.

Dyke did not answer.

At twenty-five past six a large chauffeur-driven saloon car came round the house and stopped by the porch. As soon as it appeared, Dyke pulled in his tackle quickly and threw it into the well of the launch. He started the engine and as a tall, thin figure got out of the car, was swinging the launch round swiftly to point downstream.

Then suddenly the engine spluttered and stopped.

He swore. There was a good stream running and he was in the middle of it. If he left the tiller to go to the engine he would be aground before he knew where he was. Stuck perhaps. He pressed the starter, but it whirred without any response from the motor. The sound seemed to mock him.

He threw the anchor over the stern and went to the engine hatch and raised it. What to look at first? He was not ignorant of engines, but he was in a hurry; he had to escape, and his haste flurried him. This was not an engine that broke down irresponsibly, and it had run sweetly enough in the morning. Ignition or petrol for a bet! He tried to flood one of the carburettors but no petrol spurted up between his fingers and there was an empty echo as the float knocked against the bottom.

'Damn!' he said aloud. Petrol. That means the feed-pipe or the pump. May take an age.

He was aware of someone shouting, and looked up. The arc he had turned had brought him only a very little lower than where he had fished yesterday, and Michael's voice was quite clear.

'I say, father, Sir James has arrived.'

Dyke restrained an impulse to ask Michael to tell Sir James to go to hell.

He stood up. 'I'm stuck,' he said. 'Engine won't start.'

He stooped over it again, and opened the tool locker for tools. Out of the corner of his eye he saw Michael get into the dinghy and push the oars in the rowlocks.

He was working out a fresh plan, working it out furiously. He'd insist on getting the engine working—it wouldn't take long. Then he'd try it—to make sure everything was all right—and he could stay down the river. The silly old fool would get tired of waiting. And it would seem normal—or nearly normal, barring a bit of obstinacy on his part. A good job the launch had stopped where it did. He hadn't gone far enough to look as if he were

231

running away. He began to feel elated, though he was still excited and anxious.

Michael was standing up in the dinghy holding on to the edge of the launch.

'I say, father, Sir James is waiting to see you.'

'I'll be there in a minute,' said Dyke.

'What's up?'

'Feed-pipe, I think. I'll clear it and then I'll come in. You go and talk to him.'

Michael looked uneasy. 'You may have run out of petrol.'

'No, there's plenty,' said Dyke.

'Well, you row over and I'll see what I can do.'

'I'd prefer to see to it myself, Michael, thanks.'

Michael rowed away reluctantly, then, about half-way to the landing-stage, quickened his stroke. Dyke could not refrain from looking every now and then to see how far he had gone. Once out of the dinghy he almost ran up the garden.

A few words Michael had said came floating up through his memory and suddenly he seemed to hear them again. *You may have run out of petrol.* What a ridiculous thing to suggest. The launch was never allowed to run out of petrol. That was one point he had always been fussy about, and Michael knew it as well as he did. The tank was never allowed to get half empty even.

He went quickly to the tank, took off the cap and peered in. It *was* empty, though. But that was ridiculous! He had looked—when was it—yesterday when he went in. It had been quite three-quarters full then. It couldn't have leaked—it would have stunk to high heaven. . . .

And then he knew. He heard Michael's voice again with its tentative suggestion and he understood. Michael knew. One of them, Michael himself perhaps, had drained the tank last night. They had not liked his isolation on the launch, and the feeling that he had a means of getting out of their sight easily. Of course, they thought he was mad. He must not be left alone. He might talk to somebody. He had to be watched.

He stood up, and as the house came into his line of vision he could see Michael on the verandah. Ryder was standing by him—so he had come over, had he—and they were staring over the river at him. Ryder began to come down the garden.

Dyke went to the cupboard where spares were kept. There were a few petrol cans on board. Surely he could find a gallon somewhere. He searched furiously, throwing things to left and right. Altogether there were three old cans, but not one of them contained any quantity. There might be a drop in the bottom of each.

He found an enamel jug and poured the precious drops in from each can. Together they did little more than half fill the jug. He looked at it in dismay.

By now he could hear the dinghy close at hand, so he tipped the drop of petrol into the tank and then went to the side of the launch.

It was Ryder in the dinghy this time. He backed water when he saw Dyke.

'I say, Dyke, are you coming in? Sir James is here, you know.'

'Yes,' said Dyke. 'I know Sir James is here. And I am not coming in.'

'I say, don't be a fool, man!'

'I'm very sorry to have put Sir James to so much trouble. But I have decided not to see him after all.'

'But look here——'

'So there's no point in his waiting.'

'But you can't do that. Invite the man to come——'

'I didn't want him to come. I suppose he can send me a bill for his wasted time. I'll pay it, then we'll be quits.'

'You certainly won't be quits. Why, as a matter of common courtesy——'

Dyke leaned over the gunwale. 'Thank you, Arthur, for your homily on manners. I'm very rude. You can offer Sir James my apologies as well as my refusal to see him.'

'But why won't you see him?'

'Because I don't want to. I've been thinking and I've decided I don't want to. And apparently that was a very wise decision.'

'What on earth are you talking about?'

Dyke leaned over a little further. 'Was it you put them up to the clever trick of draining the tank?'

Ryder was so confused that he knew his shaft had gone home. 'I—I don't know what you mean.'

'I think you do, Arthur.'

'I didn't suggest draining any tank. I—oh well, if you will have it, I did suggest to Caroline that you should not go wandering off alone——'

Dyke stood up straight. 'You see,' he said pleasantly, 'you'd already made up your mind that I'm off my head——'

'Oh, rubbish——'

'So you tell your Sir James and ask him to come and say the same thing. Isn't that it?'

Ryder was indignant. 'Nothing of the sort. I don't think you're in a normal frame of mind at present, that's all. Sir James could help us. You're behaving like a kid who's afraid to go to the dentist. Look here'—he pulled on one oar to turn the dinghy—'I'll come on board and we'll talk it over quietly.'

'Not on your life,' said Dyke. He picked up a boathook that lay along the side. 'You keep off, Arthur——'

'Don't be an idiot——'

'But that's exactly what I am, isn't it? I warn you, Arthur, if you come in here I shall throw you out again. So stay where you are.'

234

'My dear chap, be your age——'

'You can go back to your Sir James and tell him that I'm cracked, but just add that I prefer to remain cracked in private and without his confirmation.'

Ryder began to plead. 'Dyke, you're making everything much worse all round. If you'd only be reasonable——'

'I don't intend to be reasonable. Go away.'

'Man, I'm your friend——'

'Go away.'

Ryder hesitated. He looked at Dyke, he looked at the boat-hook, then he seemed to realize the hopelessness of his position. He lowered the oars into the water, spun the dinghy round and moved off in the direction of the landing-stage.

Dyke watched until he had gone half-way, then went back to his engine. He looked in the petrol tank again but no amount of looking would make that tiny drop more than a tiny drop. Then he had a brainwave. He went to the saloon and hunting in one of the cupboards found two bottles containing lighter spirit. One was half empty, but the other was full. He went and added their contents to what was already in the tank. Now he must have at least a quart.

His elation at this did not last. A quart! How far would that get him? He was bound to keep the launch going or she would not steer. His impulse was to open the throttle full and keep her going as fast as she would. But with the drop he had he wouldn't even get as far as the lock. Anyhow, everything was spoiled now. What could have appeared as, at the worst, a piece of cussedness had set the seal on what they all thought. And they'd talk it over with Sir James in the lounge, and Sir James would shake his head gravely and say that really something would have to be done . . .

Dyke had gone to the stern and sat on it, high up, lighting a cigarette. He was watching the house, wondering what their next move would be. It was some time now since Arthur had gone in. Perhaps the specialist would allow himself to be rowed over. Or perhaps not. Not after he had threatened Arthur with a wetting.

There was a movement around the door and some of them came out. The tall, thin man got into the car, and it started—Dyke could hear the faint whine of the low gear—and was turned and driven away slowly.

That was better. So he wouldn't wait, after all. He had another patient to see, or he was going out to dinner—or he might have thought it was all a bit too silly.

Dyke was watching, but not the house. He was watching the spot, fifty yards from the house, where the hedge had been broken. Through this gap he would be able to see the last of Sir James's car. But the car did not pass the gap. Dyke had been watching that spot since the moment the car turned the corner of the house, so he knew he had not missed it. It could not have gone the other way because that went only to the farm and there was no way out.

So that was it! They were being clever now. Sir James *was* the patient sort, after all. . . . Drive the car round the corner of the house so that if he's watching he'll think I've gone and then he'll come in. Then I can meet him. We shall have to be gentle . . . very reasonable . . . and he can't refuse to be civil . . .

They *were* determined.

Sir James had gone in again by the door on the other side of the house, and he would be having a drink. Perhaps a meal. And they would be discussing him. Sir James wouldn't say much to their speculations, but he would have made up his mind.

The house appeared very quiet. Not even Michael in the garden. Nobody came out to ask him was he coming in to dinner. He was ignored, forgotten. This was a new game, a game of waiting, of being very patient.

He remembered that by watching him through the window

with the glasses they would be able to see every change of expression on his face and he suddenly felt he was being stared at, and changed his position. He had no plan now, apart from the fact that he was determined to keep away from them all. He sat there smoking cigarette after cigarette, lighting a fresh one from the stub of the other. He emptied his case and went into the saloon and refilled it.

There was food somewhere, when he wanted it, but he was not hungry—he felt he could not have swallowed anything. But he found a bottle of whisky and had a drink.

He went back to look at the engine, over which he had now replaced the hatch. Nothing he could do about that. He could go a couple of miles, not more. That was no use. If he'd had petrol he could have got away and put up for the night at one of the riverside pubs. He had plenty of money in his pockets. Though, really, he did not want to stay anywhere but at home. Why should he let them turn him out like this?

When he looked up from the engine the light seemed to have changed. The sun had set some time ago, now the sky was darker. He could still see, but the clearness had gone; objects were blurred round the edges.

He supposed he'd have to spend the night where he was. Not to sleep, though. If he slept they'd row out and fetch him. He would have to keep awake. Anyhow, he didn't want to sleep.

Sometimes when he and Felicity had been alone at the Lodge they would come out on the river on nights like this. Sometimes they would cruise up and down a while, sometimes moor the launch, not in midstream as he was now, but at some spot near the bank where the water was deep enough. They had not talked much then. It had been enough to be out, to watch the stars appear, to listen to the movement of the water, to hear the cry of a water fowl.

The strange thing was he could not remember a more perfect evening to be out in. I wish she were here now, he thought. I wish she could be with me. And then, in a way, she was. He could imagine her laughing at the trick he was playing on the others, approving, sympathizing because they had taken the petrol out of the tank so that he had to stay where he was. He could sense her presence . . . out of reach . . . only just out of reach.

A light went on in the house and was switched off again. It was not natural for it to be in darkness. He fancied he saw a movement on the landing-stage . . . he was not sure; straining his eyes to see, he thought again he saw someone move.

Down the river road a car went with headlights full on, and then the engine was suddenly cut out and the lights went out. Why should a car stop there? It was somebody coming to watch him. Brayton, perhaps. They had rung up Brayton and said he was getting worse, and Brayton had said he must be watched.

The night was full of people watching him from the house, from the garden, from the landing-stage. There were men coming out of a car and creeping across the field to peer at him through the bushes; eyes staring greedily through the leaves of the willows and the aspens on each bank. As it grew darker they would come nearer, closing in. He felt he could not bear it. He wanted to shout out that he knew they were there, he wanted to tell them to clear off and leave him alone.

A vole went into the water with a splash, and he started violently.

He pulled in the anchor and started the engine. At the first attempt nothing happened, but at the second the motor responded throbbing like a heart full of vigour. He throttled down to a murmur and a moment later was gliding down stream. He ought to put on the lights, but with the lights on he would become a mark for their curious eyes and they would be able to follow him. For the moment he had them baffled, they did not know what he was going to do; did not know what to do themselves.

The launch swung round the bend into Masterman's Reach and he had the long straight stretch in front of him. He opened the throttle wider a moment so that the launch picked up speed, then stopped the engine altogether. The launch glided on, slowing to the pace of the current, the stern swung over a little, he corrected it with the rudder but felt her irresponsive. Better use the motor again a minute.

It would not start.

The launch, as if aware of the lack of control, struggled against the rudder to move broadside into the stream.

Down at the bottom of the reach someone on the towpath was directing the beam of a powerful torch on to the water. Suddenly it picked him up.

'Hey!' called a voice. 'Anybody on that boat?'

Dyke did not answer, but he must have been seen.

'Hey, you're out of control. Steer into the bank. D'you hear me? You're a danger to yourself and everybody else on the river. If you don't come in you'll be fetched.'

This is it, thought Dyke. They can fetch me. I'm crazy. I'm like this boat—he had let the steering go as it would and the launch was now turning to go broadside, like a very slow, heavy old waltzer—I'm crazy. They can say what they like to me now and do what they like to me. I've gone too far. I've given myself away. I told them I was a murderer and they wouldn't believe me, and when I tell them I'm sane they won't believe me.

And then Felicity was with him. Felicity, sympathizing with him and comforting him; agreeing with him about the obtuseness of everybody. Felicity. Very near. Nearer than she had been since—perhaps since he had known her. They were close at last—

and free of the body, cleansed of desire. He did not want her in the least any more, and he needed her more than ever. And when he needed her she was there.

In some strange way he suddenly felt happy—a kind of serenity took possession of him. He felt he had only to put out a hand and touch her—and yet did not want to touch her because he was so nearly a part of her.

A loud roaring filled his ears, and he thought it was something that had gone wrong in his head, and then he knew. It was Gather's Mill.

It brought a flood of memories. Here, it was, he said, just here. It started here and it ought to finish here.

He leaned over to stare into the depths and in the faint light of the stars he could see the reflection of the stern, moving and shimmering in the dancing water, so that it might have been a woman there . . . so that it might have been Felicity herself still there, waiting for him, waiting all the time since he had left her.

He got up on the stern and swung his feet over the edge. Then, grasping hold of the woodwork, he lowered himself into the water. A moment later he let go.